Love, Lacey Donovan

JILL BRASHEAR

MOMENTUM PRESS

Cover by Sarah Kil Creative

Cover Photograph by Wander Aguiar

Editing by Kristen Weber, Cyndi Sandusky, and Novel Nurse Editing

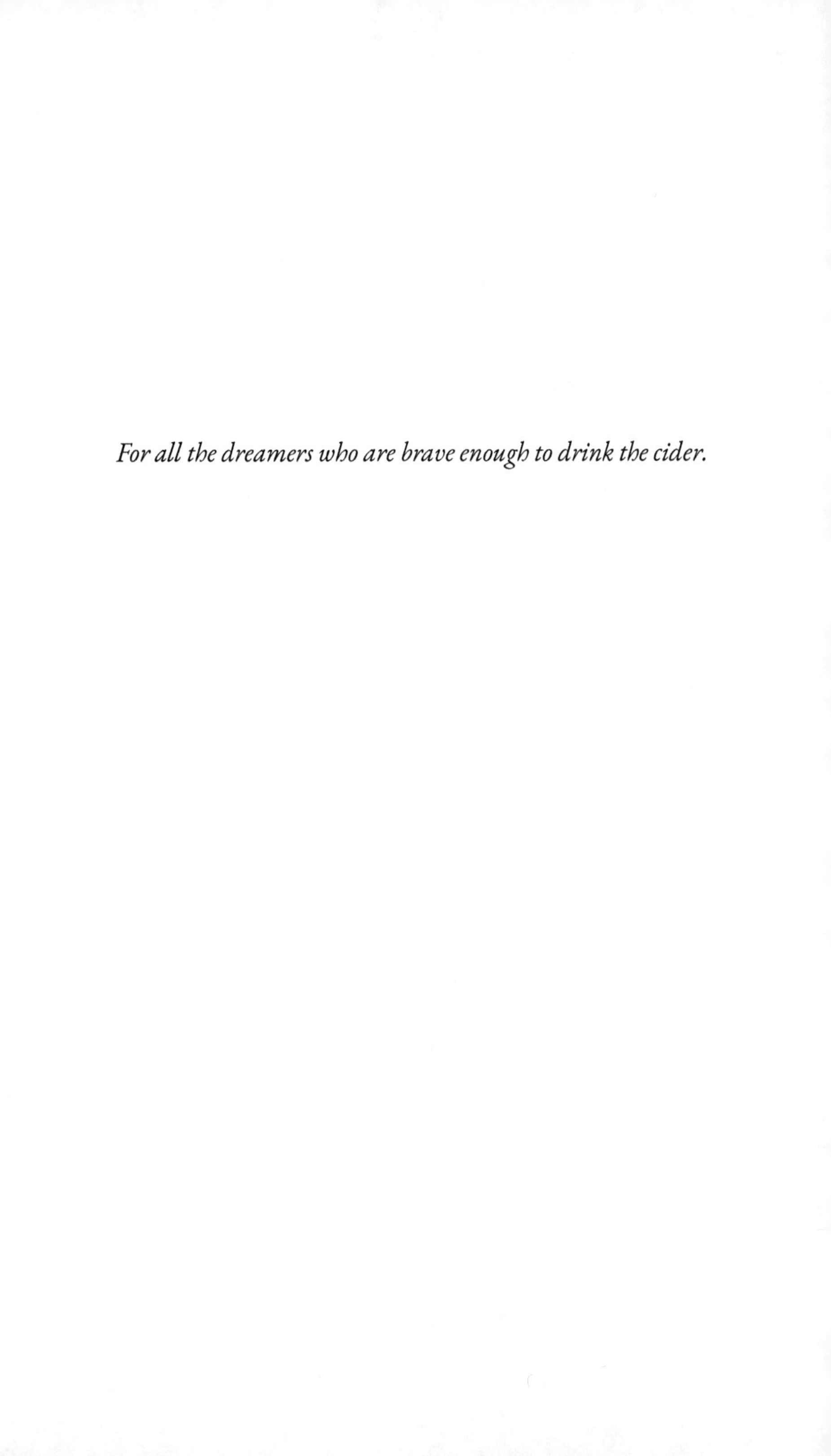

For all the dreamers who are brave enough to drink the cider.

Contents

Book Review of "Temporary" by Savannah Moone

BY LACEY DONOVAN, BLUERIDGEBOOKCLUB.COM

4 STARS

2 FIRE EXTINGUISHERS

5 BOOK BOYFRIEND BOW TIES

DEAR READERS,

Do you ever feel like reading romance has spoiled you for real relationships? Sometimes I wish I'd never picked up that copy of *Wuthering Heights* my Great-Aunt Franny left lying on the coffee table. Or that Janet Dailey novel about the sexy ranchers in Montana either.

I blame my single-hood area code on the ranchers of Blue Moon, Montana and all the other sexy heroes who raised the bar of dateable men to an unhealthy status.

What can a real guy do to compare to these brooding heroes with perfect physiques and expert kissing skills?

Nothing!

If you love a good book boyfriend as much as I do—which is impossible by the way—then run to your nearest retailer and pick up a copy of *Temporary* by Savannah Moone.

You guys know how stingy I am with my 5-star ratings, right? Well this book deserved every one of them.

Super-sexy Bently James was raised by his single father after his mother abandoned them. Bently's father taught him to treat women with respect and tenderness but warned him never to fall in love. Bently has spent his entire adult life avoiding the L-word. Instead he throws himself into his career as an actor. Never being in a relationship has backfired on Bently because now his status as a leading man has been threatened by rumors (untrue) that he is gay.

Bently James needs a woman in his life—fast.

Enter CeeCee DeMilo, a struggling actress who could use a leg up in her career without having to spread them. Fake-dating Hollywood's favorite heartthrob sounds like the perfect gig to CeeCee. If the rumors are true, there is no chance Bently will be a romantic threat. Little does CeeCee know her temporary role as Bently's sweetheart is one she will want for a lifetime.

PROS:

- Trope: I can't resist a good fake-relationship romance.
- Meet-Cute: This novel has one of the cutest first meetings I've ever read. CeeCee is working at the county DMV to pay her rent when Bently comes in to take his road test. What thirty-year-old man doesn't have a driver's license? Bently. He has ridden around in the back of limos half his life. He never wanted a license before. He never wanted a girlfriend either, but now he needs both. Unfortunately Bently is a horrendous driver, and CeeCee has to fail him.
- Secondary Characters: CeeCee's roommate Bill is the perfect best friend. Bently's dad is everyone's dream father—best friend, role model and number-one fan rolled into one.

CONS:

- Believability: I don't do spoilers, so let's just say the ending was a little bit too far-fetched and perfect. But still cute...
- Sex: Okay, get ready to fire away all your hate emails calling me a horn-dog. But really? ONE sex scene, Ms. Moone? The kissing scenes were off-the-charts sexy, but a single bedroom scene just wasn't enough for this randy reviewer.
- Clichés: *There's only one bed in the hotel room? Oh, my! Guess we'll have to share.*

THE FINAL WORD:

I loved this book! It was a quick, enjoyable read that had me laughing and crying. *Temporary* is charming, and, sexy, and oh so swoon-worthy.

I *highly* recommend the paperback edition because it has a BONUS scene written from Bently's point of view. We get to see exactly what Bently thinks about CeeCee when they meet for the first time.

SPOILER ALERT:

The Bonus Scene has something to do with her DMV uniform.

Love,

Lacey Donovan

Chapter One

I named him Aslan.

The only thing about him that deserved the lionesque name was his size. He was 120 pounds of homely looking mutt with a stubborn streak as long as *Gone with the Wind*, and I loved him with all my heart.

"Aslan! No!" I tugged his leash as he attempted to chase a soccer ball whizzing across the field.

Aslan gave the ball one last wistful glance and then trotted back to the rest of the pack.

It wasn't easy to walk four dogs at once, especially when one of them had as much energy as Aslan. But the gods had blessed me with a gift. I was a wrangler of dogs, a whisperer of puppies, a... volunteer at the Mossy Oak Canine Rescue Center, with a lime-green T-shirt to prove it.

Every Sunday I chose four lucky pups to take on a walk. I tried to rotate the dogs, but Aslan nearly always made the cut. He'd been adopted from the shelter a few times and brought back because the owners couldn't handle him. I couldn't help but sympathize with him. My parents had kicked me out at seventeen, and I'd been roaming ever since, never finding anywhere that felt like home.

Mossy Oak was a great town in the North Carolina mountains, but I was sure I'd get the itch to move soon. Moving was what I did.

Every week I walked the rescue dogs at Ginger Cake Acres—a sprawling park teeming with life no matter what the weather. After an hour spent meandering along the paths with the dogs, I felt rejuvenated.

I was a natural-born dog walker, and it was great money for a side gig. My job at the bookshop would have been enough to pay the bills if I wasn't in debt to the frizzed ends of my naturally curly hair.

"Aslan!" I cried as he tugged on his leash to chase another errant ball. "No!"

But this time, I was too late. The wiry mutt was on the loose. In a flash, Aslan was gone, tearing across the field in pursuit of the ball.

"Hey!" A woman sitting on a nearby bench scrambled to her feet. "Your dog is heading straight for my daughter!"

Aslan ran across the field, heading straight for a little girl sitting under a tree.

"He isn't dangerous," I assured the woman, who clutched her phone as if ready to call emergency services. "He's just annoying."

"My daughter is afraid of dogs."

Aslan dropped the tennis ball in the little girl's lap, and she looked up from her book, startled. Aslan stared at her, tongue lolling. The little girl's face light up, and I knew she'd fallen for his charm.

"She doesn't look scared," I said.

The girl picked up the ball and threw it. Aslan darted after it, and the sound of girly laughter floated across the busy playground.

Her mother didn't seem to recognize the sound. "She looks..."

"Happy?"

The woman nodded, watching her daughter with teary eyes. "I haven't seen her laugh in so long."

"Aslan has a way with people," I said, bending the truth a little. Aslan's way with people was to annoy the heck out of them until they couldn't take him anymore and returned him to the shelter. Three times he'd been adopted. Three times he'd been returned.

I gave a sharp whistle to call Aslan back to the pack. He trotted over reluctantly. The little girl watched him, then returned to her book, a frown reclaiming her pixie-like features.

"He's kind of funny looking," the woman said as I grabbed Aslan's leash. "What kind of dog is he?"

"Who knows?"

She arched a brow at me, eyeing me and Aslan with equal curiosity. "You have a lot of dogs."

I laughed. "They aren't mine. They're from the rescue center. I walk them every Sunday on my day off." I smiled and offered her Aslan's leash. "Wanna walk Aslan for a minute? I've got my hands full with these guys." I had a beagle, a Labrador, and a poodle waiting patiently to finish their walk. I could handle them with ease, but I had a feeling the woman needed a walk as much as the dogs did.

"Aslan?" Her eyebrow arched higher.

In response to his name, Aslan turned his head to look at her.

"He's kind of cute, I guess." She shoved her phone in her bag and took the leash. "He made Summer laugh, and I'm grateful."

We set off in a loop around the playground so she could monitor her daughter as we walked.

"She's supposed to be at a play date," the woman said, gesturing toward a group of girls about her daughter's age sitting on a blanket sharing a picnic. Under their winter coats, the girls wore full princess regalia. "Summer would rather sit under a tree by herself."

I studied the little girl under the bare oak branches. She was smaller than the other girls. Dressed in a pirate's ensemble, complete with a swashbuckling sword at her side, she must not have gotten the memo requesting royal attire.

"The invitation said to dress as your favorite character." She shook her head. "Summer is obsessed with these pirate books, *Ashes of Mooreland*."

I smiled and shoved up my sleeve to show her my tattoo. It was Princess Alaura of Marlydia's ship. "I know the series."

The woman inspected my ink from wrist to elbow. "You're even more obsessed than my daughter."

"I love books. I work at Hyperboles Bookshop and write book reviews for the website." I nodded at the dogs. "This is my side gig."

The woman trained her eyes on her daughter as we circled the playground. She sighed. "I don't mind her being a bookworm, but I hoped she'd at least try to make friends."

I transferred my glance from the daughter to the mother. "What about you? You were sitting on a bench all by yourself. All the other moms are over there."

I gestured at a group of young mothers dressed in the suburban mom athleisure uniform of fitted jeans tucked into riding boots and colorful puffy vests.

"I work too much. We just moved back here. I haven't had time..." She trailed off, her frown slowly morphing into a smile. "I sound like a walking excuse. Sorry. I didn't even introduce myself. I'm Pressly Carleton, and that's my daughter, Summer."

"Lacey Donovan."

We walked around the playground a few more times, chatting nonstop. On our last loop, our conversation dipped below the surface level of jobs and hobbies and dived in to the deep water of relationships.

Pressly told me about her painful divorce from Summer's dad and how the little girl had sank further into the fantasy world of her books since moving back to Mossy Oak a month ago. She told me about wanting to find a place closer to town so Summer wouldn't be so isolated at her brother's house in the hills near her job at Sky Valley Vineyards.

"My job doesn't leave me with a lot of downtime. I need to prove myself right now. My previous boss got fired for embezzlement, and everyone is looking at me to keep things afloat."

"Sounds like you need a night out on the town, not that Mossy Oak has much to offer."

She laughed. "Just one of the things I'm working on. I grew up here, and the only place to go was an old honky-tonk on the outskirts of Azalea Falls. I'm trying to change things at the Vineyard. I want to make the bar at the inn a place for locals as well as guests."

"I've been there once."

She raised her eyebrows at me. "Only once?"

"Once was enough. Too uppity for me."

"Exactly my point." Pressly sighed as she saw the tea party was breaking up. "I better go drag Summer away from her book. She should at least say goodbye to the others."

Aslan gave Pressly a mournful look as she passed his leash back to me, and we both laughed.

"Is he available for adoption?"

Aslan might be just what mother and daughter needed. "Are you looking for a dog?"

Pressly's nose wrinkled. "Not really. We're staying with my brother, and his place isn't exactly dog friendly."

I glanced down at Aslan, who was eying us as if he understood every word. "Does it have a fenced yard?"

"Not exactly."

I narrowed my eyes at her.

"The property is gated, but it's too big to let a dog run loose." Pressly chewed her lip, eying Aslan. "But I am looking for a place in town. Maybe one with a yard."

I transferred the leashes into one hand and pulled one of my cards from my coat pocket. "If you decide to adopt Aslan, I can help you with walking and training."

Pressly took the card with a laugh. "Looks just like you."

The cartoon drawing of a woman with a headful of curls walking four dogs at once did look a lot like me. She even had a nose ring.

"Call me if you decide to adopt him."

"I will. Bye."

"Nice meeting you."

Lots of people talked to me while I walked the rescue dogs. They were drawn to me like I was some kind of entertainment. Many promised to adopt dogs. Some followed through on their promises. Most didn't. I watched Pressly hurry up the hill to get her daughter, and I wondered which category she would fall into.

Chapter Two

I made it all the way to the other side of the park before I found out. My phone rang, and I shuffled the leashes into one hand to dig it out of my coat pocket. I pulled out my trusty "dumb" phone and flipped it open to see an unfamiliar number with an out-of-state area code.

"Hello?"

"Lacey, it's Pressly."

"Hi."

"I've thought about it, and I want him. You'll help, right?"

"Of course." A skateboarder flew past me on the bridge, and the dogs surged forward. "I can come over every day if you need me."

"This is going to cost me a fortune, isn't it?"

"Nah. I'll give you the friend discount." Who was I kidding? I was already walking Aslan for free. I was a sucker for that dog. I had a huge grin plastered on my face.

"When can you start?"

I laughed. "You have to adopt him first." I juggled the leashes as we neared the bridge. The dogs always got a little nervous when we crossed it. It was narrow, and people on bikes sped by in both directions. "I better go. Text me your address."

"Thanks a lot!"

"You're welcome."

"And, Lacey?"

I jerked the leashes as a woman on roller blades whizzed past. "Huh?"

"I just wanted to warn you about my brother. Don't bother him while he's working. He's pretty...intense."

"Gotcha!" Another woman on skates squeezed by. "Text me." We hung up and I folded my phone back into my pocket. "Congrats, buddy!" I told Aslan as we exited the bridge. "Looks like you've got a new home."

And I would have some extra money. I had made some decisions right after high school which had landed me in a pile of debt. After seven years of living cheaply and paying down the principal, I was finally getting my head above water. Extra money meant I could indulge in my favorite purchases—books, matching bra-and-panty sets, and mocha lattes. In that order.

We exited the bridge and came upon a field where people were playing soccer. A ball flew past, and it was too much for Aslan to resist. He yanked the leash from my hand and chased after the ball. He didn't see the biker heading toward him until it was too late. I held back a scream as Aslan darted right in front of the biker's wheel.

Tires squealed, brakes screeched, and a string of curse words not suitable for tender ears rang through the air as the biker swerved. Aslan darted off the sidewalk, free from harm, but the biker wasn't so lucky. The bike jackknifed, and he flipped over the handlebars and crashed into a row of prickly bushes.

I knew the biker was still alive from the curse words streaming from the bushes. My heart raced in my chest as I led the dogs— minus Aslan—over to the scene of the accident.

I peered into the bushes and saw the biker lying with his arms and legs akimbo. "You still in one piece? I know some first aid." I recited the basics in my mind. RICE. It stood for rest, ice, compression, and... I couldn't remember the E. And there wasn't any ice around.

The biker stuck one leg out of the bushes. It didn't look broken.

"Aslan!" I snapped, spotting him traipsing through the bushes with a popped soccer ball hanging from his mouth. I reached down to grab his leash.

The biker rolled onto the sidewalk. All his limbs seemed attached.

"Elevate!" I exclaimed, remembering what the E stood for.

The biker stared up at me. Dark sunglasses hid his expression, but I could only guess it was thunderous. I braced myself for more cussing, this time aimed at me, not the bushes.

Unexpectedly, he burst out laughing. He pushed to his feet and pulled off the sunglasses. Tears streamed from his eyes.

"You okay?" Despite the fact that he wore a helmet, I thought he might have knocked something loose in his head. He was having trouble standing he was laughing so hard.

He finally caught his breath. "I wonder if anyone got that on video," he said. "Had to be hilarious."

"I'm glad you're not hurt." A giggle escaped my mouth. Now that I knew he was okay, it was hard not to laugh.

He pulled off his helmet and ran his fingers through long black hair that had been made for a shampoo commercial. His long tresses had gotten a little disheveled during the tumble, but the rest of him seemed unharmed.

"Those all your dogs?" he asked, binding his hair in a low pony-tail at his neck.

"No." I tightened my grip on the leashes. "None of them are mine. I volunteer at the rescue center."

He pointed at Aslan. "He looks like a handful."

Aslan ignored the biker's disapproving tone, tongue lolling in blissful oblivion.

"You don't seem hurt." I crossed my fingers this was true.

"I'm fine," he said, plucking a leaf from his shirt.

"And your bike? I can pay for any damages." There went my extra income. *Easy come, easy go.*

He crouched over his bike, running a hand over the frame and inspecting the tires. "We've been through worse." He straightened to his feet and wiped his sunglasses off on the hem of his shirt, revealing a swatch of tanned, toned abs. "The major damage is to my ego," he said.

My shoulders relaxed, and my heartbeat slowed back to normal. He was good looking, and he knew it. He had a wide smile, and all that long shiny hair probably got him tons of attention from the ladies. "Your ego looks fine to me."

"It was worth crashing to get the number of the prettiest girl in the park."

"I didn't give you my number."

"Ouch." He winced. "That hurt worse than the crash." He patted down his left arm. "I think something's broken." He showed me his elbow, which looked perfectly fine under his fitted jacket. "I should probably get your number just in case," he said.

"If something's broken, call a doctor. Not me."

He grinned. "So that's a no?"

"It's a small town," I said. "I'll probably see you around."

"I can only hope." He replaced his sunglasses and reached for his bike.

"Sorry about making you crash."

"No worries."

He flashed a wave as he rode his bike off along the trail. I waved back, watching him until he disappeared around the corner. He had a cute smile and gorgeous eyes. And he'd laughed at himself. I liked that. But I didn't feel any flutters in my heart or elsewhere. Nothing. *Nada.*

I was more excited about the next Miranda Lockhart romance novel than I was about meeting a hot guy in the park. Book boyfriends were much better than the real thing.

Chapter Three

A week passed, and Pressly hadn't returned Aslan. Every day when I went to walk him, I sighed in relief as I saw him sitting in his gated room waiting for me. He had a plush bed, plenty of toys, food, and water—everything he needed. My only concern was that he missed his friends at the rescue center.

Today I planned to take him back to town with me to walk around the park with my afternoon dogs. It would give him a chance to socialize and see his old turf.

Pressly hadn't been kidding when she'd said her brother's place wasn't suitable for a dog. All the furnishings were a shade of white, and the only color was in the paintings on the walls.

A long winding road separated the house from the surrounding hills of Sky Valley Vineyards. An intimidating stone wall deterred visitors.

I pulled up to the gate and entered the security code.

"Entry is incorrect," a pleasant female voice informed me. "You have two remaining tries."

I tried again, careful to enter the same code I'd been using for a week without any problems.

"Entry is incorrect," said the voice again. "You have one remaining try."

I leaned out the window, steeling myself against a cold blast of mountain air and tried the code again.

"Entry is incorrect. Goodbye."

I got out of the car and slammed the car door. Huddled in my coat, I bent over the keypad and stabbed the code again.

As soon as I touched the screen, a high-pitched wail pierced the air. My heart raced, and I tapped the screen frantically. I glanced toward the street, half-expecting a security team to jump out from behind the cedar trees and tackle me. I covered my ears with my hands to muffle the siren and grabbed my ringing phone. Thank God, it was Pressly.

"Hello?" I shouted over the noise of the alarm.

"I forgot to tell you the new code!" Pressly shouted back. "My brother just got back, and he changed it. Security reasons."

I added "security freak" to the list of things I knew about Pressly's brother. So far, the list was short. All I knew was that he was stinking rich, his favorite color was white, and his job kept him away from home a lot.

I didn't even know his name.

The siren changed pitch, becoming a steady irritating beep.

Pressly rattled off the new code, sounding distracted. "I gotta go," she said. "I'll text you the new door code in a second."

I punched in the new code and the noise ceased. A moment later, the gate slid open to reveal a cobblestone driveway weaving between tall cedars to the mansion on top of the hill.

A light snow fell as I walked up to the front door. The forecast had been for sunny skies, and I wasn't dressed for snow. I huddled in my coat, waiting for the text with the new code. Flustered and shivering, I peeked through the glass front door into the foyer.

White walls, bleached floors, ivory console table—who knew there were so many shades of white.

I was freezing by the time Pressly texted me the new code. I punched it in with numb fingers and braced myself for the alarm to sound again.

After a moment I heard the mechanical click of the locks opening. I opened the door and walked inside. I walked through the foyer and then froze as I stepped into the living room.

My jaw fell open as I glanced around the room. Heat flashed through my body, followed by an icy chill in my veins.

The normally pristine room was trashed. White was no longer the predominant color. Coffee grounds were scattered across the floorboards, chip wrappers were strewn across the sofa, crumpled cereal boxes littered the hallway, and feathers floated down from the ceiling fan.

I gritted my teeth as I recognized the signs of a dog gone wild.

From the corner of my eye, I spotted the culprit: Aslan digging in the dirt of a rubber tree turned on its side.

"Aslan! Come!" My sharp voice pierced the silence.

The green leaves parted to reveal Aslan's shaggy face covered in dirt. When he saw me, his ears perked up and he bounded across the room. He skidded to a halt at my feet.

I bent down to his level and stared into his eyes. "What have you done?"

Aslan rolled over on his back and exposed his belly. I dusted the dirt off his face and paws, then took him by the collar and escorted him outside.

After Aslan visited his favorite bush, I called him back inside and secured him in his gated room.

He lay down in his plush dog bed and settled in for a nap.

I'd warned Pressly about making sure Aslan was confined when he wasn't getting attention. Aslan couldn't handle free rein in a house, especially a house as stark as a museum. It wasn't Aslan's fault his human couldn't follow directions.

If only people were as trainable as their pets, everything would be so much simpler.

Last week there had been no problems. Aslan had behaved like the perfect dog. He and Summer and Pressly were on their way to becoming a family unit.

Would Aslan's adventures in the trash can send him back to the rescue center for good? I couldn't let that happen.

I rummaged in the pantry until I found cleaning supplies and got to work. I righted the rubber tree, trapped the feathers, and swept the floor. The sofa was in need of a deep clean, but anyone who bought a white sofa was begging for trouble.

A loud thump sounded from overhead, and I remembered the brother. He was the one stupid enough to purchase white furniture. He must have been the one to leave the gate open.

The faint pulse of music drifted down from above. I glared at the ceiling, my anger mounting. After I finished cleaning, I marched up the stairs, straight to the source of the problem.

Chapter Four

I knocked, but there was no answer. He probably couldn't hear me over all the horrible noise that hardly passed for music. I knocked again, harder this time.

The music stopped and a muffled voice called, "Yeah?"

I tried the knob, but it didn't open. I leaned against the door. "Can you unlock the door?"

There was a loud thump and then a mechanical whir as the locks released. I pushed the door open, hoping I wouldn't be greeted by Quasimodo.

I knew nothing about him. When I'd asked where he'd been all last week, Pressly had shrugged and said, "Working." There were no family pictures around the house, no personal touches. No clues to the owner's identity.

The room was empty. It smelled of candle wax, cigar smoke, and sweat.

A whoosh followed by a clang sounded to my left. I pivoted and saw another door, which was cracked open.

"I told you not to bother me while I'm working," he said, sounding as annoyed as I felt.

I glanced around at the wasteland of an office. The only light came from a burning candle on the desk. It didn't look like he was getting much work done, and the candle was a safety hazard. There was enough loose paper littering the room to make the whole house go up in flames.

I marched over to the desk and blew out the candle, then threw open the door to the adjoining room.

Presley's brother lay on his back on a weight bench, straining to push up a loaded bar. My first instinct was to help him, but I stopped mid-stride as I took in the amount of weights on the bar. As a spotter for so much weight, I'd be useless.

He finished his set, then dropped the bar to the rack with a loud clank. The noise was deafening in the quiet room.

He sat up and aimed a glare in my direction. My heart lurched and then skipped back to life. Heat flooded my cheeks.

This man was no Quasimodo.

He belonged on the cover of a romance novel ripping bodices. He had one of those broad male chests that looked like it had been hewn from stone and polished to a high sheen. A light smattering of dark hair covered his flat, hard pecs and then thinned to a line bisecting his distinctly carved abs. Not one ounce of fat dared to cling to his body.

Dark hair curled in damp hanks over his forehead, and his skin shined with sweat.

Fire streaked down my spine, and my heart leaped into my throat. I didn't usually go for the jock types, but this guy would get anyone's heart pumping. I shut my mouth before the drool could escape.

He grabbed a towel to rub the sweat from his eyes. "You're not Pressly," he said, his tone both disapproving and Southern genteel. "You're the one who tripped the alarm?"

My skin tingled at the sound of his rich baritone. His voice was just as sexy as the rest of him. "You changed the code."

His body was a work of art. Lean chest, muscular thighs, rounded calves, and...bright pink socks emblazoned with yellow rubber ducks? *What the hell?*

I bit back a laugh. "What's up with the socks?"

He tossed the towel to the floor and glared in my direction. Ignoring my question, he asked, "What do you want?"

My temper flared, and I remembered how angry I'd been while cleaning up the mess downstairs. "You're a jerk," I said.

Pressly's brother stood from the bench and began loading on more weights as if I hadn't spoken. My eyes dropped over his chiseled torso in a slow perusal, and all the blood rushed from my head. I felt dizzy, as if I'd forgotten to eat. His voice had sent a tingle of awareness straight to my belly, and even the smell of his sweat heightened my senses.

He didn't spare me a glance as he finished loading the weights and lay down on the bench. He grunted his way through another set, counting under his breath.

Up, down, up, down went the heavy bar. Up, up, up went my temperature. The flex and strain of his bulging biceps hypnotized me. He could easily pick me up without even straining. Toss me onto the bed, the floor, the weight bench...I bit my lip.

"I'm the jerk?" he asked. "You're the one setting off my alarm, interrupting my work, and insulting my style."

I glanced at at his socks again. The ducks were wearing sunglasses. A guy who wore socks with ducks on them couldn't be all bad, *could he*?

"You left Aslan out. He can't be left out."

He sat up and swung his leg over the bench. "Who are you?"

"I'm the dog walker, Lacey Donovan." Not for the first time, I wished my parents would have given me a more serious name. Something literary like Zelda, or Isobel, or even Matilda would have suited me much better. Lacey sounded like something my grandmother set on her coffee table so cups of tea wouldn't leave a mark... or someone who slid around on a pole.

He reached for the bar again, his muscles rippling. "We done here?"

Blindsided by my physical reaction to him, it took a moment for his words to sink in. I'd thought I was immune to good-looking men, but one look at him had me shocked to the core. It wasn't as if

I never saw handsome men. They came into the bookshop all the time, but I never felt a glimmer of interest. I usually liked my boyfriends between the pages of a book, but I wanted this man between the sheets.

I cleared my throat and tore my eyes away from his gorgeous form. "Yeah. That's it."

He grabbed his phone and tapped the screen. With a swipe of his finger, music filled the air. He nodded behind me in dismissal. "The door's that way."

Too stunned to say anything, I backed out of the room and closed the door. A moment later, I heard the whirring sound of mechanics as he locked the door.

Chapter Five

"Everyone's gone," I called to Thatcher, who was stacking books into a box behind the front desk.

"You deserve a raise, Lacey," he said. "Only you can charm Dr. Underwood. She's been coming into this shop for years and has never opened her purse for a purchase. Although she did hit me over the head with it one time."

I laughed, picturing Dr. Underwood's huge satchel flying through the air. "She's just lonely."

"You're good with those lonely types."

For some reason, people opened up to me. I was a magnet for drawing out people's personal stories, even the ones they didn't want to tell. Pressly had told me all about her marriage and divorce the first time I'd met her, and Dr. Underwood had told me all about her illustrious career as one of the first female doctors in the area. I should have been a therapist instead of a bookshop clerk and dog walker.

"You want a drink?" I asked Thatcher, on my way into the café.

"Coffee."

"Again?"

"Lay off, Lacey."

Thatcher was renovating his family's historic house, intent on making it livable after decades of neglect. Lately he'd been working all day at the bookshop, then staying up all night doing manual labor.

"You need sleep," I said, pointing a finger at him.

"Yes, Mom," Thatcher grumbled. "Heavy on the cream. I'll sleep after I get the cabinets finished."

Although Thatcher tried to keep his tone light, he didn't fool me for a minute. His lack of sleep had less to do with his renovation project than with his nightmares. Thatcher never talked to anyone about his time in the Army, but he'd let a few things slip with me.

I fixed Thatcher's coffee the way he liked it and then grabbed a beer from his private stash in the fridge for myself.

I usually went for a sugary decaf at book club, but tonight I needed something stronger. My mind had been busy all day, replaying my encounter with Pressly's brother.

Thatcher raised an eyebrow when he spied my beverage selection. "Rough day?"

I flipped off the bottle cap and tossed it in the trash, wishing I could be rid of thoughts of Pressly's brother with as little effort. I took a sip of the rich, stout beer. "I need to take the edge off."

Thatcher laughed. "Those tattoos are the only thing edgy about you."

I glared at him. "Careful."

But it was true; I was a total creampuff. It was why I loved romance novels so much. They made it okay to embrace all those fluffy feelings of hope and love—the ones that rarely happened in real life.

"What do you have for me this month?" I asked, eyeing the box full of books Thatcher carried under his arm.

"You'll have to wait until everyone gets here." He set the box on the low-slung table in the reading nook.

Anticipation burned inside me. My favorite author, Miranda Lockhart, had a new release hitting retailers next month. My copy could be in that box.

"Come on. Just a peek." I dropped onto the sofa and crossed my arms over my chest to keep from reaching for the box. "The suspense is killing me."

"You'll survive another five minutes." Thatcher took his coffee and backed through the swinging door into the kitchen.

I shot him another glare before settling back against the cushions. In an attempt to distract myself from wondering what was in the box, my mind strayed to my new favorite subject—Pressly's brother.

I was lost in thought, rehashing our encounter over and over like a brilliant passage in a novel I wanted to memorize, when Gabi plopped down onto the sofa next to me. She smelled like sweaty socks and menthol rub. Her stench instantly pulled my mind from tight abs and broad shoulders.

"How's my girl?" she asked.

"Ugh," I said. "You stink."

"Sorry." Hopping up from the sofa, she peeled off her nylon jacket and tossed it aside. She sniffed her armpit and grimaced.

"Did you run here?" I asked, eying her tights and T-shirt.

Gabi nodded. "I had to. Shane just finished a game. This was the only time I had in my schedule."

Shane was Gabi's fourteen-year-old son. A gifted athlete, Shane was the only freshman on the varsity football and basketball teams. Between all of Shane's games and her job as principal of the elementary school, Gabi barely had time for herself. She was used to squeezing in a run between work, single-mom duties, and book club.

I worried she pushed herself too hard. She and Thatcher, neither ever stopped moving.

Gabi grabbed a bottle of water from the fridge and twisted open the cap. "I was sweating my ass off at Shane's game because the new smart HVAC system they spent so much money on isn't as smart as advertised." She slapped the water bottle on the counter and righted her ponytail, which had the audacity to look sleek and beautiful after bobbing behind her head for miles. "I have smarter kindergartners!"

"Did you eat?"

She guzzled more water. "I ate at the game."

I wrinkled my nose. "Vending machine?"

Gabi shrugged. "Best peanut butter crackers in town." She pointed her water bottle at me, pinning me with her laser-sharp stare. "What's up with you? You were in outer space just now. You didn't even hear me come in." She looked at the books on the coffee table and grinned. "Thinking about the new Miranda Lockhart release, huh?" she asked and took a swig of water.

Heat crept up my chest to stain my cheeks. *Not exactly.* "Busted," I said. Gabi's eyes narrowed skeptically, but before she could comment I turned the tables on her. "How's the sexy Spanish teacher?" I asked, in an effort to take the attention off me and my new obsession with Tall, Dark, and Brooding. The Spanish teacher at the elementary school was always a good topic to distract Gabi. She hadn't stopped talking about him since she'd hired him last fall.

Gabi sighed dramatically, rubbing the cold bottle of water across her forehead. "I swear, God put Latin men, especially Mr. Morales, on this earth to torture women everywhere."

I laughed. "You're just a sucker for a sexy accent." I couldn't help but think of Pressly's brother's distinct accent. Southern charm laced with New York confidence.

"Who isn't?" Gabi asked.

"You should try a different genre for a while," I suggested. Gabi read and reviewed erotica under the pen name Valentina. She insisted that her day job as principal of an elementary school made secrecy imperative. Gabi dated even less than I did, which meant never. She said she'd already been married to the love of her life. Her husband had been killed in active duty when Shane was a toddler, and she didn't believe another soul mate was out there for her. At the ripe age of thirty-four, she was finished with men, except in books.

"Not a chance," Gabi said. "My books keep me sane. No one's climbed into my bed since Shane stopped having nightmares."

Thinking about climbing into bed with a man brought the

unbidden image of Pressly's brother back to the forefront of my mind. I was obsessed with a man whose name I didn't even know.

Sloane breezed in and sat down on the sofa across from me. "What smells?" she asked, wrinkling her nose.

"I don't stink that badly," Gabi insisted.

"Yes, you do," I said.

Gabi pouted. "I'll just stay over here, then."

"We love you anyway," Sloane said, rummaging in the huge tote bag she carried. "Here." She tossed a deodorant stick to Gabi. "Apply generously."

Gabi caught the deodorant and did as she was told.

"Pour me a glass of wine, will you?" Sloane asked Gabi. She spied the box on the table and rubbed her hands together. "Books," she squealed, leaning forward to open the box.

"Wait." I stopped her. "Thatcher wants us all here. Remember how pissed he was last time when we started without him?"

"Thatcher is such a baby," Gabi said loudly.

"I heard that," came Thatcher's muffled reply from his office.

Gabi motioned as if rocking an invisible infant, making me and Sloane laugh.

"I heard that too!"

We exchanged knowing looks as Gabi delivered Sloane's wine.

Sloane sampled the wine. "Not as good as Sky Valley, but decent."

Sloane had come straight from the vineyard where she worked as an event planner. She still wore the pale-pink button-down shirt with Sky Valley Vineyards emblazoned on the breast pocket. I looked at the logo, and an idea sparked. Sloane might be the perfect person to pump for information on Pressly, and, more importantly, her brother.

"You guys remember Aslan?" I asked, starting at the beginning.

"The mutt who caused the cute biker to wreck?" asked Gabi.

"Yes."

"The biker you didn't want to go out with?" Sloane jabbed a finger at me. She was always after me to sign up for online dating, but her disastrous experiences were more of a deterrent than an advertisement.

I took a sip of my beer. "Never mind the biker," I said. "I'm talking about Aslan. His new owner is Pressly Carleton." I aimed my question at Sloane. "You know her?"

"Sure," Sloane said. "Pressly Vinroot-Carleton."

My forehead wrinkled and understanding dawned. "Pressly's a Vinroot?" The mansion in the mountains overlooking the rolling hills of grapevines suddenly made sense.

Even I, the newest resident to Mossy Oak, knew about the Vinroots. They were the wealthiest people in Mossy Oak. Their name was on the library, the courthouse, and the art gallery. The Vinroots owned half of Main Street as well as Sky Valley Vineyards, which attracted visitors from all over the world.

Was it possible that the painting I'd spied in the living room of Pressly's brother's house really had been a Picasso?

Sloan leaned forward to fill me in on the dirt. "Pressly took over last fall. Right after Tamsen got fired."

I vaguely recalled Sloane being worried for her job when the manager of the vineyard was fired.

"That big mess with the embezzling," Gabi said. "Right?"

"Right. I guess they only trusted family after that because that's when Pressly started."

"She's a single mom like you," I told Gabi.

"I remember her from middle school," Gabi said. "Cheerleader type. With great hair."

Gabi had grown up in Mossy Oak and had come back home after her husband died. She knew everyone in town.

"She has a shoe collection to die for," Sloane said.

"Pressly's staying with her brother," I said, trying to look nonchalant even as my blood heated to an uncomfortable level. "Do you know anything about him?"

"Not really," Sloane said.

"He was a few years younger," said Gabi.

My heart plummeted. "Oh."

"I did meet him once when all the shit was hitting the fan," Sloane said. She raised both eyebrows and gave a low whistle. "I can't remember a thing he said during the whole meeting. I was too busy staring at his perfect jawline."

I blew out a puff of breath. "You should see him shirtless."

"You saw Beckett Vinroot shirtless?"

Beckett Vinroot. A tingle ran down my spine at the sound of his name.

"The name rings a bell," Gabi said. "We should look him up."

"No," I said. "We can't."

"Not on your phone, we can't," Gabi said. "That thing is from the last century."

Sloane took her phone from her bag.

"I remember him playing little league with one of my cousins," Gabi said. "He was the only kid with glasses."

Sloane swiped her finger over her phone. "Nope, nope, nope. He's not on Facebook, Instagram, or Twitter."

Swipe, swipe, swipe. Her mouth dropped open. Bingo. She'd found him.

"Oh!" Sloane covered her mouth.

Gabi grabbed the phone and finished Sloane's sentence. "My. God."

I scrambled up to look over Gabi's shoulder and saw a picture of Pressly's brother fill the screen. My mouth watered. That was him all right. He wore a tuxedo and rectangular black glasses. I pulled the phone closer, trying to determine the color of his eyes. Were they brown or green? All I could tell was that they were dark and stormy. *Intense.* Just as Pressly had warned me.

"Beckett Anderson Vinroot," Gabi said, reading his name under the photo. "My, my, my. You turned out real nice. You grew into those glasses all right."

I jerked the phone from Gabi's grasp and scanned the article below the photo.

Thirty-three-year-old Vinroot plays a vital role in the success of his family's multi-million dollar company.

The article went on to detail Vinroot Enterprises' hostile takeover of a tech company in the UK.

Mia came in as we were passing around Sloane's phone to gape at Beckett. She smelled like cigarette smoke, and my first thought was to remind her of her New Year's resolution to quit, but one look at her bloodshot eyes and disheveled hair and I cut her some slack. She worked longer hours than Thatcher and Gabi combined.

"Who's that?" She grabbed the phone and used her thumb and forefinger to enlarge the photo of Beckett.

"Some guy Lacey is stalking," Gabi told her.

"I'm not stalking him."

"And he's my boss," Sloan said. "Sort of. More like my boss's boss's boss…"

"Just as long as he isn't joining the book club." Mia took off her coat and draped it over the counter. "Thatcher threatened to find a guy for the group."

"We already have a guy," said Thatcher as he walked into the room. "Me."

"You don't count." Gabi leaned forward to dive into the box of books on the coffee table. "Can we look now? Everyone's here."

"Not Kennedy," Mia said, rolling up her sleeves and untucking her blouse.

"Kennedy's at a yoga retreat in Asheville," I said.

"Again?" Mia rolled her eyes. "She works more than I do."

"She's killing it," Sloane agreed.

"Hey, why don't I count?" Thatcher asked. "Last time I checked, I was a man."

"You're too nice," said Gabi. "You definitely don't count."

Thatcher took a seat in the only club chair, pretending to be offended. We all knew he secretly loved the attention we gave him.

"I've become irrelevant in my own bookshop," he complained.

"You're not irrelevant." Mia kicked off her heels and perched on the arm of Thatcher's chair. She ruffled his hair. "But you need a trim."

"I'm getting another guy for this group," he threatened.

"Don't you dare," Mia said. "I mean it. I'm tired of men," she told Thatcher.

"Thanks a lot."

Mia sighed and pulled her feet from her high heels. "I have to get back to work," she said. "If we're going to talk books, we'd better get started."

"Back to work?" I asked. "It's so late."

"Crime never stops." She dove into the book box and started handing out the advance reader copies. "Not even in Azalea County."

Mia was an assistant district attorney and she was always catching up on a case, trying to manage a witness or convincing an unruly detective to cooperate. She lived and breathed crime and punishment. Even the novels she reviewed were thrillers.

When Mia handed me Miranda Lockhart's latest novel, *Beneath the Stars*, I forgot Beckett for a moment. I couldn't suppress a squeak of excitement as I laid eyes on the cover for the first time. Ms. Lockhart tortured her fans by only publishing once a year.

Everyone began talking at once, discussing their upcoming reads, the latest releases, and other book news.

"Brace yourself, Lacey," Thatcher said.

"Why?"

"Guess who's coming to Hyperbole's to promote her latest release?"

My jaw dropped open, and I clutched the book to my chest. "Miranda Lockhart is coming here?" I'd dreamed of meeting her for years. "Are you teasing?"

"No, I'm not teasing. I just got the confirmation today."

I jumped up and threw my arms around Thatcher. He stood up just in time to catch me.

"You're the best boss in the world!" I hugged his neck.

Thatcher laughed and patted my back. "You're only saying that because I give you a good discount."

"Don't forget the free coffee." I hugged him harder.

"Thanks for the compliment, but I didn't do anything. Her agent set it up. Said they were doing a small-town tour."

"Thank God I live in a small town!" I'd never been happier to live in Mossy Oak. This news was exactly what I needed to forget about Beckett Vinroot for a while.

I cracked open the book, eager to meet my new book boyfriend.

Chapter Six

The next day my phone rang while I was walking Aslan. It was Pressly, and she needed a favor.

"Is there any way you can pick up Summer from school today?"

I could hear the tears of frustration in her voice. "I know it's a lot to ask, but I don't have anyone else—"

"Absolutely," I said, cutting her off. "But what about your brother? Can't he help you?"

"I think Beckett's in New York, or maybe Los Angeles. I can't keep up with his crazy schedule."

Curiosity flooded me. "What exactly does your brother do?"

Pressly paused. "Nobody knows," she said. "If there's a problem in the company, Beckett fixes it. He's a genius. Did you notice how the entire house is electronic?"

I'd noticed. I'd had a hard time finding the refrigerator the first time I was in the kitchen. A keypad on the wall controlled seamless cabinets that opened to reveal all the appliances. His kitchen was like a stark spaceship decorated in shades of white.

"Beckett wired the house for fun one weekend because he was bored. I think he changes the security code for the same reason."

"Sounds riveting."

Pressly laughed. "He's the same annoying little brother he used to be, except now he towers over me."

Aslan tugged me to a halt at the top of the hill. We were in the habit of stopping here. Aslan had his favorite tree, and while he peed I looked out on my favorite view of the rolling valley of grapevines.

"Summer gets out at three thirty," Pressly said. "And ballet class is at four o'clock at Blossom's. I'll pay you for your time."

"No need," I said. "What are friends for? I just need to check with my boss and make sure I can leave to go get her."

Pressly sighed. "I would send the hotel courtesy van, but Summer threatened to stop talking to me if I did that again. Things are difficult enough as it is between us."

"It's no big deal. My boss is a sweetheart. He won't mind."

"Thanks Lacey," she said. "Let's get drinks this weekend. First round is on me."

"Sounds good."

"There's a live band at the Inn on Friday. We could meet there. Bring your book club friends. It's time I met some new people in this town."

"Damn right." I was proud of Pressly for making the effort. Since I'd known her, she'd been immersed in work or mom life.

"Gotta go," Pressly said. "Summer's ballet bag is in the mudroom. Don't forget to grab her snack."

"Okay, as long as I can figure out how to open the fridge."

We shared a laugh and then hung up. I stood staring out at the view for a long moment, watching a patch of smoke rise from the rows of grapevines. Crews of workers crawled through the valley, trimming vines and stacking the prunings on trucks.

I'd come to Mossy Oak on a whim, craving small town life. After a year of living in Cincinnati, Ohio, I'd become restless. The man I'd been dating casually had wanted more, but I couldn't give it. My job at a college bookstore had paid peanuts, and the weather was too unpredictable to have a good dog-walking service on the side. I'd needed a change, and Mossy Oak had been the perfect choice.

A year had gone by as quickly as turning a page. My lease was up in a few months, and I didn't have a plan. I'd never stayed this long in one place before, but I couldn't imagine leaving Mossy Oak. The thought of starting over—finding a new job, new dogs to walk, new friends—had always excited me in the past, but now it had never seemed so unappealing.

Aslan tugged on the leash, and I tore my gaze from the view to glance down at him. I would miss Aslan more than anything when I left Mossy Oak.

"Summer does ballet?" I asked him.

He answered me with a crooked grin and a soulful stare.

We finished our walk, and I secured Aslan back in the mudroom before venturing into the kitchen. The house was eerily quiet. I missed the horrible music Beckett blasted while he was "working."

The house seemed too big and empty without him.

* * *

I pulled up in the carpool line at Pinewood Elementary behind a Chevy Suburban with a stick-family decal in the back window. One of the stick figures was delivering a high kick to the face of the basketball-toting figure next to it. I guessed either this family had a sick sense of humor or their kid liked martial arts.

Putting my car into park, I laid the seat back and prepared for a few blissful minutes of uninterrupted reading. Usually I would have already finished the new Miranda Lockhart romance, but I was having a hard time falling into her latest story. Maybe it was because I couldn't picture anyone other than Beckett Vinroot as the leading man.

I grabbed my book and flipped it to the front cover. The cover model was a dark-haired man in a suit carrying a bouquet of roses. His perfect jawline was dusted with just the right amount of beard scruff. His eyes blazed, promising sinful nights more romantic than the Paris backdrop behind him. He was hot enough to make my cheeks burn, but he had nothing on Beckett.

The memory of Beckett pumping iron, his chest muscles rippling with each movement, had me rolling down the window to let in some fresh cold air.

"Hi!" Came a high-pitched voice from the other side of my window.

"Shit!" I jumped when I saw a woman standing outside the car.

"I didn't mean to scare you," she said. "I thought you saw me." She smiled, revealing a row of perfect white teeth. "You rolled down the window."

I dropped the book into my lap and turned to face her. Dressed for the cold weather, she wore a puffy coat, a knit hat, and gloves. Oversized sunglasses covered the top half of her face.

"I'm Chelsea." She extended a gloved wave. "Kaylee's mom?"

I nodded as if I knew who the hell Kaylee was.

"Are you a nanny?"

"A nanny? No. I'm just doing a favor for a friend."

"The new kid?"

"Um...yeah."

"It's too bad her mom has to work such long hours. Kaylee told me Summer's mom never volunteers or brings snacks." She gave me an appraising look. "I can't imagine handing off my responsibilities as a mother to anyone else. This time is precious, you know?"

I shook my head. "Not really," I said. "I'm not Summer's mom, but I know she is doing the best she can."

"I didn't mean Summer's mom is doing anything wrong. But it won't be long until the girls are off to college. I don't want to waste a moment. I'm not judging or anything." She pointed to her perfect-toothed smile. "This is a judgement-free zone."

Her eyes slid over my face, lingering on the diamond stud piercing my nose. It was probably good she couldn't see my tattoos under my jacket.

"How old are you anyway?"

"Twenty-five."

She blew out a relieved breath. "I'm only thirty-two. And hold-ing." She tugged the glove off her right hand and pulled a phone out of her coat pocket. "Let me get your number."

"Why?"

Her finger hovered over the screen, and her eyebrows bunched together. "So we can arrange for a sleepover," she said. *Duh.*

"You had better call Pressly for arrangements."

"Okay." She swiped her finger over her phone a few times. "What's her number?"

Knowing Pressly wouldn't want me giving her number to a stranger, I offered to take hers instead.

"Have her call me ASAP," she said. "If Summer can't come for the sleepover, I'll have to invite someone else," she warned.

"I'll be sure to tell her."

Chelsea took a few steps back from the car. "By the way, you have to cut your engine."

"What?"

"Our kids breathe here," she said, spreading her arms as wide as her smile.

I pressed the button to roll up the window, then turned off the car. Chelsea gave me the thumbs-up sign as she opened the door to the Suburban and stepped up on the running board. I smiled and returned Chelsea's thumbs-up gesture, but I'd rather have been giving her another finger.

She'd just cost me precious reading time.

* * *

"Did you bring Aslan?" Summer asked when she opened the car door.

"No," I said. "Sorry."

"It's okay," she said, as if expecting to be disappointed. A frown settled over her delicate features.

"Hungry?" I offered her the healthy snack her mother had packed.

Summer shrugged and stared out the window.

"We can stop for ice cream if you want. There's enough time."

Summer didn't spare me a glance. "I'm not allowed to eat ice cream before ballet," she said. "It's junk food."

"Oh? I thought it was one of the major food groups."

Summer shook her head, entirely too serious. "I don't think so."

We were quiet for a minute as I maneuvered the car through after-school traffic. "So. Ballet, huh? You like it?"

Summer shrugged again.

"I took dance as a kid, too," I said. "I was horrible." I had been worse than horrible. I'd been terrified of the dance teacher, Madame Newberry, who used to crack our knuckles with a ruler if we missed a step. "Are you any good?"

"Not really."

"Do you like it?"

"No."

"What do you like?"

Another shrug.

"You like reading?"

She glanced at me warily. "I guess."

"Me too." I was struck with an idea as we turned onto Main Street. "We have a little time before ballet. Would you like to stop at Hyperbole's?"

"The bookshop? Can we?" Summer's eyes lit up, and I recognized the gleam of book lust. Being with Summer was like taking a trip back in time to my childhood when I'd escaped into my bookshelf to hide from my problems.

I slowed the car as we pulled up to Hyperbole's. Summer spied the window display, and her eyes went wide.

"Oh!" She pressed her nose to the window. "It's Obsidia."

"You know the books?"

"Sure. Doesn't everybody?"

I laughed. "Everybody who counts."

Summer looked at me from under her bangs, and I swear I saw the glimmer of a smile.

"What else do you like to read?" I asked, maneuvering into a parking spot.

Summer listed out her favorite books as we headed into the best bookshop in the world. I wasn't biased just because I worked there. The shop was a slice of heaven for any book lover. Tucked between a yoga studio and a chocolate shop, Hyperbole's Bookshop rose tall and narrow from the herringbone sidewalk of Main Street. The gleaming windows featured ever-changing displays of book worlds, inviting readers to step inside and escape between their pages. Comfy reading nooks nestled between the aisles, begging bookworms to curl up for a page or a dozen.

I'd worked at bookstores across the country, but none of them compared to Hyperbole's.

As we strolled over to Thatcher's latest window display, Summer finished her long list of books she liked to read. Things had sure changed a lot since I'd read middle-grade fiction.

"My mother would have freaked out if I'd read apocalypse stuff when I was your age," I told her.

"My mom doesn't pay attention to what I read. I mostly check books out at the library, or Uncle Kit gets them for me. He got me the best Christmas present last year," she said. "Signed copies of the Warrior Clan series. All eight books!"

"Uncle Kit?" A tingle raced down my spine at the thought of her uncle. "Is that what you call him?"

Her cheeks turned pink. "It was easier to say when I was a kid," she admitted.

I refrained from pointing out that she *was* still a kid. "Your uncle likes to read?"

She gave me a strange look. "Doesn't everyone?"

Summer couldn't suppress her smile when she saw Thatcher's masterpiece up close. Thatcher went all out for his displays, going so far as to replicate entire fictional towns complete with functional fountains and shooting stars.

His latest display depicted the craggy lilac mountains and cloudless fuchsia skies of Obsidia, home of the clan of Cat Warriors. The middle-grade series featuring battle-ready cats willing to defend their realm at all costs dominated the best-seller list.

"What do you think?"

I turned and saw Thatcher standing a few feet away. Eyes pinned on Summer, he barely acknowledged me. Thatcher took his window art so seriously that a negative review from his target audience could ruin his day.

Summer transferred her wide eyes to Thatcher. "It's amazing."

"Thanks." Thatcher studied his masterpiece with a critical eye. "I couldn't decide if I should add the lake or not," he said. "What do you think?"

"You've read the books?" Summer's eyes were brighter than the cat's eyes in the display.

Thatcher nodded. "I've read every book in here."

Summer's mouth dropped open as she surveyed the crowded shelves climbing to the ceiling.

"Don't listen to him," I said. "Thatcher wishes he had time to read all these books, but he has to work for a living. This is his shop."

Summer's eyes fixed on Thatcher with renewed admiration. He'd just been elevated to superhero status.

"Have you ever shopped here before?" he asked Summer. When she shook her head, Thatcher reached into his pocket and pulled out a card. "Here. This is good for one free book of your choice."

"Any book?" Her eyes were huge in her tiny face.

"Sure." Thatcher made a sweeping gesture to encompass the entire store on his way back to the register. "Anything you like," he called over his shoulder.

Summer took the card and clutched it to her chest.

"Do you want to use it now?"

She shook her head. "I'll save it to use with Uncle Kit."

"You should come on Saturday." My heart beat double-time at the thought of seeing Beckett again. "I'm working all day."

Chapter Seven

"Be careful up there, Miss Lacey!"

I was standing ten feet up on a rolling library ladder, reaching for a book. At the sound of my name, I looked down and froze.

An emotion so acute I could only describe it as panic surged through me at seeing him again. *Beckett.* He made me feel hot and tingly and vulnerable, as if every dirty thought I'd had about him was printed across my chest.

He looked different when fully dressed. I couldn't see those tight abs, but I knew they were under there. His neatly combed hair and black glasses lent him the look of a superhero in disguise.

Oh God. The way he was looking at me made me feel like I was bursting into flames. He probably remembered me scolding him. I was embarrassed for both of us. My cheeks flamed.

"I'm fine."

I forced my voice to sound that way, but I was anything but fine. I was on fire. Those fantasies I'd been having every time I closed my eyes rushed back to haunt me. I'd dreamed about Beckett just last night.

I tore my gaze away from him and reached for the book.

Ah. That was better. When my hand closed around the slim

volume, I relaxed, drawing comfort from the words within the leather binding. *Wuthering Heights* was one of my favorites. Heathcliff had been my first love, Catherine my first strong heroine.

I pulled the book from the shelf and glanced at it briefly, appreciating the leather cover engraved with flowing script before slipping it in my bag. One glance down told me Beckett was still staring up at me as I descended the ladder. I was nervous as a twice-jilted bride on her wedding day to see him again, but at least I was wearing my good-butt jeans.

"Weren't you scared up there?" Summer eyed the ladder with huge blue eyes.

"Not at all." I pulled the Emily Brontë novel from my bag and showed it to Summer. "Check it out. This is what I was reading at your age."

Summer took the book and flipped through the first few pages, a frown creasing her brow.

"Isn't she a little young for Brontë?" Beckett asked.

His voice was as I remembered it, significantly Southern with a touch of raspy gravel.

I couldn't help challenging him. "Have you read it?"

Beckett nodded. "In school," he said. "Not for pleasure."

A sudden flush of warmth spread through me as I pictured Beckett reading—or doing *anything*—for pleasure. He was close enough I could smell the spicy scent of his aftershave. His skin was smooth and January pale, with a faint shadow on his chiseled jaw. A thrill ran through me to discover the color of his eyes— brown with flecks of mossy green, rich and earthy like the forest floor.

Summer handed *Wuthering Heights* back to me. "I'm here for my free book. Can I really choose anything I want?"

"None of that apocalypse crap." I shook my finger at her. "It will warp your brain."

"But romance novels are better?" Beckett asked, teasing me.

"*Much* better."

I hadn't meant for the words to come out all husky. Embarrassed, I cleared my throat and looked away from Beckett's knowing gaze.

"Are those real tattoos?" Summer asked.

"Summer." Beckett shot her a warning look.

Color bloomed in Summer's cheeks. "Sorry."

I reached out and patted her shoulder. "It's okay, kiddo." I'd prefer people ask about my tattoos rather than just gawk. "They're all real. They all have a story."

Her eyes lit up as they roamed over my arms. "Do you have them all over?"

"Nah." I shoved up the sleeve of my T-shirt to show the bare flesh of my shoulder. "Just the sleeves."

Beckett's green-brown eyes traced the intricate lines of my tattoos, stirring the flame inside me.

"I want to go upstairs," Summer said, grabbing his hand.

"Go on up. I'll be there in a minute."

"Don't take forever," she whined.

"I won't."

Summer skipped off, leaving us alone in the crowded store. I clutched the Brontë novel to my chest as if it would protect me from Beckett's scrutiny.

"You're the dog walker," he accused.

Adrenaline shot through me as his eyes slowly raked over me, lingering on the bookshop name spelled across my chest before jumping back to mine.

"That's me."

His lips curved. "I thought you'd be..." His grin widened. "Never mind." He shook his head.

I should be used to people judging me. They took one look at my tattoos and nose ring and thought they knew what kind of person I was.

"You thought I'd be what?" I blasted him with an icy squint.

"I don't know." A laugh bubbled through his words. "A granny?"

I froze. Confusion scrunched my face. "A what?"

He pointed to his glasses. "I don't wear these when I lift. I couldn't really see you." His eyes moved over my hair, then down my body. "Your voice reminded me of this granny librarian we had at school."

I patted the curls that had escaped my bun. Tucking them back into place, I started walking again. My heart was doing a crazy pitter-patter, and I needed to move in an attempt to keep up. "I'll take that as a compliment," I told him. "I love libraries."

"So, you're Lacey Donovan?"

I shot him a glare. "I think we established that, Mr. Vinroot."

"It's Beckett."

"Okay, Beckett." His name on my lips tasted sweet. I savored it for a moment, getting lost in those mossy eyes. After a moment, I snapped out of my trance. "How's Aslan?"

Beckett frowned. "Annoying."

"But adorable?"

One eyebrow raised over the black frames of his glasses. "That's debatable," he said. "Where did he get that name? He's a lot more like the Cowardly Lion from Wizard of Oz than a C. S. Lewis creature."

I couldn't help being impressed that Beckett knew *The Chronicles of Narnia*. The reference to Aslan went right over most people's heads.

"I named him." I planted my hands on my hips. "You're not thinking of returning him?"

Beckett shook his head. "He's not mine to return. Summer is happy, and Peppy adores him." He lifted his shoulders. "It doesn't matter what I think. I'm never home anyway."

I looked up at the children's loft where Summer sat on a beanbag surrounded by books. She seemed happy there. *Who wouldn't be?*

Beckett followed my glance. "I should go," he said. "I promised to help her pick out the perfect book." He glanced around the store, taking in the elaborate display tables and the reading corners tucked at the ends of the aisles. He blew out a breath. "We might be here all day."

I laughed. "I can't think of a better way to spend my time."

Beckett's eyes dropped to my inked sleeves, scanning every inch of my exposed skin. "You like to read?"

I raised both eyebrows. "Who doesn't?"

Beckett's mouth moved in a brief smile when he realized I was teasing him. "Not everybody."

"Really? I don't see any of those people." I made a show of glancing around the crowded aisles. Hyperbole's was a magical place, vibrating with energy.

Beckett glanced around the bustling bookshop, then up at Summer. "I like this place. If you have a minute, maybe you can show me around?"

Heat crawled up my chest at the look in his eyes. The image of him lying on the weight bench, muscles gleaming as he pumped iron, flashed before my eyes. A man who looked like him and liked to read? Beckett was honestly too good to be true. A warning bell blasted in my head, but I ignored it. He was so tall that I had to tilt my head back to fix my curious eyes on him.

"I thought you grew up here," I said.

Green fire sparked in his eyes. "How'd you know that?"

I was no good at lying, so I didn't even try. "I Googled you."

One dark eyebrow raised, bringing my heart rate with it. "Why'd you do that?"

I crossed my arms over the book at my chest, remembering the origin of my anger. "I wanted to see who'd yelled at me."

His mouth thinned. "I didn't yell at you."

His eyes were so gorgeous. And he smelled yummy. It was hard to remember what had made me so mad the first time we'd met. Then, I recalled the way he'd told me to find the door behind me. "You were rude," I mustered.

"That's not the same as yelling."

"Close enough."

He smiled—a genuine smile that reached his amazing green-brown eyes, and made my belly shimmy in a little happy dance. His mouth in full smile mode was so distracting that I nearly plowed over a lady crouched in front of the self-help shelf. I apologized and forced myself to focus on reality. This wasn't one of my romance novels where a gorgeous man swept a woman off her feet at their first meeting. This was real life, and I had books to gather. I started off toward non-fiction.

Beckett caught up to me in one determined stride. Did I mention he was tall? Those long legs only needed one step to my three.

"How about that tour?" he asked.

I smothered a sigh. He was entirely too distracting. That mouth. Those eyes. That scent, like a walk through the forest on a rainy day.

"This is the local section." I kept my tone professional as we strolled through the aisles. "We have signed copies by resident authors and books on hiking trails and other Blue Ridge Mountains attractions." I was all business as I led Beckett around the store. "Hyperbole's is the best bookshop in the world, and I'm not just saying that because I work here."

We stopped at the end of the aisle to let a mother pushing her stroller walk by.

Beckett reached out and took my elbow as I started to walk again. "What would I find out about you if I Googled you, Lacey Donovan?"

My name on his lips sent a shiver through me. "Nothing at all." The breathless quality of my voice surprised me. "I don't do social media."

Beckett's dark brows slashed together. "Not at all?"

"Only my book reviews for the BRBC."

But Beckett wasn't listening. He was looking at the romance section where an employee stood on a ladder hanging paper-mâché hearts from the ceiling. There was a life-size cardboard cutout of Miranda Lockhart with her arms looped around the neck of a very attractive shirtless man. She was wearing a man's white dress-shirt, her signature scarlet lipstick, and nothing else. The dark-haired man wore only a pair of plaid pajamas, and his face was covered in kiss marks that matched Miranda's lipstick. Behind the cutout, a ten-foot-tall Eiffel Tower constructed of gold mylar stretched to the ceiling. It was so big and bright, Beckett had to shade his eyes.

"Miranda Lockhart is coming next month to promote her latest book," I said, laughing at his pained expression.

"You're a fan?"

"I live and breathe Miranda Lockhart. I can't wait to meet her."

He raised a brow at the display. "That's a lot of fuss," he said.

From the look on Beckett's face, I assumed he thought romance novels were a waste of paper. "You probably like mysteries or true crime?"

His shoulders lifted in a shrug. "I read a bit of everything," he said. "I like romance too." He gestured at the hearts falling from the ceiling.

My insides did a little jig at the suggestion in his tone, but I did my best to ignore it. "Romance is great between the pages, but not so much in real life."

Beckett's eyes narrowed on me. "You don't really believe that?"

"I really do. Love is just make believe—the creation of an imaginative mind. Kind of like alternate realms in a science-fiction novel, love is a tool writers use to tell a story."

Beckett made a strangled sound. "That's... blasphemous."

I laughed at his dramatic reaction. "It's true."

Beckett looked offended. "You adore *Wuthering Heights*, but you don't believe in love?"

"Romance is different in books," I said. "There's always a happy ending. And besides, guys like Heathcliff don't really exist."

Beckett took a step closer. The way he looked at me made me feel as if he could see all the way inside me. I felt exposed, and I clutched the book tighter to my chest.

"Go out with me," he said. "I'll show you Heathcliff."

I should have laughed at the cheesy line, but my throat was too tight for any sound to escape. I shook my head instead.

Beckett's eyebrows drew together, and his eyes flicked to my left hand. "Are you married?"

"No."

"Serious boyfriend?"

I bit my lip. "No." *Not for a very long time.*

Beckett's eyes lingered on the small diamond stud in my right nostril. One dark eyebrow ticked up. "Serious girlfriend?"

I shook my head. "You think I'm a lesbian because I have a nose ring?"

His eyes crinkled in the corners. "Are you?"

I rolled my eyes. "Not that it's any of your business, but no. I'm not gay. I just think romance is for books."

Beckett's mouth curved in a half smile that had one dimple popping. "I'm officially making it my mission to prove you wrong."

My heart raced, and my belly performed a gymnastics routine. "No thanks," I said. "I'm not interested."

Beckett studied me, and my cheeks flamed bright pink. I was the world's worst liar. My face gave everything away. My mind was definitely on board with dating Beckett. As were other parts of my body. But my heart, the most important part, was not into it. My heart was terrified.

Don't do it, my heart advised. Each pulsing throb in my head reminded me of the ache I'd endured. The pain I didn't want to repeat. It was so much safer not to get involved with a man.

"We could be friends," I suggested.

The heat in Beckett's eyes dimmed. "I don't do friends. I'm too busy."

My blood stopped rushing, my heart immediately calming. I'd listened to the right body part. I'd made the right decision.

"Good thing I said no." I turned on my heel to leave. "If you don't have time for friends, you don't have time to date me."

I walked away, hoping he enjoyed the view of my good-butt jeans.

Chapter Eight

A few days later, I picked Summer up from ballet. Pressly was working late, and Beckett was MIA, but I didn't mind. I wanted to see the kiddo. I even brought her a surprise.

"It's not really from me," I said, watching Summer's eyes catch fire as she slid the book from the bag. "It's from Thatcher. He gets a lot of advance reader copies..." My words trailed off and emotion choked my throat.

Like a blossom unfolding to the first ray of dawn, Summer's smile beamed. "The new Clan series? But it doesn't come out for months."

"Thatcher is magic like that."

Her smile grew and then faded as she became serious once again. "I wish I could start now."

I reached over and flipped on the light above her visor. "There you go."

"But my mom says it distracts her too much."

"My dad never let me either."

We exchanged a knowing eye roll, then Summer grinned and turned her attention to her book. I heard her surprised gasp and knew she'd seen the author's signature on the title page.

"It's signed!" Summer squealed again, examining the page.

"I know." Having a signed copy of a book was worth more than gold. I only had a few, but they were some of my cherished possessions. I packed my signed books carefully with each move. Someday, when I settled down permanently, they would occupy a shelf of their own.

The remaining ride to Beckett's mountain house was quiet, filled only with Summer's sighs and bursts of laughter.

I'd told Pressly I would stay until she got off work. After taking Aslan for a walk, Summer and I settled down for some serious reading.

The L-shaped sofa had been cleaned and was back to being ivory. I was reluctant to sit on it.

"Why is everything in here white?" I asked Summer.

She looked up from her sprawled position in the corner of the sofa with a shrug. "I dunno. Uncle Kit isn't good at decorating."

I laughed, knowing full well Beckett had paid someone a lot of money to cultivate the white-on-white aesthetic.

Who has a white rug? Someone who is never home to walk on it.

After a moment's hesitation, I joined Summer on the sofa. It was surprisingly comfortable. Sinking into the cushions, I stroked Aslan's coarse fur and felt a sense of calm wash over me. Maybe there was something to the lack of color.

Beyond the windows, the snow-capped peaks of the mountains gleamed in the moonlight. I bet the sunsets were amazing from this spot.

Did Beckett ever make time to sit and watch the sunset?

No, he seemed more of a sunrise kind of guy. I could imagine him waking early and padding out onto the eastern-facing deck with a mug of coffee in his hand.

Did Beckett drink coffee? I had no idea. I hadn't seen any evidence of a coffeemaker. Then again, it had taken me nearly a week to locate the refrigerator hidden behind the seamless cabinet.

I decided, for the sake of my fantasy, that Beckett did drink coffee, and he took it black. A no-nonsense man like him wouldn't want his caffeine laced with milk or sugar. He'd want it strong and bitter, serving its purpose as a morning wakeup call. Then again... He did wear socks with rubber duckies. Maybe he liked cream and sugar after all.

In my fantasy, Beckett was shirtless. He wore a pair of pajama bottoms that hung off his lean hips and no socks. Bracing his elbows on the railing, he leaned artfully, watching the sun rise over the horizon. His hair would be tousled from sleep, his jaw dusted with the shadow of his dark beard, and his eyes bright. He would smell of clean sheets, and he would turn to me, opening his arms...

"Uncle Kit!" Summer cried.

My pulse hammered, and I was pulled from my fantasy to see Beckett striding down the hall in a suit that probably cost more than my entire wardrobe. His eyes found me, and a tingle raced down my spine. My cheeks flushed as I recalled I was about to walk into his arms in my little dreamworld.

"Look what Miss Lacey brought me!" Summer said, waving the book at him.

Beckett walked up behind the couch and took the book from Summer. He examined the cover, which featured two sword-wielding cats in leather regalia.

"How is it so far?"

"I'm only twenty pages in." She grabbed the book and resumed reading. One flip of the page and Summer was back in the world of cat warriors—adults forgotten.

Beckett's gaze met mine, and we exchanged a smile over Summer's head. My stomach did a few cartwheels at the sight of his dimple winking.

"Hello, Lacey," he said.

A shiver rolled through me. "Hello, Beckett."

He walked into the kitchen, and I tried not to drool as he peeled off his suit jacket. He draped the jacket over a stool and loosened his tie. A shadow of beard clung to his jaw, and his eyes looked tired.

I wondered where he'd been the last few days. The house had felt so empty while he'd been gone.

"Where's your mom?" he asked Summer.

She ignored him, her eyes moving rapidly over the page.

"She's working late," I said. "I guess I can go now that you're here." Turning down the corner of the page I hadn't been reading, I set the book aside and reached for my boots.

Beckett came up behind me as I bent over the laces. "What are you reading?" he asked.

His voice sent a thrill down my spine. I turned and saw him looming close. Without waiting for permission, Beckett reached down and picked up my book.

"How is it?" His eyebrow quirked above the rectangular frames of his glasses. "Any good?"

I bent over my boots, letting my hair fall in front of my face to conceal my surprised expression. I'd expected a snide comment about my choice of reading material, or at least a jab at the cover model. Most people had no qualms in expressing their opinions about the inferiority of the romance genre, but Beckett seemed genuinely interested. When I finished lacing my boots, I peeked over my shoulder at him. He'd propped one hip on the back of the sofa and was reading a page from somewhere in the middle.

"It's not pulling me in like her books usually do," I confessed. Although I wasn't sure Miranda Lockhart was at fault. More likely my obsession with the man holding my book was to blame.

Beckett turned the book over to scan the blurb. "What's wrong with it?" he asked.

I watched his eyes drop down to the stunning photograph of the author.

"The hero," I told him.

Beckett's eyes flashed up at me, and he smiled warily. "The man's fault, is it? What's wrong with him?"

I grabbed my bag and hoisted it onto my shoulder. "He's too cocky."

Beckett grinned, making both dimples pop. "Powerful boss man with daddy issues who thinks every woman wants to go to bed with him?"

I nodded, heart thumping as our eyes collided. He seemed to know a thing or two about cocky heroes.

"What else?"

"I don't know," I said, unsure if he was teasing me.

Beckett pushed his glasses up on his nose and stood from the sofa. "I looked up your reviews on the website," he said, walking into the kitchen. "I got the impression you have plenty to say."

My cheeks heated at the thought of Beckett stalking me online. "You honestly care what I think about romance novels?" I asked.

He turned to face me. "I like to talk books," he said. "It relaxes me."

His confession had the opposite effect on me. I'd never been more turned on in my life. A hot guy wanted to discuss books? Sign me up for the conversation.

"Stay for a glass of wine and some book talk?" he asked.

It was the most appealing invitation I'd had in years, and I didn't even like wine. "Okay."

Beckett carried my book with him to the kitchen and set it down on the counter. "Red or white?"

"Either." I didn't care for wine, so both choices were equally unappetizing.

I took a seat at the counter while Beckett went into the pantry. I only had a moment to get my reaction to him under control, and I feared it wasn't nearly enough time. A year might not be enough time, and no one's pantry was that big.

I hadn't been this attracted to a man in ages. Maybe never. I'd thought my longing for him was purely physical, but now I wasn't so sure. My attraction to him was magnetic. Mind, body, and soul. My heartbreak over Julian was a long time ago and absolutely forgotten when Beckett was around.

When he sauntered back into the kitchen looking sexier than Clark Kent and Heathcliff rolled into one, my heart skipped more than a beat. He was so gorgeous, there was no way I could ignore my physical reaction to him. My chest tightened, my skin felt taut, and every nerve stood on end.

Beckett poured, standing close enough for me to get a whiff of Old Spice and everything nice. When he sat down next to me, his pants inched up at the hem to show navy-blue socks printed with tiny Union Jack flags.

I smothered a laugh. "What's up with the socks?"

Beckett reached for his glass. "What about them?"

"Is that how you express yourself? Zany socks?"

"It's one of the ways." His voice was low, flirtatiously promising more. "To romance," he said, lifting his glass.

I frowned and tapped my glass to his. "To books."

Beckett's lips tipped up in a half smile before they opened and closed around the rim of the glass. There was something wicked in that little smile, and my temperature spiked in response. Was everything this man did sexy? Heat filled my cheeks as I brought the glass to my lips, fully expecting to find the wine horrible. To my surprise, the cool, crisp liquid slid over my tongue like liquid gold with a hint of vanilla.

"This is good."

Beckett nodded. "It's one of my favorite vintages."

I took another sip and savored the pop of flavor on my tongue. "I don't even like wine."

Beckett put his glass down and started to get up. "I'll get you something else."

I put my hand on his sleeve, right above the silver watch on his wrist that probably cost more than my car. Touching him made my heart beat wildly. I swallowed the lump in my throat. "It's okay."

Beckett slid back onto the stool beside me. Capturing my hand in his, he slid his thumb along the inside of my wrist where swirling lines of ink gathered. Fire blazed through me at his touch. My heart banged in my chest, warning me.

"I thought we were going to talk books," I said.

"Okay," he said, sweeping his thumb over my erratic pulse. "What do you want to talk about?"

I tugged my hand from his grasp, unable to think when he was touching me. Reaching for the book, I pretended to study the description while my heart recovered from Beckett's touch.

"This book almost seems like she's going through the motions," I said.

Beckett slid forward on his stool, moving closer to me to look at the book. "You think the author has given up?"

Mesmerized by the fullness of his lower lip, I watched his mouth move as he spoke. His words weren't heavily accented, but their pace was undeniably Southern. Everything moved slower in the South, including Beckett's drawl.

"Maybe," I said. "This book just isn't grabbing me." Our eyes met, and I hoped he couldn't guess the real reason I couldn't escape into the book: him.

"Give it a little more time," he suggested. "I'm sure they will be forced into spending a month in Europe together any page now. With a little wining and dining they will be right on track for a happy ending."

I tensed and then realized he was teasing me about the predictability of romance novels. "I thought you were a romantic," I said.

"I am." He reached for his wine and sipped slowly. "I could show you," he suggested. "Go on a date with me."

My cheeks burned, and I looked down at the photograph of Miranda Lockhart on the back of the book. She had perfectly highlighted brown hair, every wavy strand in place. My hair was always a crazy mess.

"I'm not even your type."

His smile faded and he set his glass down with a clink. "Why would you say that?"

I gestured between us. "Isn't it obvious?"

His frown deepened. "Not to me."

"You own a winery," I said. "I don't even like wine."

His wicked grin returned. "I have other beverages."

"I should go," I said.

"You should stay." Leaning closer, he tugged on a curl that had escaped my ponytail.

I shivered as the curl snapped back into place. Beckett was too close; another inch and I would be tasting the wine on his lips. His eyes scorched mine. Having this man's full attention on me was like being set on fire. My blood roared, echoing in my head.

"Stay."

My heart hammered at the soft suggestion in his voice. My pulse thrashed against my wrist where Beckett's thumb had swept lazy circles. Longing sliced my heart, and the pain of the emotion brought me back to my senses.

"I can't." I slid off the stool. "I need to go."

Beckett stood. "I'll walk you out."

"No need."

I felt Beckett's eyes on me while I gathered my belongings and said goodbye to Aslan and Summer. When I walked to the door, he came up behind me and helped me with my coat. He insisted on walking me to my car and opening my door. When I glanced in the rearview mirror, I saw him standing with his hands in his pockets staring after me.

I didn't realize until I got home that I'd forgotten my book.

Chapter Nine

"This is different," I said, raising my voice to be heard over the live band.

It was Friday night and Mia, Gabi, and I were sitting at a table at Sky Valley Vineyards Inn. Sloane was on the dance floor letting off steam and Pressly was joining us as soon as she got off work.

"I haven't been here in ages," Gabi said, glancing around.

The last time I'd been to the bar at the inn, it had been a stuffy place with fifteen-dollar cocktails and a clientele more my parents' age. Tonight it was crowded with a healthy mix of locals and resort guests. It was an all-ages crowd, and most of them filled the dance floor.

"She looks good out there," Mia said, nodding at Sloane who was dancing her heart out.

"I'd join her," I said, "but my feet are killing me."

I'd worked a split shift at the bookshop and the hours in between had been filled with dogs. My feet were tired, but I was happy. The dogs were more to me than just a source of income; they were my loyal friends. My dogs were always happy to see me, they never held a grudge, and they never failed to make me laugh.

Whenever I moved to a new place, the first thing I did was

volunteer at a rescue center to walk dogs. It was not only a great way to get dog-walking clients but also to meet people. I could live comfortably, if modestly, on just my dog-walking salary, but I usually found another job too. Dogs were great, but they didn't talk back. I needed people in my life too. Glancing around at the friends I'd made in Mossy Oak, I couldn't imagine leaving them. I was beginning to think I'd finally found the place that made me want to put up that shelf for my autographed books.

Sloane collapsed in the chair next to mine. "Remind me why I want to get married so badly."

"Because you're crazy?" I suggested.

"Hush, Lacey," Gabi intervened, turning toward Sloane. "Because you want the love of your life. The kids. The Christmas dinners. The family vacations."

As Gabi ticked off the pluses for being in a marriage unit, Sloane's shoulders inched up to her ears. "The groom from the bachelor party keeps hitting on me," she said. She reached for my drink and took a gulp of my beer. "Ugh." She wrinkled her nose. "How do you drink that nasty stuff?" She raised her hand to wave over a waitress just as Pressly joined the table.

I introduced her to my friends.

"What book are you discussing?" Pressly asked, looking nervous.

"This is more like a drink and bitch session," Gabi said.

"Perfect." Pressly took a seat. "I have to pack up my child and drive to Atlanta for a weekend with her absentee father."

Sloane grabbed a pretzel from the bowl on the table and popped it in her mouth. "The groom from that bachelor party just asked for my number," she said.

Gabi took a sip of her wine. "My son is failing Spanish and might get kicked off the basketball team."

"The rapist I was prosecuting just walked on a technicality," Mia said.

Everyone turned to me, and I shrugged. "I cleaned up a lot of dog shit."

We were all laughing when our waitress stopped at the table.

"Hi, Becky," Pressly said.

The waitress smiled, clearly pleased the boss knew her name. "What can I get you Mrs. Carleton?"

We ordered our drinks, and when the waitress left, I asked about Summer.

"She's doing better." Pressly's tentative smile bloomed. "She's even made a friend."

"Kaylee?" I guessed, thinking of Chelsea at the carpool line. Had Summer been invited to the sleepover?

"No," Pressly said. "A little boy. It's sweet. He's another bookworm like her. I swear, between my daughter and my brother I'm surrounded by book lovers." Pressly suddenly remembered who she was talking to and smiled sheepishly. "No offense," she said to the table.

"No offense taken," I said amiably.

"Thank God Thatcher was too busy with his cabinets to come tonight," Mia said. "He might try to make us discuss books."

"Thatcher?" The color drained from Pressly's face. "You don't mean Thatcher Hayes?"

"Yeah," I said. "You know him?"

Pressly's eyes glazed over. She looked as if she was a million miles away. "I thought he lived in D.C."

"He moved to Mossy Oak to take over Hyperbole's about five years ago," Gabi said. "Before that, he was in the Army."

Thatcher was like a brother to all of us, but he and Gabi had known each other the longest. They were the closest, and they had the military in common. Gabi's husband was a soldier who had died in Afghanistan when Shane was four years old.

"Thatcher joined the Army?" Pressly asked, her eyebrows drawing together. "Did he fight?"

Gabi eyed Pressly warily. "He doesn't talk about his days in the military," she said. "How do you know Thatcher?"

Two splotches of color stained Pressly's cheeks. "Is he still sinfully good-looking?"

"Yes," we all replied at once.

Gabi pulled her phone from her purse and scrolled through her photos until she found one of Thatcher. He was sitting by a pool with a cocktail in his hand, wearing a shit-eating grin and a pair of sky-colored shorts that made his eyes look impossibly blue.

Pressly grabbed the phone for a closer look, her jaw dropping. The waitress deposited our drinks, and Pressly reached for her wine. She took a gulp, swallowed, and then looked each one of us in the eye. "This goes no further than this table."

We all nodded, leaning closer.

"I lost my virginity to him when I was sixteen years old," Pressly said.

Gabi gasped. "Holy shit."

"It was a long time ago," Pressly said, waving her hand in the air as if it didn't matter. "He was down here visiting his cousin for the summer. I was home from boarding school." She paused and drank another sip of wine, as if she needed to quench a fire in her throat. "I fell hard for him. We were inseparable that whole summer. Then he went back home. I went back to school. I never saw him again. End of story."

My shoulders sagged in disappointment. Thatcher was one of those dickwads who had used and discarded a girl. I was shocked to hear it. Pressly's story hit too close to home. *Julian.* It made my stomach churn.

"Disgusting," I said.

"No. It wasn't his fault. I didn't keep in touch either. We didn't have cell phones and internet back then." She poked a finger at me. "You're too young to remember."

I bristled. The problem with relationships had nothing to do with cell phones or internet. The problem was people making promises they couldn't keep and leaving without a trace.

"Here's to book boyfriends," I said, raising my glass. "God's apology for men in real life."

Everyone chimed in. "Cheers!"

Chapter Ten

"Let's do something other than talk about men," Mia suggested. "Come on! Let's dance!"

We shuffled onto the dance floor, joining a crowd that was drunk or well on their way to getting there. After a few songs, we were all dancing together. The band played an Irish song that everyone on the dance floor seemed to know.

Sloane grabbed Pressly's hand and they danced together, laughing. The lively music filled my body, making me want to dance, but I didn't know the steps.

Voices raised to compete with the singer on stage, and bodies bumped together as people flooded the dance floor. An arm brushed mine, and I backed into something soft and hard at the same time. A man.

He moved awkwardly and off beat, but he had nice form. My lips twitched in a smile as I watched his butt bump and grind to the wrong beat.

The beat of the song picked up pace and so did his dancing. He stumbled into his friend and then stepped closer to me, narrowly missing the toe of my blue velvet boot.

I scooted out of the way just in time.

"Sorry..." The apology froze on his lips as he turned to look at me. Recognition flashed in his eyes. "Hey! You're the dog walker chick from the park," he yelled over the music.

"You're the biker dude," I said.

"Wanna dance?"

"Is that what you call it?" I pointed to his clumsy gyrations.

He laughed and took my hand, then pulled me into his dysfunctional jig. It turned out he was even worse at dancing with a partner. But I wasn't any better. We made fools of ourselves, laughing the entire time.

The band started a slow dance and couples began forming. I took a step back, not wanting to give him the wrong idea. There was an awkward pause and then he asked, "Buy you a drink?"

I glanced over and saw Sloane and Gabi heading back to our table. Mia and Pressly were still on the dance floor. "I'm with my friends," I said, wiggling my fingers in a wave.

He lifted his hand, waving at them too. "Come on," he said. "One drink. To apologize for my atrocious dancing."

"I was bad too," I said.

"Yeah." He grinned. "You were."

He cocked his head toward the bar in question, and I nodded. Weaving our way through the tables, we made our way to the bar. I ordered my favorite beer and his dark eyebrows shot up. I thought he was going to question my choice of drink, but he surprised me by turning to the bartender and asking for the same.

"We have the same taste in beer," he said.

It wasn't as loud in the corner of the bar opposite the dance floor, and we could talk without shouting.

"What's your name?" he asked.

"Lacey."

"Nice to have a name," he said. "I've been calling you Cute Dog Walker Chick in my mind since that day at the park."

I smiled at the compliment, feeling a little guilty that I hadn't thought of him at all. My thoughts had been focused on a tall, dark, and brooding businessman.

"I'm Xan," he said. "I'm with a bachelor party. My best friend is getting married this summer."

His best friend was the guy hitting on Sloane. My skin prickled, and I dropped my eyes over him. If I had a type, which I didn't, Xan would be it. On paper he checked every box. Wiry, muscular frame. Dark skin. Messy man bun and tattoos snaking up both exposed forearms. His hipster style coordinated perfectly with my sexy librarian chic.

He had a slight edge to him that I suspected was not so much bad boy as it was introvert.

"Your friend was hitting on my friend," I said, taking a sip of my beer.

Xan scowled. "I'm not surprised. That marriage is doomed. I've told Marcus a hundred times he shouldn't go through with it."

I was taken by surprise at Xan's easy admission. I expected him to stand up for his friend.

"Does his fiancée know he cheats on her?" I asked.

Xan shrugged, taking a pull of his beer. "I don't think he's done anything. Not yet. He's wasted tonight and kind of a mess." Xan set his beer on the counter, his jaw clenched. "It's not like she doesn't have her own thing going on," he said. "She's never been faithful. Not since day one."

"Why the hell are they getting married?"

"Marcus is doing it for the money," Xan said. "Jane is loaded. He wants that life more than anything. Most of those guys in the wedding party are jerks. Family of the bride." He rolled his eyes. I can't believe Marcus wants to be rich enough to marry into that..." He trailed off, glancing up at me. "Never mind them," he said, flashing me a grin. "Tell me about you. I can't place your accent. Where are you from?"

"I moved here from Cincinnati," I said.

"Ah!" His eyes lit up. "Do you know West Chester, Ohio? It's right outside Cincinnati."

"I've been there," I said. "Small town, right? With a huge athletic complex where they have all sorts of competitions."

Xan nodded. "I go there every year with my team."

I imagined him on an adult soccer or softball league. That must be why he was in such good shape. "Team?" I asked.

"I coach a kid's triathlon team," he said, eyes lighting up. "They are already training for the race in West Chester."

I could tell by the way his smile gleamed that we were touching on one of Xan's passions. I probably wore a similar expression while discussing books.

My phone buzzed from the pocket of my dress, and I glanced across the room at my table of friends. Gabi was motioning for me to answer my phone.

"Sorry," I said to Xan. "My girls." I gestured to where my friends sat..

"Go ahead," Xan told me, nodding at the table.

I pulled out my phone, flipped it open, and saw a text from Gabi.

> Who's the hottie?

I flipped the phone shut without answering.

"I haven't seen a phone like that in years," Xan said. "I didn't think they still made those."

"They do," I said.

"Can I see it?"

I handed him my phone. It was a completely different species from the smartphones everyone carried, but it did what I needed.

"I remember texting on these." Xan grimaced. "It was painful."

"I'd rather talk than text."

"That's very..." Xan scratched the scruff of his beard. "Refreshing," he said finally.

"You were about to say something else," I said with a laugh.

"Maybe," he admitted. He toyed with my phone another moment. "Is it okay if I put my number in your contacts? Maybe we could go out dancing some time?"

I laughed, picturing us tearing up the dance floor. "I don't really date much," I said, trying to let him down easy.

He nodded, taking the rejection like a champ. "Friends, then?"

"Sure."

He smiled and entered his information. No questions. No protests. No pressure. Xan was easy. Our conversation flowed, and I wasn't on edge with him. When he handed me my phone, our fingers brushed, lingering for a moment too long. My eyes dropped to his mouth. He had nice lips. For a moment I allowed myself to think about kissing him.

My heart didn't race. My belly didn't flutter. There was nary a tingle anywhere on my body. I thought of Beckett's sensual mouth and a shiver of desire surged through me.

That was it. I was officially obsessed with Beckett. I needed to get him off my mind. I looked up from Xan's mouth to his eyes, and an idea popped into my head. I chewed my lip, deliberating.

"What?" Xan asked, raising his beer to his mouth. "Why are you looking at me like that?"

"Do you think you could kiss me?" I blurted.

Xan's eyes went round. "I thought we just agreed to be friends."

"We did. I'm kind of obsessing over someone, and I need to get him off my mind. This would be a friendly gesture."

He sipped his beer, then eyed me as he put it on the counter. He wiped the corner of his mouth with the back of his hand, not quite hiding his grin.

"What are friends for?" he asked.

It was like a moment in a novel—every element of romance in place. The handsome hero, the charming setting, the sexy slow music... This moment was so chock-full of tropes, it could fill a bookshelf.

We both leaned forward and our lips met. I closed my eyes as his mouth moved softly against mine. It was the merest brush of a kiss, a teaser of something more to come. It was sweet and sexy and almost shy.

Xan leaned back, his eyes searching mine. Even though the kiss had been nice, I had been thinking of another man the whole time. The experiment had backfired.

I took in a deep breath and then reached for my beer. "Thanks," I said and drank deeply.

"Anytime," he said, giving me a wink.

After a moment, the ease we'd had earlier returned, and Xan told me a little more about his traveling with his team.

The band broke into a popular song that everyone knew. "Friends dance, right?" he asked.

I grabbed his hand and slid off the stool. "You bet."

Chapter Eleven

"What was that?" Gabi asked.

Every eye was on me as I approached my table of friends.

"That was some kiss," Sloane said wistfully.

"Not really." I grabbed my lukewarm beer and drank.

"Who is he?" Gabi pulled out her phone. "What's his name?"

I grabbed her hand. "I don't want you to look him up. He's just a friend."

"A friend who put his tongue in your mouth," Gabi said.

I glared at her. "He *did not* put his tongue in my mouth. It wasn't like that. We are just friends."

Sloane poked me. "When are you going to give a guy a chance?"

"I'm not interested," I said.

"Name?" Gabi insisted, her finger hovering over her phone.

I glanced over at the bachelor party, looking for Xan. "He's coming over here in a minute."

"Hurry," Sloane said.

Another quick peek at the group on the other side of the bar told me Xan was still engaged with his friends. Even though our kiss hadn't sparked any chemistry between us, I was curious about him. "Xan," I said.

Gabi tapped her phone. "Last name?"

I pulled my phone from my pocket and checked his contact. "Carson." I peered at her phone as she tapped, curious about what she'd find. "He's probably not on there."

"Wanna bet?" Gabi grinned. "Xan Carson from Mossy Oak. Can't be too many of those." She turned her phone toward me. "That him?"

The screen showed a man posing on top of a Volkswagen bus, legs planted wide, arms outstretched. Behind him, a lake glistened in the setting sun and mountains framed the sky.

A smaller photo showed him on a beach, shirtless.

"That's him," I said. Grabbing the phone, I zoomed in on the photo. "Whoa..."

Xan's naked chest was a canvas of muscle and ink. Tribal tattoos curved over his shoulders and across his well-defined pecs. His long jet-black hair fanned out over his shoulders. He grinned at the camera. In person, his eyes were just as dark and full of zest.

"You have all the luck," Sloane said with a pout.

"Shh..." I glanced over my shoulder to see if Xan was coming.

"Text him and tell him to come over here," Mia said.

Gabi grabbed my phone and pressed call before I could stop her. She handed me back my phone and I flipped it shut, ending the call on the first ring.

"You guys are annoying," I told them, my words coming out a little slurred. Whoa. I sounded drunk. I felt it too. I'd only had two beers, but it felt more like five.

My phone buzzed, and I flipped it open to see a text from Xan. The restaurant was so dark that I had a hard time making out the words. I squinted at the screen, feeling more than two beers drunk.

"That was him," I said. "He's busy and might be awhile."

"Damn. I need to go," Mia said. "I have to get back to work."

"Work?" Sloane cried. "It's Friday night! And you just finished a big case."

Mia's eyes narrowed. "I just lost a big case. That can't happen again."

"I'm out too," Gabi said. "Mia is my ride, and Shane is by himself."

"Shane is fine," Sloane said. "He's a good kid."

"It's not him I'm worried about. It's his friends. All those older kids on the basketball team are teaching him stuff I'd rather he not know about yet." Gabi got up from the table and nodded at a group of women at the bar. "I just spotted Kaylee Andretti's mom over there. I don't want them to see me."

"I'm sure they know their principal cuts loose every once in a while," Sloane said.

"Well, I'm not about to advertise it." She grabbed her purse. "Let's go, Mia. I know you're dying for a smoke."

"I quit, remember?"

Everyone turned to gape at Mia. We all knew she was lying. She'd smelled like an ashtray when I'd hugged her.

"Give me a break." Mia got up from the table. "I just let a rapist walk. It wasn't a good time to quit smoking."

Gabi ushered Mia out of the bar.

"Let's get another round." Sloane signaled the waitress. "We can Uber back to town together."

"Beckett can come for me," Pressly said. "He's at home with Summer."

A slow smile tugged at my mouth. "How's Beckett doing?" I couldn't resist asking about him.

Pressly lifted her wineglass. "He's broodier than usual. Must be all the traveling he does for work. Or maybe he's having woman problems."

My shoulders sank. Beckett probably had a girl in every major city. I needed to get drunk. I pushed to my feet, wobbling a little. I leaned on the tabletop for balance.

"You okay?" Pressly asked.

"I'm fine. A little drunk, but that's the point."

"We need some food," Sloane said.

"Have some water," Pressly insisted.

I sank back to my chair. My eyelids drooped. I hadn't realized how tired I was.

I grabbed the menu and squinted. My vision doubled and I focused harder on the words. They danced in front of me and I laughed. The noise sounded funny to my ears. "Or maybe s'air?" I tried to stand up, but my knees buckled.

Sloane scraped her chair back from the table. "What's wrong with you?"

"She's drunk," Pressly said, grabbing my other arm.

"I need s'air," I said, slurring my words.

I stumbled out of the bar into the lobby of the hotel. Pressly and Sloane each took an arm and helped me outside. Once the doors closed behind us, I filled my lungs with the cold air. My head cleared, and for a moment I felt better. I glanced around at the twinkling lights in the trees, marveling at the beauty of the vineyard. Then the lights blurred as my vision doubled. The air chilled my heated skin. The tunnel in my vision closed in around me.

Sloane wrapped her arm around my waist, and I heard her voice from far away.

"I've never seen her drunk before," she said. "She can usually drink all of us under the table."

Pressly's hand was cool on my forehead. "We need to get her out of here."

"I can't drive," Sloane said.

"Me either."

I tried to take a step, but my feet were rooted to the ground. Everything felt heavy, most of all my sluggish thoughts. They weighed a ton, and my head ached with the extra burden of holding them.

"I'll call Thatcher," Sloane said. "He'll come."

"No!" Pressly's sharp voice rang out. "Please don't. I'll call Beckett."

I groaned. Trying to protest, I opened my mouth, but no words came out. I swayed on my feet, and Sloane helped lower me to the ground.

I could hear Pressly on the phone, more than likely talking to Beckett. I tried to plead with her, but it was no use. My mouth wouldn't work. Feeling exhausted, I sank against Sloane. A moment later, the narrow frame of my vision closed completely, plunging me into darkness.

* * *

Xan Carson [10:55pm]: LACEY! ru ok?

Xan Carson [10:57pm]: Wtf?

Xan Carson [10:59pm]: Plz answer me!!!!

Xan Carson [11:08pm]: Obvs u don't want 2 talk 2 me????

Xan Carson [11:22pm]: Can u plz talk 2 me????

Xan Carson [11:56pm]: Call me ASAP!!!!

Xan Carson [11:56pm]: Plz!!!

Chapter Twelve

A persistent ringing brought me back to life. Groaning, I cracked my eyes open only to shut them again. Sunlight scorched the backs of my eyes and my throat burned when I breathed. The ringing noise sounded again, and I realized it was in my head. It was loud enough to split my ears apart. I gritted my teeth, trying not to move.

I was lying on something firm, and I knew it wasn't the soft mattress in my apartment. Confusion fogged my brain.

Something wet tickled my cheek, so I opened my eyes and saw a furry snout in my face.

Aslan.

I must be at Pressly's place. Beckett's.

Patchy memories came back to me through the fog in my brain. I remembered the cold air in my lungs, the twinkling lights of the vineyard. Then, nothing.

Frustration settled over me as I searched for more memories and found them missing. Last night was a blank page. The harder I tried to focus on remembering, the more elusive the memories became.

I glanced around the room, hoping something would ring a bell, but I recognized nothing. The furniture was oversized but minimal. Shades closed over the windows, shrouding the room in darkness. I pushed the sheets down to see that I was wearing a baggy T-shirt and a pair of pink sweatpants. I didn't own a pair of pink sweatpants.

My stomach churned and my head spun. I pushed up from the bed and leaned on the nightstand for support. My hand landed on something cold and metallic. A pair of glasses. Rectangular, black-framed glasses. Beckett's glasses. Under the glasses was a copy of *Beneath the Stars*. *My* copy of *Beneath the Stars*.

I was in Beckett's room.

I groped my way along the wall until I reached the open door-way. Nausea warred inside me as I stumbled into the bathroom to the toilet. Every movement hurt. Every muscle ached.

Last night's memories had disappeared into a black hole of nothingness. The last thing I could remember was Sloane wrapping her arms around me as I sank to the stone walkway.

I used the counter to pull myself up and looked in the mirror. A hideous creature confronted me. With its wild hair, black-rimmed eyes, and ghostly pale skin, the thing looked like it had crawled out of a swamp.

I gasped, realizing the creature was me. My knees gave way, and I sank to the tile. Tears sprang to my eyes, and a sob ripped from my throat. I wrapped my arms around my knees and hugged them close, desperately wishing I could remember what had happened last night.

This was much worse than any hangover I'd ever had. I'd had some crazy nights, but I'd never forgotten whole chunks of time.

My stomach rolled and I crawled toward the toilet. I retched, but I had nothing left in my stomach. My throat burned with bile.

I figured it was safer to stay put in the bathroom than try to make it back to the bed. The last thing I wanted was to vomit on Beckett's thousand-thread-count sheets. I curled into a ball and rested my hot cheek on the tile.

The click of nails on the tile warned me of Aslan's approach a moment before he nudged his face against my shoulder. He circled me, then lay down against the hollow of my belly. I put my arm around his back and closed my eyes.

* * *

Strong arms wrapped around me. Hard muscles flexed and lifted me from the floor.

"You awake?"

Beckett's voice penetrated my ears. I remembered his smell—clean and woodsy like a forest trail in the summer. I turned my face into his sweater and laced my fingers around his neck. My mouth didn't seem to want to move, which was fine by me because my brain was too tired to formulate a sentence.

"Hang on, I'm taking you back to bed."

Any other time, that phrase coming from Beckett's mouth would have sent a thrill through my body. But right now, all I wanted to do was to sleep.

Beckett lowered me onto the bed. "Shh." He reached up and smoothed my hair from my face. "Sleep."

I rolled onto my side and let my eyes drift shut. When I woke the next time, Beckett was sitting in the chair by the fireplace, his legs extended out in front of him, his eyes closed. He'd removed his glasses and had them clutched in one hand, a book in the other.

He woke slowly, stretching his legs and then squinting across the room at me. He replaced his glasses and saw that I was awake.

He pushed up from the chair and came to stand next to the bed. "How do you feel?"

"Like someone hit me over the head with *War and Peace* a few times."

Beckett made a face that said he didn't think I was funny. "I'm getting the doctor back over here."

"What?" Confusion and shame settled over me. I didn't remember a doctor.

"She came to look at you last night, remember?"

I shook my head, causing a riot of pain between my ears. "I hate doctors," I groaned.

"Too bad." Beckett whipped his phone out of his pocket.

"Please don't call the doctor," I begged. "I'm fine now."

"You don't look fine."

I glanced down at my T-shirt and pink sweatpants, then raised my eyes to Beckett, cheeks heating. "Who changed my clothes?"

"Your friend," he said. "The one who works at the winery."

"Sloane?"

He nodded, and my shoulders relaxed. The thought of Beckett having anything to do with taking off my clothes made my skin heat. I cleared my throat, and it was like gargling nails. "Can I have some water?"

Beckett strode from the room, and I took a moment to collect my thoughts. I smoothed my hair and glanced around for my purse. Beckett's room was twice the size of my apartment. My purse was on a dresser on the other side of the room, but it may as well have been in South Carolina. I didn't have the energy to swing my legs to the ground, much less trek across the room to get my purse.

I sat up and scooted to the edge of the mattress. My head spun, and I rested it in my hands. Aslan nudged my thigh, whimpering.

"What are you doing?" Beckett's sharp voice cut the air.

I lifted my head to see Beckett scowling at me from the doorway, looking dreamier than Heathcliff on a foggy moor.

"My purse," I croaked.

Beckett grabbed my purse from the dresser and brought it to the bed. He fluffed the pillows against the headboard. Once I was in an upright position against them, he handed me the water. I sipped, easing the fire in my throat. Beckett's eyes roamed over my face, and I remembered that I looked like a cat dragged from hell. I raised a hand to my wild halo of hair and Beckett's frown twitched.

"Thank you." I reached for my purse and found my phone. I flipped it open only to see a black screen. It was dead. "Do you have a charger?"

Beckett eyed my phone. "Sorry, nothing from the previous

millennium." Pulling his phone from his pocket, he offered it to me. "You can use mine."

With a sinking feeling, I realized I didn't know anyone's number. Even if I did, I wouldn't know who to call. I didn't want to worry Gabi. Sloane and Pressly knew I was safe with Beckett.

"Never mind." I shook my head. The slight movement caused pain to ricochet through me. I sank further into the mattress.

"Are you cold?" Beckett tucked a blanket around me. "I could start a fire."

I blinked up at him, noticing his messy hair and beard scruff for the first time. Behind the glasses his eyes looked tired, like he'd been up all night.

"What happened last night?" I asked.

Beckett's eyes narrowed on mine. "You don't remember?"

I started to shake my head but stopped myself in time. "No," I said.

Beckett paced across the room, turned around, and came back to the bed, eyes blazing. "That asshole got you wasted, then tried to play it off like he didn't know what was happening. I punched him and then brought you here."

"That asshole? What asshole?"

"The guy with the man bun."

"Xan?" I asked, putting the pieces together with difficulty.

Beckett snarled. "That's his name? Xan?"

He crossed his arms over his chest, and I saw that the knuckles on his right hand were bruised and swollen.

"You punched Xan?" I asked, horrified.

"I got one good one in before Peppy pulled me off him."

"Why'd you punch him?" I asked, trying to picture Beckett losing his composure in a fight. The image was electrifying. All dark hair flying and muscles bulging.

"He fucking drugged you, Lacey."

I sat up straighter against the pillows and fired an angry glare at Beckett. "Don't cuss me."

Beckett sighed and reached up to rip off his glasses. He

massaged his eyes with the heel of his hand. "I'm not cussing you," Beckett said, lowering his hand. "I'm cussing him. That little shit with the man bun."

"Xan wouldn't drug me." Even though I couldn't remember the details from the night before, I knew this was true. "We were dancing," I said, trying to piece things together.

"You were doing more than that." Beckett's voice was an angry growl.

My eyes snapped open. "What?"

"Peppy said you were kissing."

Heat burned my cheeks as I remembered. Xan had smelled like nutmeg and cinnamon. "It was just one kiss."

Beckett scoffed.

"Maybe I got food poisoning."

"No, Lacey." Beckett's lips thinned. "I don't think you got food poisoning." He flexed his bruised fist. "I think that asshole drugged you."

I didn't have to know Xan well to know he wasn't that man. He was sweet and funny. His eyes were full of light and his smile was one of the most genuine I'd ever seen. He wouldn't resort to criminal behavior to get a girl. I knew it in my bones.

Chapter Thirteen

"**X**an wouldn't do that," I said.

Beckett stood abruptly. The mattress shifted, and the drum in my head pounded.

"Stop saying that prick's name," Beckett said. "I never want to hear it again. He fucking drugged you, Lacey."

I rubbed my temples and shot Beckett a glare. "Stop cussing me."

Beckett's brows drew together, and he stepped closer. "Let me call someone for you. Sloane? What's her number?" Beckett's finger poised over the phone.

I shook my head, then winced. Every movement hurt. "I don't want to talk to her."

"Someone else then?"

Gabi or Thatcher would be there for me, but I was too embarrassed to call them. There was no one else. I'd been on my own since high school.

"No. There's no one."

Beckett swiped a finger over his phone, then held it to his ear. "I'm calling Peppy," he told me. "I promised her updates." Beckett walked to the fireplace and sat on the chair where he'd spent most of the night. "Hey," he said into the phone. "She's fine. Finally awake."

Beckett's eyes met mine, and he forced a smile. My cheeks flushed. His glasses were a little crooked. I studied him, trying to decide if he was cute or sexy. The final verdict: both.

"Can you call Sloane and let her know Lacey is fine?" Beckett asked. "I've got her. She's resting."

I tried to get up again, but Beckett jabbed a finger at the bed. I sighed and sank back into the pillows.

"Hi, Summer." Beckett's voice softened. "How's it going so far?" Beckett paused, listening. "Aslan's fine. He's been a big help this morning."

I reached down and patted Aslan's head.

Beckett said good-bye and came back to stand over the bed. "Peppy has been worried about you. She thinks it's her fault this happened."

"It's not her fault."

"I know," he said. "It's mine."

"What?"

"That's my bar." He tossed his phone on the nightstand. "My hotel. If people think they can come into an establishment owned by the Vinroots and drug a woman, something needs to change."

I suppressed a laugh. "You're not arrogant at all."

"And you're not sarcastic."

The air sizzled between our stares.

"I'm sure you own a few bars."

Beckett raised an eyebrow.

"More than a few?"

He gave a terse nod.

"You can't control what people do in a bar."

"We need to step up our security at the Inn." He pushed his glasses up his nose. "Bouncers at the bar. More valets."

I held back another laugh. "Bouncers at Sky Valley Vineyards?" I pictured muscle-bound men dressed in black, sitting on stools in the elegant lobby. "I can't imagine that working. I think you're over-reacting. We don't even know what happened."

"Don't tell me you still think you got food poisoning."

I closed my eyes, suddenly tired again. "I don't know what happened."

"What's the last thing you remember?"

I scrolled through my memories. I remembered kissing Xan. It had been a lovely kiss, even though it didn't make my heart race like the mere thought of Beckett's sensual mouth anywhere near mine did. We'd danced some more. We'd drunk some more. Gabi and Mia left. The cold air outside the inn. The hard stone of the tile. Beckett's jacket under my cheek. His arms around me...

My eyes popped open. "I don't know."

"Were you drinking?"

I glared at him. "It's perfectly legal. I guess somebody could have slipped something into my drink." I squeezed my eyes shut, remembering leaving my beer on the bar while Xan and I were dancing. What if the drug had been meant for him? Or what if it was random? What if I never found out? The questions hurt my head.

"You want me to get the doctor back? She's an old friend, and she owes me."

"No." I didn't want to think about the favors a female friend owed Beckett.

"If you want to press charges, you need to get checked out. Maybe even go to the hospital."

"I don't want to press charges." I glared up at him. "I don't even know what happened!"

Light burst through my head as my voice rang loud between my ears. I groaned and massaged my temples. My stomach rolled, threatening to get violent with me if I didn't shut up and sit still.

I could feel Beckett hovering over me, and I risked a glance through slitted eyes to look up at him.

"What are you doing?"

"I'm not leaving you." He crossed his arms over his chest.

"At least sit down. You're stressing me out, looming over me like that."

"God forbid I stress you out." The mattress shifted under his weight as he sat beside me. "This okay?"

I scooted over to give him more room. "Yes."

Beckett stretched his legs beside mine. He grabbed his phone and tapped the screen. There was a clicking sound, then the shade lowered, shutting out most of the light. He pulled a quilt over our legs and sat back against the headboard beside me. In the dim light coming in from the hall, I could see the shapes of our legs beneath the quilt—Beckett's long and powerful, mine much smaller.

Aslan settled between us, his head in my lap, his tail on Beckett's legs. I reached down to pet him. The darkness and the quiet relaxed me, and I grew sleepy again.

My thoughts drifted, settling in place for a moment before flitting off again. Beckett's hand brushed mine as he scratched Aslan behind the ear in his favorite spot. Aslan's tail thumped against Beckett's leg. It made me smile to see Aslan so happy in his new home.

I remembered Summer was visiting her dad in Atlanta. "How's Pressly?" I asked.

Beckett's hand stilled. "Did she tell you why she went to Atlanta?"

"Yes. She mentioned her ex."

Beckett's mouth thinned. "Jeff."

"I take it you don't like him?"

"I love Jeff. Everyone loves Jeff. He's the kind of guy who will get last-minute tickets to the World Series and take everyone he knows. He parties with rock stars, skis with dukes, surfs with YouTubers."

"Sounds like a fun guy."

"He's great. Just not for my sister."

Beckett's hand brushed mine again, and this time I didn't move away. Beckett's hand was big and square, the knuckles swollen. I studied the bruised skin in the dim light. No one had ever fought for me before. My heart squeezed.

"Did you sleep in the chair last night?" I asked.

"I didn't want to leave you in here alone."

"I'm sorry I stole your bed. You must be tired."

"Not really." He smothered a yawn.

We both laughed softly.

"I'm sorry."

Beckett's hand covered mine. "For what?"

I turned my hand over and our fingers linked. "For making you hurt your hand."

"I was glad to do it," he said.

He took off his glasses and set them on the nightstand. He looked younger without them. More vulnerable but just as handsome. It was hard to decide which way I liked him better—with or without glasses. It was a tie.

"Are you reading my book?" I asked, glancing at my copy of *Beneath the Stars* on the nightstand.

"What?"

"*Beneath the Stars*. I left it here."

"I wanted to make sure you got it back."

I studied his face in the darkness, tempted to lift my hand and caress the line of tension from his jaw. "You don't have to be embarrassed," I said. "Lots of men read romance."

He squeezed my fingers. "I'm not embarrassed. I don't get embarrassed."

"Everyone gets embarrassed."

"Not me." Beckett shifted closer and then eased an arm around my shoulders. "This okay?" he asked.

A streak of fire raced down my spine as I leaned into him. The hard lines of his body under the soft cashmere of his sweater made my skin tingle. "It's fine."

We fell silent, and our breathing synced. I was almost asleep when Beckett asked, "Do you like limericks?"

I lifted my head. "You mean the poems we wrote in elementary school?"

"Yes. I write them to relax. Do you want to hear one?"

"Okay."

Beckett cleared his throat and began. "There once was an old man named Keith. Who often misplaced his false teeth." He paused dramatically. "Imagine his face, when he sat on the chaise, and was suddenly bit from beneath."

I held back a chuckle. "That was horrible," I said.

"That's the idea." He rubbed my arm. "You want another?"

I nodded and closed my eyes.

"There once was an ice skater named Chuck," he said. "Who thought he was good with a puck..."

Even though it made the pain in my head explode, I laughed.

Chapter Fourteen

In my dream, I climbed a ladder with dozens of rungs. As soon as I neared the top, I slid right back down to the bottom and began the process again. I woke slowly, feeling as though there were a dozen things I'd left undone.

It took a moment to adjust to the darkness of the bedroom, but as soon as my vision cleared, I knew I was in Beckett's bed. And I was alone.

Beckett had probably gone to another room to get some sleep. I could hardly blame him. Not when I lay outstretched on his bed like a starfish. I wasn't used to sharing a bed with a man, and I was a cover hog.

I sat up and yawned, then shuffled into the bathroom. Moonlight streamed in from the tall windows, casting a glow on the white tiles.

A set of fluffy towels and a note sat on a chaise lounge in front of the shower door. My heart skipped as I grabbed the note and unfolded it to see Beckett's elegant handwriting sloping across the paper.

* * *

BAV

TThere once was a dog walker so fair
Her beauty was awfully rare.
Her eyes were alight
With a spirit so bright.
And her hair you couldn't compare.

Make yourself at home...
Beckett

A laugh bubbled up in my chest, and I lifted my hand to my hair.

Beckett had called me beautiful. And he liked my hair.

Sure that my hair was a sight to behold at the moment, I took Beckett up on his offer to make myself at home. I wore his shirt and had slept between his sheets; I might as well use his shower.

And what a shower it was...

The glass enclosure occupied the entire back wall of the room and had more nozzles and spigots than a car wash. After a moment of hesitation I hurried to lock the door and strip out of my clothes. I laid my clothes on the bench and stepped inside the shower.

Heated tiles warmed my feet, and a soft light glowed overhead. Dispensers lined the tiled walls, but there were no knobs. No handles. No way to turn on the water. I groaned, remembering how I'd spent twenty minutes trying to figure out how to open the refrigerator in Beckett's kitchen.

"Good morning." A woman's voice filled the glass enclosure.

I jumped and whirled around. My heart slammed in my chest. Hands covering my bits and pieces, I scanned the bathroom for the source of the voice.

"What temperature would you like?"

On the back wall, a keypad lit up, offering a selection of temperatures ranging from sixty-five to one hundred twenty degrees. I tapped the keypad to select an option somewhere between a polar plunge and the rivers of hell. Warm water rushed from panels in the ceiling and sprayed from nozzles on the walls.

"What pressure would you like?"

The soothing voice filling the shower was the same one that had calmly informed me I was out of tries at the gate before the sirens had blared.

I flashed an irritated glance at the keypad. "Can you shut up?"

"Have a wonderful day," she said. "Good-bye."

Blissful silence ensued. I lifted my face to the cascade of water and sighed as the tension in my muscles released. I pumped shampoo out of a dispenser and massaged it through my hair. Beckett's scent filled the air, and my belly quivered at the thought of sharing this decadent shower experience with him. With his scent in the surrounding steam, it wasn't hard to imagine him standing under the waterfall wearing nothing but a wicked grin. His skin shiny with soap. His hair slicked back from his face. His eyes naked and vulnerable without his glasses. He would reach for me...

I rinsed the shampoo from my hair, wishing I could rid my mind of Beckett so easily. My imagination wouldn't let up. It insisted on wondering if Beckett tasted as good as he smelled, and if his abs were as hard as...

I needed an intervention.

"Hey, lady in the keypad?" My voice reverberated in the silence. "Hello?"

"How can I be of assistance?"

Can you make me stop thinking about Beckett's sexy body, naked? "Can I get colder water, please?"

"What temperature would you like?"

The keypad lit up with selections, and I chose the Arctic blast. A torrent of icy water rained down over my head and blasted from the nozzles on the walls.

"Too cold!"

"What temperature would you like?"

I sputtered as freezing water soaked my hair and body. "Hotter!"

The temperature rose to a tolerable level, chasing away the goose bumps that covered my skin. I shivered and cursed under my breath. "Damn machines."

"Do you need further assistance?"

"No."

"Have a wonderful day. Good-bye."

I don't think I imagined the smirk in her voice. I finished showering in blessed silence. At least the cold water had taken my mind off Beckett.

Dammit. Now I was thinking about him again.

Powerful thighs. Lean hips. Abs I wanted to lick clean...

I swiped my finger over the keypad to turn off the water. The spray fizzled to a stop, and a fine mist fragrant with eucalyptus and lavender released into the air. I stepped out of the shower onto heated tiles and wrapped myself in one of the world's fluffiest towels.

A girl could get used to this.

I made myself at home in Beckett's luxurious bathroom. I discovered he used eye cream, sunscreen, and leave-in conditioner. His shaving gel smelled like a walk through a cedar forest, and he had an entire drawer full of new toothbrushes.

Either he was big on oral hygiene or he had lots of sleepovers. The thought of another woman in Beckett's bathroom left a nasty taste in my mouth. I ripped open one of the toothbrush packages and scrubbed my teeth.

I slicked lotion on my skin, combed product through my hair, and dabbed cream that probably cost more than a month's rent under my eyes. When I finished, I felt like a pampered princess.

A girl could get very used to this.

Wrapped in the towel, I hesitated before getting dressed. I was too clean to wear yesterday's underwear, so I went without. I glared at the scrap of silk and lace.

When I was little, I'd crashed on my bicycle, and every time I'd walked past the bike in the garage I relived the accident. When I looked at those panties, I remembered the craziness at the bar. I scooped them up and shoved them in the trash. Might as well add the bra too. They were a matching set that I'd blown a lot of money on, but I never wanted to wear them again.

I promised myself a trip to Mossy Oak's finest boutique on my next payday. I'd buy something sexy that made me feel strong and beautiful. Perhaps in white—Beckett's favorite color.

I dressed in the borrowed clothes and dried my hair as best I could with the towel. On my way back to the bedroom, I walked past the open door of Beckett's closet and paused.

I might need a sweatshirt. Especially since I'd gone braless. If I got a little cold, or if Beckett looked at me a certain way with those smoky brown eyes, there would be no hiding the high beams.

I poked my head into the closet and flipped on the light. A

petite blonde woman stood across the room. She had a cloud of wet hair curling around her shoulders, and she wore pink sweatpants. I blinked and recognized the orchid blossoms inked on my left arm and the pirate ship belonging to Princess Alaura of Marlydia on my right. It was me. And I was wearing pink sweatpants.

I did not wear pink, but if I did, it would be fuchsia.

My gaze drifted from my reflection to the custom shelves and cabinets built into Beckett's closet. The man owned more clothes than a department store. There was an entire wall of shoes that looked identical from afar but upon closer inspection had subtle differences.

I ran my hand along a panel of silk ties arranged by color and pattern. I imagined Beckett getting ready in this closet, selecting a suit from the dozens that marched across the back wall, checking his tie in the mirror.

I plucked a pair of tortoiseshell glasses from a display case and set them on my face. My reflection in the mirror became a huge pink and white blob. I pulled the glasses off and blinked to clear my vision. Beckett hadn't been lying when he'd said he was blind without his glasses.

The drawers lining the walls were sleek and knobless. I pressed my hand against the flat surface of a drawer and it slid open soundlessly. Beckett's collection of socks filled the drawer. I picked up a pair of turquoise socks emblazoned with unicorns and laughed.

Beckett always dressed impeccably. Every hair in place. Every detail down to his watch and glasses on point. Beckett's suits were the epitome of sophistication, but his socks looked like he'd bought them at a gag gift store. Each pair was more outrageous than the next. It made me wonder what his underwear looked like.

Ashamed that I was even considering snooping around in Beckett's underwear drawer, I replaced the pair of socks and pushed the drawer closed.

I crossed the room to the casual section of the closet and ran my hand down a stack of neatly folded cashmere sweaters. I remembered the feel of Beckett's hard body beneath the soft fabric of his sweater when he'd held me in his arms.

My chest ached, and I rubbed a palm over my heart. I felt funny, but not the same funny that I had felt earlier when I thought I would get sick on Beckett's luxurious sheets. This was more of a tingle that started in my chest and bounced through me, pinging every nerve along the way.

Maybe I was hungry. I couldn't remember my last meal. I should be starving. The thought of searching for a bite to eat in Beckett's kitchen didn't excite me nearly as much as the thought of finding him. Where was Beckett? And where was Aslan?

The traitor. Who would have thought Aslan would choose Beckett over me?

I grabbed a sweatshirt and went in search of Beckett and my favorite rescue dog.

Chapter Fifteen

I found them in Beckett's office.

I pushed open the door at the top of the stairs and saw Beckett sitting at his desk, his back to the door. He was bent over his keyboard, a pair of headphones covering his ears. Aslan lay at his feet in a plush doggie bed. His tail thumped when he saw me, but he made no move to get up.

"Traitor."

Beckett didn't turn around. I guessed he had the volume turned all the way up on the headphones. He couldn't hear me over the noise.

A gust of cold air blew through the room, and I was glad I'd found a sweatshirt. A window was open somewhere, and the blast of air rustled papers and blew wrappers across the floor. The smell of cigar smoke permeated the air.

Beckett paused in his steady typing to take a few puffs of his cigar and blow smoke above his head. His fingers tapped his leg in time to the beat of the song and then returned to the keyboard.

As I watched him type at a pace a notch below frantic, I remembered Pressly's warning. She'd told me to steer clear of her brother while he was working. He was intense. He was a genius.

I did not understand what Beckett did for his family's company, but whatever role he played, it was a vital one.

I could sense the tension radiating off his hunched shoulders from the doorway. I crept into the room, watching him with fascination. His body vibrated with tension. His fingers flew over the keyboard. His passion filled the air, pulsing all the way across the room.

Was he firing someone in a different time zone? Orchestrating a takeover of a rival company? I was dying to know what he was doing. I stepped closer, not stopping until I stood directly behind Beckett. I didn't mean to read the words on his computer screen, but after scanning the first sentence, I couldn't stop.

She sank the knife into his chest. The hilt stopped at the barrier of his skin. Blood gushed over her hand, warm and tingling. His essence...

My heart beat faster with each word I read. This was no business correspondence; this was prose. Beckett wasn't writing a letter or an email. He was writing...

The screen slammed shut, the sharp noise echoing through the silent room. Beckett ripped off his headphones. The driving bass of rock music poured out of them.

A blast of wind ripped through the room, and I shivered. Beckett burst from the chair, stalked to the wall of windows, and slammed one shut. His profile was rigid, the blade of his nose unforgiving. "Your hair is soaked. You'll catch a cold."

I wrapped my arms around myself. "What were you typing?"

"Nothing." Beckett's eyes dropped over me. "You look better. How do you feel?"

I darted a glance at the laptop on his desk. "What are you writing?"

Beckett winced. "It's nothing."

"It didn't look like nothing. It looked like a story. Or a novel."

"Lacey." He shook his head. "It's nothing. Really. Forget about it."

I scanned the room, noting the piles of papers, the stacks of reference books, and the pictures pinned to the cork boards on the walls. My jaw dropped. This was a writer's office. "Is that what you've been doing up here?" I glanced toward the gym. "I thought you were just working out."

Beckett turned to look out the window. A flush spread over his neck, and his shoulders tensed. The sound of his shallow breathing filled the air.

I crossed the room to stand next to him. Beckett stared out at the magnificent view of the Blue Ridge Mountains bathed in moonlight. But I don't think he saw a thing. I reached for his hand. He let me weave our fingers together. I squeezed his hand, and his eyes flashed to mine.

"You're writing a novel."

Beckett's shoulders slumped as he let out a breath. "Yes."

My heart leaped. "That's wonderful. What's it about?"

Beckett's mouth tightened. His fingers squeezed mine. "You don't understand." He sounded like he'd swallowed a cup of tacks.

I narrowed my eyes at him. "I'm sure you're worried that it isn't any good. I'll bet every author thinks the same thing."

"I'm not worried it isn't good. It's good. It's fucking great. Dark and gritty, which is different. But great. I've written shitty novels before, and this isn't one of them."

My jaw dropped. "You've written shitty novels before?"

His lip twitched. "I've written some good ones too."

"But…" I glanced around at the office, more curious than ever. "Where are your books? Why didn't I know?"

Beckett shoved his glasses into his hair and pinched the bridge of his nose. "No one knows."

I wrinkled my nose. "I don't understand."

"You can't tell anyone."

The skin around his eyes was tight, and he clutched my fingers. I felt the panic pouring off him.

"I won't tell anyone."

His shoulders relaxed an inch. "Thank you." His tight grip on my hand loosened, and he turned to face me. "I thought you'd sleep until morning."

"You thought you could sneak up here and get some writing done?"

Beckett nodded.

"How do you find the time?"

He checked his watch and raised an eyebrow. "I don't sleep."

"I want to know more," I said. "How many books have you written? Is that a thriller? Can I read it?"

Beckett laughed. "Slow down."

"I'm dying of curiosity."

"I can see that." His eyes dropped to my chest. "Nice sweatshirt."

"You said make yourself at home."

"And I meant it." His eyes grew more serious. "I'm glad you did." His eyes darted between mine. "Thank you."

My eyebrows rose. "For what?"

"I was in a funk," he said. "Unable to write anything at all. My last book was shit. The one before that not much better. But since the moment I saw you standing up on that ladder..." He shook his head, searching for the words.

My throat went dry as I waited for Beckett to finish. His eyes burned into mine, and his hand slid up my arm to my shoulder. The air between us pulsed with energy.

"You inspired me." His eyes bored into mine. "You're my muse."

Goose bumps broke out over my skin. "That's the nicest thing anyone has ever said to me."

"It's not flattery. It's the truth."

"I can't stop thinking about you," I blurted.

Beckett's soft laugh ruffled the air. "It sounds like I'm a disease you caught."

"Maybe you are." I smiled up at him.

"Hmm. Maybe we've infected each other, because I can't stop thinking about you either."

I lifted up on my toes, wanting to feel the soft puff of his breath on my skin. He cupped his hand around my neck, urging me closer.

"Are you ready to admit you want to date me?" His mouth lowered an inch. Closer. So close.

I hadn't thought it was possible to want Beckett any more than I already did. But finding out he was an author who created stories —whether they were terrible or fucking great—made me want him even more. I craved Beckett like the sequel to my favorite novel. He was better than any book boyfriend I'd ever read about. Too good to be true, but I didn't care.

I linked my arms around his neck and pressed my mouth to his.

Chapter Sixteen

The kiss was soft, achingly sweet. Full of promises of what could come. His kiss invited me to lean in. His hands cupped my face as his lips moved against mine, tasting me as if I were a delicate treat.

The muscles in his shoulders flexed, and I felt the restraint in his body as he pulled away. He inched back. But I was having none of it. I threaded my fingers through his hair and pressed my body against his.

Beckett hesitated for a heartbeat before his arms locked around me, and his mouth crashed down on mine.

His tongue dipped into my mouth, and heat flooded my body. Stars exploded behind my eyes.

This kiss had been building in my head since I'd first laid eyes on Beckett. I'd thought about him endlessly, and now that his mouth was finally on mine, I wasn't letting him go.

My arms tightened around his neck as I pressed into his chest. His tongue coaxed mine into a wet, sensual dance, at which he was an expert. Every rational thought flew from my mind as he slanted his head, deepening the kiss from passionate to all-consuming.

Need raced through me, and I ground my hips against his. He groaned and pulled me closer.

The cold metal of Beckett's desk bit into my hip when he backed me against it. He swept me off my feet and deposited me on top of the desk. My body ignited as Beckett pinned me to the desk, kissing me with unrestrained passion.

Hooking my legs around his hips, I pressed against him and felt the hard length of his erection. Beckett's moan filled my mouth. I clung to his neck, aching to get closer.

He leaned over me, pushing me back until I was lying flat on his desk. Something sharp jabbed into my back, but I barely felt the bite of pain as Beckett's mouth ravaged mine.

It didn't surprise me to know the man could kiss. Beckett did everything thoroughly, and he kissed me breathless.

I was panting by the time he released me. He backed off me, gently helping me sit up.

He came to stand between my legs and cupped my face in his hands. His eyes went soft behind his fogged glasses. "Forgive me."

"For what?"

"I just attacked you." He brushed a thumb over my bottom lip. "I'm sorry."

I kissed his thumb, swirling my tongue around the tip. "I'm not."

His eyes blazed, and he traced the seam of my mouth with his thumb. His jaw tightened. "You've had a hell of a time." A muscle in his cheek flexed. "I shouldn't have touched you."

"I kissed you." I hooked my leg around him, scooting closer along the cold metal desk. "I've wanted to for weeks."

His eyes turned smoky. "This isn't how I planned it."

"You don't have to plan everything."

"I wanted to take you out on a date, prove to you that romance exists outside the world of books."

My chest tightened. "I don't...." I was going to say I didn't want that. I didn't need that. I didn't believe in love. What I wanted was more of Beckett. More of his lips on mine, wreaking havoc on my senses. "I..."

His mouth hovered over mine, then lowered to nibble at my

bottom lip. He kissed me with an aching tenderness. He tasted of the wine he'd been drinking, the cigar he'd been puffing, and a darker, spicier taste that was all his own.

The chemistry that had been zinging between us since the minute we met caught fire. This kiss was what I'd been waiting for ever since I'd cracked open my first romance novel.

A flash of fire roared to life in my belly, then spread lower, electrifying me.

This kiss was going to end me.

But it was just the beginning.

My hands slid from Beckett's neck to flatten against his chest. I felt the hard planes and ridges of his muscles beneath the cashmere of his sweater. His taste flooded my senses, seducing me to open wider, to let him inside places I'd thought were locked forever.

He cupped the back of my neck. "Is that a yes?"

I'd forgotten there was a question. All I could think about was feeling the sandpaper scruff of his beard on my cheeks and the hard muscles flexing under my touch.

Yes. The answer was yes.

I would not say no to more of this man. To more of his mouth, his tongue, his hands, his words...

The thought of reading Beckett's words had me tossing away my excuses like cargo off a sinking ship. The bricks I'd so carefully laid to protect myself crumbled. I watched them fall as if from very far away. It wasn't safe here in Beckett's arms. I'd get crushed. But all I wanted was to get closer.

Beckett gripped my shoulders. "Saturday night? Are you free?"

My brows knitted. "What day is it?"

"Sunday."

"I have to walk the rescue dogs on Sunday."

His smile curved. "It's four in the morning." He backed up, pulling me with him until my feet rested on the ground. "Will you go out with me or not?"

I tilted my head back to look up at him. In my bare feet, he towered over me. "I'll think about it."

"Lacey." His voice was a frustrated growl. "Why won't you take a chance on me? It's been obvious since the moment we saw each other, there's something between us."

I raised an eyebrow at him. "You didn't even remember me when we first met."

"If I had seen you, I guarantee I wouldn't have forgotten you."

I swallowed hard, unable to look away from Beckett's intense gaze. I still felt woozy, and my head hurt like hell.

He pushed his glasses up onto his head and pinched the bridge of his nose. "I know my timing sucks," he said. "Forgive me for pushing."

I imagined him bent over his laptop, churning out stories, and my pulse raced. "I'll go out with you," I said. "On one condition."

He replaced his glasses and peered down at me. "Name it."

"I want to read your book."

Beckett blew out a long breath. His hands dropped to my shoulders. "I don't think you understand. My writing is private. I don't talk about it. With anyone."

I stepped away from him, feeling hurt. I'd gone from being his muse to being "just anyone."

His hand snaked around my arm, and he tugged me gently until I turned to face him. "It's not like you think." He shook his head. "Being an author isn't glamorous. It isn't romantic."

"Then why do you do it?"

"I don't know." He weaved our fingers together. "It started out as something I did between classes and studying for the bar."

"You've been writing since law school?"

He nodded. "My first novel got published because of a dare. One of my friends thought I wouldn't have the balls to submit it, but I did." He shrugged. "It ended up being a bestseller."

My jaw dropped. "A bestseller?"

Beckett's mouth thinned into a line. "It isn't all it's cracked up to be. After I hit all the lists, the shitstorm began. There was pressure from the publishing house, my agent, my editor." Beckett ticked off his complaints. "I got caught up in this life I'd never intended for myself. I never meant to be a writer. I meant to work for my family, do what everyone expected of me. But these stories… they wouldn't stop. They begged to get out, and I burned myself up trying to tell them."

I shivered as if the window was still open. I could hear the passion in Beckett's voice, the rawness of his need.

"And then everything dried up. The stories in my head stopped."

"Maybe you just needed a break." I squeezed his fingers. "You can't keep working around the clock without paying a price somewhere in your life."

Beckett laughed, but the sound fell far short of mirth. "What life?" He brought my hand to his mouth and brushed his lips over my knuckles. The skin around his eyes tightened as he met my eyes. "When I saw you standing on the ladder at the bookshop, everything clicked into place. You were like an angel up there. An angel with a perfect ass." He grinned, making one dimple pop. "I wanted to write again. I wanted to create something new, and different, and worthy of your beauty."

"Beckett." My cheeks burned with a blush.

"I mean it." He tugged on a damp curl, pulling it down and then releasing it. "You inspire me." He scrunched a handful of my hair in his fist. "This hair inspires me."

I laughed. "My hair has a mind of its own."

"That's what I like about it."

"Does my status as muse entitle me to special treatment?"

His hand cupped my neck, fingers caressing my nape. "What would you like?"

The question, asked in Beckett's low rasp, made a tremble rush through me. My skin tingled, and I leaned closer, reaching up to kiss the underside of his jaw.

"I want your words."

The admission made me tremble. I'd never said something so intimate to a man. I was asking Beckett to let me see his bared soul.

"Then you'll have them."

He turned his head to take my mouth. His kiss was magic. I tumbled under his spell.

"You must be hungry," he said, pulling away.

"Are you gonna cook?" I couldn't imagine Beckett puttering around in the kitchen.

"I don't cook." He rubbed a hand down my back. "But I'm an expert at ordering delivery."

"Isn't it a little late—or early—for takeout?"

"You like omelets?" He went to his desk to retrieve his phone.

"Sure."

Beckett stepped away, speaking into his phone. He ordered a spread of food as if it were a perfectly ordinary thing to do in the middle of the night. He lifted his chin at me. "Coffee?"

When I nodded, he ordered a pot of French press, then ended the call with a swipe of his finger.

"After we eat, I'm sending you back to bed."

Chapter Seventeen

When I woke later, my head still ached, but I felt a bubble of something light in my heart that hadn't been there before. I think it might have been hope, but I couldn't be sure.

Beckett strolled into the bedroom looking impossibly handsome in dark slacks and a button-down shirt.

"You're up." He fastened a silver watch on his wrist.

God, the man could wear a watch. "Why are you so dressed up?"

"I have to leave for the airport," he said. "I can give you a ride home now, or you can stay as long as you like and call the courtesy van from the resort to take you home when you're ready."

"Where are you going?"

"London."

I regarded his perfectly styled hair and imagined a woman running her hands through it. "Do you have a girlfriend in London?" I asked.

Beckett raised an eyebrow at me. "What do you think?"

I slid my legs to the floor. "I'm sorry. It's none of my business."

Beckett crossed the room and sat down on the bed beside me. "I'd like to make it your business," he said, reaching for my hand. "I told you I didn't have a life. I don't have a woman in London." He picked up my hand and kissed my fingers. "But I'd like to have one here." He tugged on a curl and watched it spring back to my shoulder. "What do you think?"

My chest squeezed and I felt dizzy. "I don't like to be tied down."

"I'm not looking to tie you down. I just want to see where this goes."

I pried my hand away and stood up. "We should go. I don't want to make you miss your plane."

Beckett watched me gather my stuff with his arms crossed over his chest. When I started to take off his sweatshirt, he stopped me. "Keep it," he said. "It looks good on you."

I mumbled a thank-you as I bent to lace my boots.

"Can you do me a favor?" Beckett asked.

I glanced up at him from under the curtain of my hair. My heart thundered as our eyes met. When he looked at me it felt like he was turning my soul inside out. "What?" I asked.

"Can you keep Aslan until tomorrow?" he asked. "Peppy called and said she won't be home until late, and I hate to lock him up."

Aslan gave me a look that I couldn't refuse. He sat in the tiny back seat of Beckett's car on the way home. Well, the back half of him did. The front half of him was wedged between me and Becket.

He tried to climb over me to the window as we passed Ginger Cake Acres. I heaved him off my lap as we turned into Frog Level, the oldest part of Mossy Oak and my neck of the woods.

My place was a studio apartment over a garage. The whole place was roughly the size of Beckett's bathroom. Convenient to everywhere in town, my tiny apartment was cozy and cheap—perfect for me.

Beckett parked his car in my driveway and peered up the stairs at my apartment. "This is it?"

"Were you expecting a castle?"

He laughed. "No, but I wasn't expecting a dorm room either."

Beckett unfolded himself from the low-slung car and came

around to open my door. I was too tired to protest as he helped me from the car and grabbed Aslan's supplies from the back seat.

We walked up the stairs together, and I dug in my purse for the key. I struggled with the lock, my mind stuck on the fact that, besides the pizza delivery boy, Beckett was the first man to enter my apartment since I'd lived in Mossy Oak.

Beckett placed his big hand over mine, steadying it. "You okay?"

I took a breath and let it go. "I've never had a man here before."

Beckett's hand flexed over mine, his bruised knuckles stretching. "I'm the first?" When I nodded, a slow smile spread over his face. "I'm honored."

I turned the key, and we stepped inside. Beckett stalked into the living room, casting his sharp gaze into every dark corner. I wondered what he thought of the place. It was a far cry from his luxurious mansion.

He strode to the bed, which was tucked under the A-frame of the roof. "Don't you have a security system?"

"Why would I? No one in Mossy Oak even locks their door."

Beckett bent and checked under the bed skirt.

I laughed. "No one's hiding under the bed."

He straightened and pushed his glasses back up his nose. "Are you sure you're all right here alone?"

The serious look on his face made tears burn in my eyes. I hadn't relied on anyone in years, but I suddenly wanted to beg him to stay.

Beckett saw my glassy eyes and gathered me in his arms. "I can postpone my trip."

I pressed my face into his starched shirt and swallowed my tears. "I'm fine."

His hands spread over my back, molding me close. "I can't leave you here alone."

"I'm not alone, Beckett." I breathed him in, filling my lungs with his spicy scent. "I have Aslan."

Beckett leaned back to glance down at Aslan. "He's not much

of a guard dog, but he's decent company. You'll call if you need anything?"

"Yes."

"Don't forget to charge your phone."

"Okay."

Beckett curled a hand around my neck and pulled me in. His mouth closed over mine. There was a spark and then the kiss turned to a raging fire. We kissed for a long time, then Beckett pulled away, checked his watch, and kissed me again.

"Saturday," he murmured, lips feather soft against mine.

I watched Beckett jog down the stairs and fold himself into his car. The little bubble of hope in my chest expanded until I had to open my mouth and sigh it out. A buzz of anticipation hung in the air, where I knew it would grow for six more days.

Until Saturday.

Chapter Eighteen

I lingered in the shower, scrubbing my skin under the hot spray of water. I felt better after a good meal and lots of rest, but the remnants of a raging headache remained, and my throat was raw with unshed tears.

Beckett was right about me being drugged. I was kidding myself to think it was food poisoning. Someone had put something in my drink, but who? And why?

I stood under the scalding spray until the water became lukewarm and then finally turned cold. Shivering, I stepped out of the shower, careful not to disturb Aslan, who was snoozing on my bath mat.

I wrapped my body in one towel and my hair in another and went to check my phone. I'd missed over a dozen calls. Three of them were from Xan.

I called Gabi first, knowing she was probably sick with worry. I was sure Sloane had told her all about my misadventure.

Gabi answered on the first ring. "Spill it, Lacey," she said. "I want details. Every juicy one."

So much for worried out of her mind. Gabi sounded more curious than concerned.

"Where are you?" I could hear loud noises in the background, and her voice was muffled.

"I'm at Shane's basketball game. Can you hear me?"

My headache flared to life as her voice rang over the line. "I can hear you."

"Tell me what happened."

"What do you know?"

"Everything. I saw the video."

My blood ran cold. "What video?"

"Of Mr. Sexy punching out Man Bun and carrying you off."

"How is there a video?"

"That guy who was hitting on Sloane sent it to her."

I cringed at the thought of a video circulating.

"What's going on between you guys?"

"Nothing's going on between us." *Not yet.*

"Are you okay?"

Her voice finally sounded worried. I tried to answer, but no sound came out.

"Emergency book club meeting tonight?" she asked.

"Yes."

"Okay, honey. I'll round everyone up. Hyperbole's at five o'clock?"

Too public. "How about my place instead?"

We hung up, and Aslan came to my side with his leash in his mouth.

I'd nearly forgotten about the shelter dogs. I jumped up and grabbed my coat. The dogs were counting on me, and they were just the distraction I needed.

* * *

The weather had turned cold again, and the gray sky promised snow. Four dogs trotted happily at the ends of their leashes, oblivious to my heavy thoughts.

My phone rang as we entered Ginger Cake Acres. Shifting the

leashes to one hand, I dug it out and flipped it open. When I saw Xan's name scroll across the screen, I slapped it shut without answering. I couldn't deal with Xan right now.

We had walked all the way to the bridge when my phone rang again. I juggled the leashes and pulled my phone out of my pocket. It was Xan again. I couldn't avoid him forever.

"Hello?"

"Lacey!" He sounded breathless. "Don't hang up!"

"Why not?"

"I need to talk to you." He panted into the phone. "I'm here at the park," he said. "I can see you on the bridge. Don't go anywhere."

He disconnected, and a moment later, I saw the flash of a bicycle skirting around a group of women pushing strollers. Xan pedaled fast, then stopped with a skid less than a foot from my nearest dog. He dismounted and let the bike crash to the ground.

"I've been so worried about you," he said.

"That's funny, considering you might have been the one to drug me!" My voice was loud enough to attract attention, and the ladies with their strollers swung in a wide berth around us.

"I didn't drug you," Xan said, lowering his voice. "I swear."

He held his hand over his heart and looked down at me solemnly, his eyes pleading. Xan looked as miserable as I felt. His left eye was a pitiful site. Bloodshot and surrounded by a ring of black bruises, it was nearly swollen shut. It looked horribly painful.

"If you want to talk to me, you have to walk."

"Fine." He fell into step with me.

"What are you doing here? Are you following me?"

Aslan tensed at the tone of my voice, his entire body on high alert.

"I came here hoping to see you," Xan said. "Please believe me— I didn't drug you. I would never do that. My mother raised me better."

Aslan growled at Xan, and I tightened my hold on his leash. "If you didn't drug me, then what happened?"

"I don't know. But I swear to you it was not me."

My shoulders sank. "I believe you." I glanced over at him. "We were drinking the same beer. Do you think someone tried to drug you and got me by mistake?"

Xan froze. His mouth dropped open. "Those fucking assholes." He reached into his pocket for his phone and began tapping angrily. "I think you might be right. Jane's cousins were at the bachelor party. They're idiots. They probably thought it would be hilarious to slip me a roofie."

"Oh my God."

Xan finished his text and shoved his phone back in his pocket. "If that's what happened, I can't apologize enough.

"Your friends are jerks. One of them took a video and sent it to Sloane."

Xan rolled his eyes. "Marcus thought me getting punched by a guy in a business suit was the funniest thing he'd ever seen."

I looked at Xan, my eyes shooting daggers. "It wasn't funny for me."

Xan flinched. "Believe me, it wasn't funny from my end either." He rubbed his eye. "I really am sorry. I don't want you to hate me or think I did anything to harm you. I've been hanging around the park all day hoping to catch you." Xan stopped walking. "That's all I wanted to say. I won't bother you anymore."

I stopped walking and watched Xan wheel his bike around on the bridge.

"Hey," I called, stopping him.

Xan's head whipped up, and his eyes went round. "What?"

"I'm sorry I left my beer on the bar. I'm sorry you got in a fight over me... I'm—" Tears clogged my throat, making it impossible to finish.

Xan dropped his bike for the second time and pushed his way through the dogs to get to me. He wrapped his arms around me and pulled me against his chest.

"I'm sorry too. Are you going to be okay?"

I nodded into Xan's jacket, breathing in his outdoorsy scent.

The dogs danced impatiently around us, unconcerned with the moment we were sharing. I sniffed back tears. "I should go. These dogs aren't going to walk themselves."

Xan turned and walked back to his abandoned bike. "Take care, Lacey." He picked the bike up and threw his leg over the crossbar. "Call me if you need anything. I already have three sisters, but there's always room for one more."

Chapter Nineteen

When I got back to my apartment, I fed Aslan and changed into my favorite jeans and Beckett's Emory baseball sweatshirt. The doorbell rang as I was tucking my hair into a messy bun. I pulled open my door and saw Thatcher, balancing a pizza box and a six-pack of my favorite beer in his hand.

I couldn't help looking at Thatcher differently after Pressly's confession. I wondered what he'd been like as a teenager.

"I heard there was a book club meeting here tonight," he said.

Aslan abandoned his kibble at the enticing smell of pizza and ran across the room. He stopped just before taking Thatcher down.

"Who's this guy?" Thatcher asked, bending down to scratch Aslan under the chin. "I would have brought Daisy if I'd known you invited canines."

I walked into the kitchen and got a glass from the freezer. A beer snob, I liked my beer as thick and rich as molasses and served in a frosty glass.

"This is Aslan, and he's on loan from a friend."

I poured the beer into the glass, watching as Thatcher held his hand out for Aslan to shake. To my surprise, the dog responded.

"Good boy." Thatcher gave Aslan's paw a firm shake. "You do

look like a lion," he said approvingly. Thatcher raised his eyes to me. "Aslan, huh?" He narrowed his eyes at me. "Which friend?"

I cleared my throat, finding a lump of emotion there just thinking of Beckett. Remembering Pressly's confession about her crazy summer with Thatcher, I thought it better not to mention the Vinroots.

The doorbell rang, saving me from answering Thatcher's question. Mia and Gabi joined us. A few minutes later, Sloane and Kennedy arrived, and the book club was complete. When every member of the Blue Ridge Book Club sat in my living room, beverage in hand, Gabi started in on me.

"How are you, honey? You sounded terrible on the phone."

I sat with my ankles tucked under me on the floor next to Aslan, absently running a hand across his fur. I felt my cheeks burn as everyone turned to look at me. We'd had these emergency meetings before, but usually Sloane was the one calling them after she'd been on one of her terrible dates. This was my first time as the center of attention, and I didn't like it one bit.

"I'm fine," I said, reaching for a handful of nuts. Everyone had brought food, and my table was overflowing with an assortment of appetizers and desserts.

Gabi scowled. "Bullshit."

Gabi was like the sister I'd never had, Thatcher like the brother, and the other women like close cousins. All of them were here for me, but still I couldn't open up.

Sloane looked at me, and I gave an imperceptible shake of my head. I didn't want to talk about it, especially after seeing Xan at the park.

Thatcher put his hand on my shoulder and gave me a gentle squeeze.

"We are here for you," he said. "Whether it's a big emergency or just the need for pizza, beer, and conversation—we have your back."

Tears filled my eyes, and I blurted the first thing on my mind. The thing that hadn't left my mind since it happened. "I kissed him," I said.

There was a collective intake of breath.

"We already knew that," Gabi said.

"I'm not talking about Xan," I said. "I'm talking about Beckett."

"I'm not surprised," Sloane said. "Watch out for him though."

"Beckett's all right," Thatcher said.

All eyes turned to him. Everyone except Kennedy knew something about Thatcher that we hadn't known last week.

"What?" He scrubbed a hand over his dark beard scruff.

"Nothing," Sloane said, smirking.

Kennedy looked at us all as if we'd lost our minds. "Can somebody please clue me in?"

Sloane popped a few nuts in her mouth and raised an eyebrow at me for permission as she chewed. I nodded, and she summed up the evening for everyone. "Somebody slipped Lacey a roofie," she said. "Mr. Vinroot swooped in to save her. Punched a guy out, then carried Lacey off." She munched another mouthful of nuts. "I have a video."

"We are not watching the video," I squeaked. "You'd better delete it now."

Mia and Kennedy wore similar expressions of shock. Thatcher's fingers tightened on my shoulder.

"Do I need to kill someone for you?" he asked.

Thatcher was Army. He knew how to use deadly force.

"No. Apparently Beckett handled it."

"He was always a good kid," he said. "Glad to know he turned out all right."

"He's scary," Sloane said. "Intimidating as hell. The one time I met him, he sat at the head of the table with this look on his face—" Sloane adjusted her face in a damn good impression of Beckett's icy expression, and I giggled.

"He's not that bad," I said. "He's actually sweet." I thought of him carrying me from the bathroom to his bed and staying with me to hold my hand.

"He did look pretty gallant in the video," Gabi said.

"He likes limericks," I said. "And he let me borrow his dog when I didn't want to be alone."

They were already all staring at me, but that admission made their eyes widen.

"What?" I asked, feeling self-conscious as I reached for my beer.

"You love being alone," Thatcher said.

"Yeah," Kennedy said, looking confused.

"I need a cigarette," Mia said.

"You quit." Gabi pointed a finger at Mia. Then turned to glower at me. "And you didn't even want company on your birthday."

"That's different."

"And you giggled a minute ago," Kennedy said. "You actually giggled."

"Yeah," Mia agreed. Mia argued before of a courtroom for a living and was normally the most eloquent among us, but even she was lost for words. "I really need a cigarette."

Everyone's eyes were glued to me, waiting to hear more. I swallowed, but it did nothing to loosen the lump lodged in my throat. The longer I sat in silence, the less I felt like explaining myself.

Thatcher came to my rescue. "I think it's great Beckett loaned you his dog. And he likes limericks. There was this guy in Freetown." A nostalgic expression crossed his face. "A local. He used to come up with the craziest poems to make us all laugh." Thatcher's eyes flashed with humor, then dimmed as he went inside himself, no doubt revisiting his Army days in Sierra Leone. A moment later, he shrugged off his memories and smiled at me. "I get you don't want to talk about what happened. You don't have to tell us anything you don't want to. We're still here for you, right?" Thatcher glanced around the group, giving them that big-brother eye-lock he'd perfected.

"Absolutely," Mia said. "We completely understand. And we are here for you no matter what. I'm going to look into cases of date rape and see if there are any suspects on the loose."

"You don't have to do that." I hugged my knees to my chest. "I think it was just a silly prank."

"It wasn't very funny. I'm glad to check into it. I have to go back to the office anyway."

"It's Sunday," Gabi said.

"You're the only one who doesn't work on Sundays," Kennedy said, pointing at Gabi. "I taught a workshop this morning for four hours." She rolled her shoulders with a grimace. "Thatcher was at the store, and I'm sure Sloane had a brunch or something."

Sloane nodded, reaching for a carrot stick. "A fiftieth anniversary party." She crunched into the carrot, looking wistful. "It was so sweet," she said.

Kennedy patted Sloane's knee. "You'll find the perfect man someday. Don't worry."

"Hopefully, I won't be eighty years old when I find him. These eggs aren't getting any younger."

"You're only twenty-eight," Gabi said. "You have plenty of time."

"Easy for you to say." Sloane pointed a carrot stick at Gabi. "You had a ten-year-old son when you were my age."

"I didn't exactly plan it." Gabi grabbed a carrot stick for herself and dredged it through the bowl of hummus. "You never know what will happen."

"You could meet the man of your dreams tomorrow," Kennedy said. "You just need to make sure you're open to receiving him."

Sloane laughed. "I'm on every dating site known to man. If I was any more open, my vulva would be wearing a vacancy sign."

"You should really try those Ben Wa balls I told you about," Gabi suggested. "Make sure you don't dry up."

Thatcher groaned and smacked his beer on the coffee table. "I really need to get another man in this group."

"You didn't seem to mind being the only man at the yoga retreat last month," Kennedy said.

Everyone erupted in laughter.

As the attention transferred away from me, my shoulders relaxed. Aslan settled his head against my leg, and I scratched behind his ear. As everyone chatted, my mind drifted back to Beckett, where it seemed determined to dwell.

Book Review of "Beneath the Stars" by Miranda Lockhart

BY LACEY DONOVAN, BLUERIDGEBOOKCLUB.COM

2.5 STARS

4 FIRE EXTINGUISHERS

2 BOOK BOYFRIEND BOW TIES

DEAR READERS,

My review of *Beneath the Stars* by Miranda Lockhart might surprise you. As you all know, I am obsessed with this author. I would read her to-do list if she published it. I've been holding my breath waiting for her latest novel, but *Beneath the Stars* kinda makes me wish I would have passed out from lack of oxygen instead. I swear, my air-deprived dreams would have been better than this book.

It rips my heart out to give a book written by the fabulous Miranda Lockhart anything less than four stars. I almost gave it three stars out of pity, but then I remembered my duty as a BLUE RIDGE BOOK CLUB member to give it to you, my devoted fans (Hi, Janice!) straight. I have an obligation to provide my fellow romance novel junkies everywhere with the truth no matter how much it hurts. If I was a superhero, my super power would be brutal honesty, so here it is...

Don't waste your time or money on this book. Read one of

Miranda Lockhart's earlier works instead. I'm always up for a trip down memory lane, and a re-read of *Heaven on Earth* is always worth it.

Beneath the Stars was my biggest disappointment of the year. It being February, that doesn't say much, but trust me when I say the hype on this book is a scam. Don't fall for it.

A few chapters into the book, I began to wonder if someone was impersonating Ms. Lockhart. Maybe she left her laptop at Starbucks, and someone else took over the story.

PLOT OVERVIEW:

Eight years ago, Linda Charles was driving the car that killed her best friend and paralyzed her cousin. Even though the accident wasn't her fault, she can't forgive herself. A brilliant student, she throws herself into college and graduates top of her class at Harvard Law. Her life is steeped in routine, but one day she goes into a Cuban café on the other side of town and spills coffee on Greg (a.k.a. douchebag). He proceeds to sweep Linda off her feet, showing her a side of Miami she's never seen before, and then offering her a dream job which includes a month in Europe —with him.

PROS:

- Writing: witty banter, crisp dialogue, surprisingly fresh sentence structure
- Setting: I could practically see the sunsets on Miami Beach and the twinkling lights of the Eiffel Tower.
- Sex: Hot as hell sex scenes—I was fanning myself. NSFW!!

CONS:

- Trope: Insta-love. Not. A. Fan.
- Formulaic: I've read this novel before, *haven't I?*

- Horror Movie Heroine: Linda would have gone into the basement. I HATED Linda. I rolled my eyes every time she swooned over Greg, who was a total bag of dicks. Couldn't she see that???
- Book Boyfriend: Greg was a total bag of dicks.

THE FINAL WORD:

Miranda Lockhart, if you happen to be reading this review, PLEASE get your laptop back from the lost and found at Starbucks and write another masterpiece like *Heaven on Earth*.

Love,
Lacey Donovan

Chapter Twenty

As I turned onto my street, I saw a black stretch limousine parked in front of my landlord's house. I slowed my car as I passed it, trying to look into the back seat, but the windows were too dark to see inside.

My stomach fluttered as I turned into the driveway that wound behind the main house to the matching carriage house with a three-car carport on the ground floor and my studio apartment above. By the time I parked, I trembled with anticipation. I glanced in the rearview mirror.

It couldn't be Beckett. Could it?

He wasn't due to pick me up for another two hours; however, he had threatened to ply me with romance. Showing up in a limousine was about as romantic as it got. I'd seen *Pretty Woman* like the rest of the world.

The back door of the limo opened, and my heart lurched as Beckett emerged. What was even more romantic than arriving in a limo? Your date stepping out of the limo with a bouquet.

Desire thrummed through me as Beckett started down the driveway. His dark hair burning russet under the sun, he was a vision in merino wool and cashmere carrying a bright bouquet of yellow tulips.

My stomach clenched as I watched his long-legged stride eat up the gravel. Evidently Beckett had more than one superpower. Not only could he melt panties with a single glance, but he could also explode ovaries with a flash of his smile.

My hands flew to my hair, pinning hastily. I'd just finished working in the stockroom all day, and I was a bit of a mess.

I hopped out of the car, grabbing my coat and purse. When I straightened, Beckett was only a few feet away. He smiled, and my heart squeezed. Did he have to be so handsome it hurt to look at him?

"Hey, Princess."

"Princess?" I asked with a laugh. I wasn't exactly the princess type. Princesses didn't usually have sleeves of tattoos and piercings. "I don't think I've ever been called that before."

"Hmm..." Beckett reached for me, and I thought he would take me into his arms, but he pushed aside the sleeve of my sweater instead. "Princess Alaura of Marlydia," he said with a nod at the pirate ship etched on the inside of my wrist. "That's her ship, isn't it?" he asked. "The *Renata*?"

I swallowed hard, loosening the knot in my tongue. "Yes," I confirmed.

Beckett stepped closer, sliding his hand up my arm. "You remind me of her," he said.

My eyes shot to his. "Why?" I breathed. Princess Alaura was a warrior. A hero.

"You're so brave," he said.

Holding the bouquet aside so we wouldn't crush the flowers, he pulled me close. I had a moment to appreciate the way the green flecks sparkled in his eyes as his mouth covered mine, and I closed my eyes.

I hadn't imagined how great the kisses we'd shared had been. Beckett's kiss was sweet and sensual, making me crave more of him. His fingers cradled me closer as he tasted my mouth like I was something rare and delicious. His breath puffed against my lips, and lightning streaked down my spine.

Beckett released me slowly, and I eased down off toes I hadn't known I was on. "You're early," I said when I could speak.

"I missed you." He held out the flowers. "I'm sorry I'm early. I'm all messed up. Still on London time."

"Did you bring me something to read?" I asked.

Beckett's cheeks flushed. "I don't back out on a deal."

I salivated at the thought of devouring his words. "Where is it?"

"After dinner." He reached up and touched a curl dangling from my rebellious ponytail. "I want to be sure you don't run out on me. Sneak out through the bathroom window or something."

"You've seen too many movies. I don't back out on deals either." I pointed at my hair. "I need to do something with this."

He leaned in to press another kiss to my mouth. "Take your time. I'll wait in the car. Dress warmly."

"Why?" It was in the fifties, and the air was dry.

"It will snow," Beckett promised, looking at something in the Carolina sky that I didn't see. "Don't rush. I have a book."

I sighed. I'd never heard anything sexier.

* * *

"Do you like champagne?" After setting aside his book, he pulled a bottle from a cooler.

"Yes." My eyes flickered to the book he'd just set aside, and I wondered about the one he was working on. I'd been dying of curiosity all week. I'd been sorely tempted to snoop through his office while he'd been gone.

"You look gorgeous," he said, handing me a plastic flute full of bubbling champagne.

I was wearing a deep-blue sweater that hung off my shoulder and jeans tucked into a pair of cowboy boots I'd bought in Boulder, Colorado. I'd pulled my hair up into a bun, and it was already doing its best to escape.

"How was London?"

Beckett sighed and leaned back in his seat with the champagne.

He crossed his ankles in front of him, stretching. "I'm glad to be back."

"What were you doing over there?"

I sipped my champagne, trying to act casual when I was dying of curiosity. I really knew nothing about Beckett. His work. His writing. His history. A nerve thrummed inside me, insisting I find out everything about him. Absolutely everything.

"Fixing things," he said.

I eyed him skeptically. "I need more."

His hand squeezed mine, and he laughed. "Okay." He paused as if searching for the best way to explain. "When things are broken, I fix them."

My mind whirred, trying to figure him out. "Are you in the Mafia? Is that what fixing means?"

He laughed. "I don't rough people up. I never even punched anyone until..." His words drifted off, and he cleared his throat. "My father taught me to use my brain to solve problems, not my fists. I fix companies. Not people. When companies fall apart, I figure out why. And if I can fix them, I do. If not, we restructure them until they work again." The last part he rattled off without emotion, as if he was reciting a company tagline.

"And if they don't start working again?"

He took a sip of his champagne. "That doesn't happen if I can help it." He turned toward me. "This is not a very romantic conversation," he said. "What book are you reading now?"

He knew just what to say to turn me on. "The latest Eileen McKinnon."

He tucked his flute of champagne into a holder and turned toward me. "You finished *Beneath the Stars*?"

Lust streaked through me. He'd remembered the name of the book I'd been reading. I reached over him to place my champagne next to his, then took him by the shoulder. That was it, I couldn't be so far away from this man. I had to kiss him. I slid closer.

Beckett put his arm over the back of the seat and cupped my

shoulder, pushing the sweater off my shoulder to sear my skin with his fiery touch.

"What did you think of it?" he asked.

His fingers brushed my skin, and I shuddered, liquid pooling between my thighs. Gorgeous, smart, and wants to talk books? I was melting. Were there no limits to how sexy this man could be?

My tight throat made it difficult to speak. "You can read my review. It posted yesterday."

Beckett bent his head to kiss my collarbone exposed by the drape of my neckline. "Hmm..." he said. "You smell good."

Goose bumps broke out over my skin. "Did you get any writing done in London?"

His hand came to my hip, and he pulled me closer. "Mm-hmm." He sampled my neck where it met my shoulder, causing a ripple of shivers down my spine. He curled his hand around the back of my neck, and his lips shifted up to my ear. I could feel the heat of his palm everywhere he touched.

"You didn't say if you missed me." He spoke against the sensitive shell of my ear.

My belly fluttered. I turned my cheek against his so that our mouths met. We kissed long and deep. A bolt of desire sparked through me, and I had to get closer. I shifted, hooking my leg over his. He grabbed my waist and lifted me to straddle his lap.

Our bodies pressed together, and his hands spread up my back. I opened my mouth, desperate to taste the champagne on Beckett's tongue. I couldn't get close enough.

We kissed as if we had all the time in the world to do nothing but explore each other's mouths. I tasted the sweet champagne on his tongue and breathed in the spicy scent of his aftershave. We didn't come up for air until the limousine slowed to a stop. The back door opened, and I glimpsed the black-clad legs of the driver.

I scrambled off Beckett's lap, embarrassed to have been caught making out in the back seat like a teenager. However, Beckett seemed unfazed. He reached past me for our pile of outerwear and exited the car.

"Are we here already?" I climbed out of the limo to join Beckett.

I had assumed our destination would be a restaurant, maybe in a small town similar to Mossy Oak, but we had stopped in an empty gravel parking lot in the middle of nowhere. The sun had sunk behind the mountains, splashing its last burst of orange across the ink-blue sky.

Beckett had been right about the temperature. It was much colder now than it had been when I'd left work a few hours ago. Snow dusted the narrow lane that led to the highway and coated the top boughs of the fir trees that surrounded us. Trees were everywhere, filling the air with their earthy spice. They marched over the hills in rows of green triangles, pointing at the sky.

Beckett peered into the rows of trees alongside the parked limo, his feet planted wide. A faint smile crossed his mouth as he scrutinized the view. He held his hand out for me to join him. I took his hand and stepped up beside him. I became concerned for his sanity. There didn't seem to be anything to see but rows and rows of trees.

What was he smiling at? Then I saw it—a flash of red gliding between the green trees. A faint jingling noise filled the air. Bells?

The limousine pulled back onto the road, leaving us in the gravel lot.

"I thought we were going to dinner," I said.

"We are." He pulled me toward a gap in the rows of trees. "We have to wait on our ride." He pointed through the trees. "It's almost here."

The sound of horse hooves pounding the ground grew louder, and in a flash of silver and red, a sleigh glided through the row of trees.

Chapter Twenty-One

Beckett climbed into the sleigh and reached down to take my hand. I placed my gloved hand in his and stepped up beside him.

"I would have settled for a plate of barbecue and a beer," I said.

Beckett tugged my hand and pulled me close. "That's not very romantic."

I pressed against him, sliding my arms around his neck. "You're determined to prove me wrong, aren't you?"

His hands shifted to my lower back. "Are you impressed?"

"I'm not sure yet."

Beckett bent his head and touched his mouth to mine. He wrapped his arms around my waist. His hands spread over the back of my winter coat as the hard steel of his thigh nudged my legs apart. He pulled me closer, and I felt every inch of his hard body pressing into mine.

Okay, I was impressed.

The man had a body sculpted by the gods, and a mouth made for sinning.

He slanted his head to dip his tongue into my mouth, and my pulse soared. I tasted the sweetness of the champagne and the dark hints of spice that were pure Beckett. I arched closer, sliding my fingers through the crisp hair above his collar. My breasts flattened against the iron wall of his chest, and I wished there weren't so many layers of clothes between us.

Beckett broke the kiss and trailed his lips over my jaw. "I'll keep trying," he whispered against my ear. "We better sit down though, before the driver gets tired of waiting and pulls off."

When Beckett kissed me, I forgot the world. I glanced at the driver, who sat looking at his horse, waiting patiently for us to sit down, and felt a flicker of embarrassment. My cheeks flamed pink, and I took a seat on the bench. Beckett joined me and tucked a blanket around our legs.

"You're sexy when you blush." Beckett placed a kiss behind my ear where my knit hat held back my hair.

The driver turned around to greet us. "Welcome to Azalea Falls Farm. Would you like some hot cider?" He offered us a thermos and two cups, and Beckett leaned forward to take them. "I should warn you—this cider is known for its magical properties. Those who drink it are more likely to fall in love."

Beckett poured two cups of cider as the horse trotted through the rows of trees. He handed a cup to me and put the thermos on the bench beside us.

"Are you going to try it?" he asked, his voice teasing.

My heart lurched, and my pulse went haywire. I didn't believe in enchanted cider any more than I believed in real-life happily ever afters, but suddenly I wanted to.

"Sure." I lifted the cup to my mouth. "Why not?"

Beckett raised his cup and joined me.

The taste of tart apples, spicy cinnamon, and sweet honey flooded my mouth. It was delicious. Just what I'd expected from a recipe for love.

"I can feel it working already." Beckett smiled and put his arm around my shoulder.

Warmed by the cider, the fur blanket, and Beckett's heat, I felt pleasantly drunk on life. "It's probably the champagne," I said.

Beckett cupped his hand around my shoulder and tucked me against his side. "It was a good vintage, but not that good."

We sipped the cider as the carriage cut a path through the Christmas trees. Snow sparkled in Beckett's hair and dusted his coat. I studied Beckett's profile as he gazed out at the scenery. The blade of his nose was straight and proud, but his mouth was soft and sensual. When he smiled, his face transformed from a brooding hero into a charming playboy. When his dimples popped, my blood heated. Snug under the blanket with Beckett's arm around me and his hard thigh pressed against mine, I felt like a princess in a fairy tale.

I leaned closer to him, taking in the scent of his spicy aftershave. "Tell me something about you that I don't know," I said.

His eyes found mine. "You already know something about me that only a handful of people know."

I couldn't contain my curiosity. I wanted to know everything about Beckett the author. "Who else knows?"

Beckett took our empty cups and set them aside. "My editor. My agent. My PA. You. And Summer."

"Summer knows?"

Beckett nodded. "It was an accident. She found out last year."

"What about Pressly? Does she know?"

"No."

"Are you sure? I wouldn't think a kid Summer's age would keep such a secret from her mother."

Beckett's jaw clenched. "You'd be surprised. Summer keeps a lot from her mother. She hardly talks to anyone these days."

I frowned up at him. "What's the big deal?" I asked. "Why don't you want anyone to know?"

Beckett reached up and cupped my cheek in his hand. His thumb scraped over my bottom lip. "Your mouth is distracting me." He placed a soft kiss on my top lip, then shifted to kiss the spot where his thumb had been. "Such a pretty mouth."

I leaned in for his kiss. His tongue met mine and began a slow dance of seduction. My insides melted as fire streaked from my lips through my entire body. When we broke apart, I was dizzy with lust but still curious.

"You didn't answer me." My mouth brushed against his as I spoke.

"Hmm? What was the question?" His lips nibbled mine.

"Why don't you tell anyone you're a writer? Why the secret?"

Beckett pulled back with a heavy sigh. "My family wouldn't understand."

I bristled at the familiar feeling. My choices had led to a bitter rift in my family. "Fuck your family," I said.

Beckett shook his head. "It's not like that. I enjoy my job with the family business. I thrive on it. Writing is a hobby. My job is my life. From the time I was ten years old, my father started grooming me for a role in the company. It's my legacy."

"It's not as if you aren't doing your job. Can't you have a hobby too?"

"I'd be the selfish, ungrateful son who brought attention to the family."

My eyebrows rose. "That's pretty heavy."

Beckett laughed, easing the tension in the air. "The Vinroots are the oldest, heaviest family in Mossy Oak."

"Secrets aren't good, Beckett," I said. "They have a way of getting out. You told a nine-year-old kid. You told me."

"*My niece* isn't going to tell anyone. *You* aren't going to tell anyone."

I felt dizzy with the weight of that burden. I clutched the blanket in my lap. "You hardly know me. How can you trust me already?"

Beckett pried the blanket from my fingers. "You put yourself out there for the entire world to see. I see you." His hand curved around my shoulder and squeezed. "I know you won't betray me."

My mouth fell open as realization dawned. "You didn't have the door locked for a reason," I said. "You wanted me to find out."

Beckett's eyebrows drew together as he considered my accusation.

He looked out at the rolling hills for a moment before his eyes came back to mine. They burned behind his glasses. "You may be right. I wanted the woman responsible for inspiring me to see the results."

My heart squeezed. I cupped Beckett's smooth jaw and brought him close for another kiss. Our lips clung together, tongues intertwining as our bodies swayed together.

Beckett's arms tightened around me. "You don't know how hard it was to leave you so soon after what happened."

"I was fine."

"The thought of what could have happened to you at my bar keeps me up at night. If I ever see that prick with the man bun again—"

"I saw him," I said, interrupting.

Beckett's body went rigid. "Where?"

"At the park."

"When?" His eyes turned glacial.

"Sunday afternoon."

"Why didn't you tell me?"

"I wanted to tell you in person, not on the phone while you were on the other side of the Atlantic Ocean."

Beckett's jaw tightened. "Tell me exactly what happened."

I relayed the encounter at the park with Xan as best as I could remember, trying not to leave anything out.

"He didn't touch you?"

"He just apologized and swore he was innocent."

Beckett's eyes flashed. "And you believed him?"

"Beckett, you don't understand..."

"I understand fine." His eyes shot daggers at me. "That douchebag drugged you, and you want to forgive him."

"I believe him. He was very sincere. He waited all day for me in the park because I wouldn't answer his calls."

Beckett's eyes widened almost comically. "*He waited for you?*"

My anger surged. It wasn't Beckett who'd been drugged—it was me. And it was up to me to forgive, not him. "Why shouldn't I believe him? Whether or not you want to admit it, Xan had no motive to drug me."

Beckett's entire body went still, and his eyes turned smoky with anger. "I can't believe you are saying this right now. I can't believe we are even talking about that creep with the man bun, or that you're defending him."

Anger bubbled over inside me, spreading like spilled ink that couldn't be re-bottled. "It's my choice."

Beckett said nothing for a long time. He looked out at the rows of trees, his stare so cold it could give the branches goose bumps.

"I just thought you should know," I said. "I don't know what's going on with us, but whatever it is, it can't start with lies."

"Talking about him drives me crazy."

I brushed my lips against his. "Then we shouldn't talk about him anymore."

Chapter Twenty-Two

We talked about everything else. Our conversation hardly stopped on the twenty-minute ride. I found out about Beckett's favorite things: what food he liked, what movies he watched over and over, and what books he couldn't live without.

We didn't stop talking until the sleigh came to a stop in front of a red-and-white barn draped in twinkling lights. A handful of cars were parked in a grassy lot, but other than that, we were alone.

"We're eating in a barn?" I asked.

Beckett hopped down from the sleigh and held his arms up for me. "Trust me?"

The last time I'd trusted a man, he'd broken my heart. Trust wasn't something I offered freely. But this was just dinner. *Dinner in a barn.* My lip curled at the irony. Beckett wore thousand-dollar suits, but he'd taken me to eat in a place that had once housed cows.

Still not sure if I trusted him, I braced my hands on Beckett's wide shoulders and let him swing me to the ground. He tucked my hand in his as the sleigh pulled away. "You hesitated a little too long for my liking," he said, walking me to the front door. "You have the power to upend my life, but you don't trust my choice of dining establishments?"

Beckett's voice sliced me to the core. I knew more about him than almost anyone, and I'd given him nothing in return.

He squeezed my hand. "I'm teasing you, Princess."

I glanced up and saw the dimple popping in his cheek.

"The food better be good," I warned.

"Azalea Farms was lucky enough to snag five-star chef Helmut Stromberg. His food will send you straight to Munich. Have you been to Germany?" he asked.

"Not yet." It was on the list. Germany and many other European countries. "I figured I would get through the United States first, then head overseas."

Beckett stopped in front of the door. "How many states so far?"

I ticked them off in my head. "I've lived in eleven."

Beckett's eyebrows rose. "That's seven more than me."

I shrugged. "I move around a lot. I never stay anywhere too long before I'm off to the next adventure."

Beckett's eyebrows lowered and drew together. "How long have you been in Mossy Oak?"

"A long time. Nearly a year."

Beckett reached for the door and pulled it open. The smell of roasting meat and fried bread wafted out the door. My mouth watered at the scent. Inside, the restaurant looked like it belonged in a cosmopolitan European city, not a farm. White tablecloths draped over secluded tables under low-lit chandeliers. The tinkle of piano music drifted up to the high ceiling.

The hostess took our coats and led us to a private booth in the corner. Once we settled across from each other at the table, Beckett reached for my hand.

"We should get away for the weekend." Beckett squeezed my hand. "I haven't been on vacation in forever, but spending time with you makes me want to go somewhere. Have you been to Littlecloud?"

My heart skipped a beat. Littlecloud was a famous inn and bookshop on a private island off the coast of Florida. Owned by one of the most famous authors in the world, the inn was a dream destination for a bookworm like me.

"You would want to visit Littlecloud?"

"I've been there a few times. It's a great getaway."

"This is our first date. Maybe we shouldn't talk about weekend getaways."

Beckett smiled. "I'm not asking you to move in with me." He reached for my hand. "Although, my house is big enough."

"Beckett!"

He laughed. "What?"

"You're going too fast."

"I know." He squeezed my hand. "Sometimes I have a hard time slowing down. My life moves so fast, I always feel like I'm a step behind. I'm always chasing the next thing. But when I met you, I knew I wanted you in my life."

His confession made my skin tingle. I'd wanted him from the moment I'd seen him too. Even though I hadn't wanted anyone in years. Even though he'd been a jerk.

The waitress came over to get our drink orders. I ordered my favorite beer, and Beckett ordered a whiskey on the rocks. I'd never known anyone who drank whiskey before, but it suited Beckett.

We flirted through dinner, holding hands across the table and feeding each other bites of our food. Before we knew it, we were the last ones in the restaurant. Lingering over coffee and dessert, we discussed books and other important topics.

"Tell me something I don't know about you," Beckett said.

I thought for a moment, trying to come up with something that we hadn't touched on yet. I took a bite of the chocolate cake as I stalled for time.

"I like sexy underwear," I said, swallowing.

Beckett's eyes turned smoky, and he raised his hand in the air to signal the waitress. "Check please."

I laughed. "One more thing, I don't put out on the first date."

Beckett took the fork from my hand and helped himself to a bite of the cake. "I don't either."

I'd expected more of a challenge, maybe some pleading. I found myself a little disappointed. I took long breaks in between men, and being in such close quarters with such a man as Beckett made me realize how long it had been. There hadn't been a man in my life since I'd moved to Mossy Oak.

Beckett flashed a wicked grin. "You look disappointed."

"No. I'm just surprised."

"That's not my idea of romance, Lacey."

He cut another bite of cake and offered it to me. I leaned forward and closed my lips over the fork.

"Romance is different than sex. Until you mentioned your sexy underwear and made me picture ripping them off you, I hadn't even given much thought to sex tonight." He laughed at the incredulity on my face. "Okay, well maybe a little when you climbed on my lap in the limo."

The waitress deposited the check just in time to hear Beckett. She gave me a wink as she turned to leave.

"I did not climb on your lap," I said in a low voice when she'd gone. "You put me there."

"You stayed. And you liked it."

I recalled how hard he'd been pressing against me and smiled. "You liked it too."

"I sure did." He pulled out his phone. "What's your email?"

"Why?"

"You didn't sneak out the window, so I'm sending the chapters."

I took a business card from my purse and passed it across the table to Beckett.

"It looks just like you." He peered down at the business card, then looked up at me with a wicked gleam in his eye. "You don't actually own an outfit like that, do you?"

The girl in the cartoon picture was wearing a black mini-skirt, knee-high boots, and a tight crop top.

"I might." I tapped my finger against my lip. "There is something I'm dying to know about you," I said.

"Oh?" Beckett peeled four hundred-dollar bills from his wallet and tossed them on the tray with the bill. "What's that?"

I eyed the money, wondering how expensive this dinner had been and how much of that was tip. When I glanced back at Beckett, he was waiting for my answer.

"Your socks," I said. "What's the story with them?"

Beckett burst out laughing. "You want to know about my socks?"

"Admit it, they are unusual. They don't really go with the rest of your vibe."

"What vibe is that?"

"The boss-man vibe."

His mouth curved in a smile. "Did you know I have seven sisters?"

"No." I wondered what that had to do with anything.

He nodded. "My parents have been married nine times between them. My dad five. My mom four. There are eight of us siblings total, including halves and steps. I'm the only male."

"Wow." I was an only child who hadn't talked to my family since I left Milwaukee years ago. My parents had been married forever and had hated each other for about as long. "Holidays must be fun."

He nodded. "My sisters started giving me socks as gifts a few years ago. The crazier the better." He pulled up his pant leg and showed me his black-and-white zebra print socks. "Now I get socks for every holiday."

I smiled. "Valentine's Day is in a few weeks."

"Now you know what to get me." He got up from the table. "I hate to cut this short, but I have an early flight tomorrow."

"But you just got back."

"I left a few things unfinished so I wouldn't miss our date."

My jaw dropped. "You came back from London to take me on a date?"

He cocked an eyebrow at me as I climbed out of the booth to stand next to him. "Trying too hard?" he asked.

I laughed. "Definitely." I'd never been out with a man who tried half as hard. "You didn't have to do that. I would have waited."

He slid an arm around my waist and pulled me close. "Maybe you could have. But I couldn't."

Chapter Twenty-Three

I read Beckett's chapters as soon as he dropped me off at my apartment. With his kiss still lingering on my lips, I devoured his words.

From his first sentence to his last mark of punctuation, I was enthralled. Beckett weaved a setting full of life and characters so real, I could picture having coffee with them. His words made my skin crawl, my breath hitch, and my heart race.

I read the last sentence and wanted more.

I scrambled to my phone and scrolled down to Beckett's name. He answered on the second ring.

"Hello?" The deep gravel of his voice made my belly clench.

"Hi."

"Everything okay? Did you forget something?"

"Is Michael going to come back?" I blurted. "It's the only thing that will save Isobel."

Beckett's low laugh rumbled. "You read it so soon?"

I pulled in a breath, trying to get my words to slow down, my heart to quit racing. "Beckett, this is..." I scrolled back to the first page and read the first line again. *The floor bled.* I stood up and went to my door. "I'm locking my door right now."

"You should have done that as soon as I left."

His voice sent a shiver down my spine. Beckett hadn't been exaggerating when he'd said his novel was dark and gritty. My skin tingled, and my heartbeat drummed in my chest.

"You were right," I said. "This book is scary. But it's so great. It reminds me of Perry Griffin's early novels." I waved a hand in the air that Beckett couldn't see. "Not the last one. It was commercial crap."

Beckett's deep laugh rumbled over the line. "You read *Woven Uprising?*"

I gripped the phone tighter. "Don't try to change the subject. You do that every time I ask about your writing. Or you kiss me and I forget what we were talking about." I couldn't think straight when Beckett kissed me.

"I wish I could kiss you right now."

My lips tingled. We'd kissed the whole ride home in the limo and kissed again at the door. It had been hard not to invite him in for more, but we'd both agreed to wait.

"I can't wait to read more," I said.

"Does that mean I'm getting a second date?"

"Do I have to wait until then to read anything else?"

"Is that a yes?"

My belly tightened and my chest ached from the drumming of my heart. "Yes."

"I'll send you something as soon as I write it."

"Hurry."

"Good night, Lacey."

"Good night."

* * *

Beckett sent me chapter after spectacular chapter. I devoured his words and looked forward to more. When he sent the emails with the files, he would always include a limerick. They were witty and charming and just as well-crafted as his chapters. His writing style reminded me of an author I'd read before, but I couldn't pinpoint who. His writing was funny and smart, dark and intriguing. I couldn't read it without making sure my door was locked and dead bolted.

Beckett had been gone five days and had sent me forty pages. When I asked him how he managed to get that much writing done while he was working, he said he thrived on being busy. He was a self-confessed workaholic. It was the only way he could have what he wanted and give his family what they expected.

His busy schedule exhausted me. I could barely stay awake past 10:00 p.m. Walking the dogs and working at the bookshop kept me on my feet all day, and when I got home, all I wanted to do was curl up on my couch with a good book.

I'd drifted off reading Beckett's work but woke with a start when my phone rang. My chest tightened and chills broke out on my skin. I'd just finished reading a suspenseful twist in Beckett's novel where a ringing phone prompted a murder, and my first thought was panic.

I pulled my phone from where it had fallen between the cushions of the sofa and saw Beckett's name scroll across the screen. It was 11:30 p.m., which meant it was 4:30 a.m. in London.

I flipped the phone open. "Hello?"

"Hey, Princess."

His voice sent a tingle of awareness down my spine. I shivered and reached for the blanket. "You scared the crap out of me."

"Sorry. Did I wake you?"

"I fell asleep reading. Isobel has me spooked."

"I told you it was dark."

Beckett's book was about a female serial killer who would not rest until she'd taken vengeance on everyone involved in her mother's death. She should have been terrifying, but I couldn't help sympathizing with her.

"What time is it in London?"

"I'm not in London anymore. I'm in New York. I flew in a few hours ago."

I heard clanging metal and recognized it as the sound of weights.

Only Beckett would work out so late at night. The man lived by his own clock. "Are you in the hotel gym?" I asked.

"No," he said over the noises in the background. "I have a place in New York."

"I've never been there. What's it like?"

"My place is in Chelsea," he said. "It's on the top floor of a new building. I bought it for the amazing views. I can see the Hudson River from my bedroom. It's..." He paused. "Lonely." His tone was resigned, mocking. "I'm used to having more people around. Summer. Pressly. Aslan—even though he's a pain in the ass. Then there's you." He grew serious. "I miss you."

A tremor of longing streaked through me. I missed him too. How was it possible to miss someone you hardly knew? I pictured Beckett in his Chelsea apartment—his hair damp, a towel around his neck, and quirky socks on his feet.

"I called because I want you to come away with me this weekend. We can leave Saturday morning. It's nice in Florida this time of year; let's go to Littlecloud."

Every part of me wanted to say yes. My heart and head were in agreement, but I couldn't do this weekend. "I can't. I have plans."

Beckett was quiet, and I knew he wasn't used to being rejected. "I see." Metal clanged in the background. "Do you have a hot date?"

He didn't sound happy about the prospect. I considered letting him think I was going on a hot date for about a hot second before admitting the truth. "It's not what you're thinking. I have plans for Sunday at Hyperbole's." Even though Beckett had overshadowed everything lately, I'd had this date on my mind for nearly a month. "Miranda Lockhart is coming."

"Oh."

"I'm sorry. I have to meet her. She's my favorite—"

"I know," he said. "She's your favorite author. I wouldn't ask you to miss meeting her. I'm sorry. I didn't think."

"It's okay."

"I'd much rather Miranda Lockhart be my competition than another man."

I swallowed the lump in my throat. "There isn't another man."

"Good," he said. "There isn't another woman."

My heart beat wildly. "I thought a man like you would have a girlfriend in every city he visited." The thought made me nauseated.

"A man like me does nothing but work."

I heard a whirring sound in the background. "You sound like you're on a treadmill," I teased.

"I work out when I'm stuck on an idea. It frees up my mind. That's what I was doing the first time we met."

I remembered the day I'd seen him the first time, and my cheeks heated. He'd been so gorgeous. He'd been wearing only a pair of shorts and those rubber ducky socks.

"What socks are you wearing?"

His low chuckle sounded across the line, making my belly clench. "Are you asking me what I'm wearing?"

My cheeks flushed, and my stomach clenched. I squeezed my thighs together as a thrill shot through me. Even though my question had been innocent enough, now it felt dirty. "Yes," I confessed.

"Lacey Donovan, are you trying to have phone sex with me?"

I swallowed. "Maybe."

Phone sex was unfamiliar territory for me. It had always seemed silly and desperate. I didn't even like reading about phone sex in books. I usually skipped those scenes. But now I understood the incredible draw of a smooth, sexy voice over the phone. It was private, safe. No witnesses. No risks. Nothing but Beckett's cultured voice with that faint trace of Southern sweetness seducing me from far away.

I might have some re-reading to do.

"Ever since you told me you love sexy underwear, I've been thinking a lot about undressing you." Beckett's low murmur caused fire to streak down my spine. "I'd press my mouth to the hollow of your neck and feel your pulse on my tongue."

I lay back on the couch and closed my eyes. It wasn't too hard to imagine Beckett's firm lips trailing kisses across my shoulder.

"Where are you right now?" he asked. "In your bedroom?"

My apartment was one big room. My "bedroom" was at the far end, tucked under the A-frame of the roof. I got up and padded across the room to the bed, then sat down. "Yes."

"Lie back."

I did as he told me.

"Unbutton your shirt," Beckett said.

I had changed into Beckett's T-shirt. "It doesn't have any buttons."

"Are you wearing my T-shirt?" he asked.

"Yes."

Silence ensued, then I heard his low growl. "Send me a picture."

"My phone doesn't do that."

I heard his muffled curse. "You're killing me with that ancient phone," he said. "Please tell me you're not wearing a bra."

I smiled. "I'm not wearing a bra."

He groaned. "I never wished I was a T-shirt more in my life. What about your pants?"

"Leggings."

"Slide your hand under the waistband."

He waited a beat for me to oblige. Imagining it was Beckett's hand gliding over my belly, I slid my hand lower.

"I'll bet you taste as sweet as a peach," he whispered. "I want to taste you. I'm going to insist on it first thing when I see you."

Warmth spread through me, and my breath quickened.

"A little lower." His words were raspy. "All the way."

Arching my back, I did as I was told. A moan escaped my mouth as I imagined Beckett's long fingers slipping inside me.

My body pulsed, throbbing to be touched. The tips of my breasts strained against Beckett's T-shirt.

"I've wanted to touch you since the first moment I saw you." His voice was strained. "And this isn't the first time I've jerked off thinking of you."

I pictured Beckett touching himself while thinking about me, and a pang of longing shot through me to my core.

"Slide your finger inside, Princess. Find that sweet spot. The one that makes you feel good."

Hearing the growl of need in Beckett's voice made me so hot I thought I would combust. I delved one finger inside and shuddered at how good it felt. Beckett's voice directed me to push another finger inside, to stretch myself for him.

"I'm going to rip off your sexy underwear and kneel between your legs. When I slide my tongue inside you, I'm going to make you mine. Do you want that? Do you want to be mine?"

My blood heated, and my breath came fast and hard. Beckett murmured his approval as he heard the change.

"I need you to say it. When I lick your sweet clit, you're going to be my woman. All mine. I'm going to fuck you with my tongue until you come in my mouth." His breath was ragged. "Do you want that?"

I panted. "Yes."

"Say it. Say my name."

I thought of Beckett's tongue licking along my slick seam. I wanted it. I wanted him. I wanted to run my tongue over every dip and ridge of his abdomen. I wanted to move aside his hand and take him into my mouth. I needed to feel his hard length. I wanted to know the shape of him. The taste...

My fingers glided over the tight bundle of nerves at the apex of my thighs and I gasped.

"Are you close?" Beckett's sexy voice filled my ear.

I was so close, I was about to catch fire. I tried to answer, but my voice failed me. Every nerve was alive and pulsing. Every breath brought me nearer the edge. I could only moan into the phone, and the sound of raw desire coming from my throat was too much. I flipped over the edge, shuddering as I found release.

"Yes." I moaned.

"Say my name," Beckett commanded.

I said his name, not once, but over and over, until my apartment echoed with the sound of my pleasure.

I don't know how much time passed as I lay there, blissed out and clutching my phone to my ear.

Turns out phone sex had been just what I needed. I felt relaxed and tingling all over. And I was alone. There would be no cuddling, no excuses, no reason to run before morning came.

"Lacey?" His voice sounded husky, and I pictured his flushed face.

"Yes?"

"Never say you're not my type again," he warned. "We were made for each other."

Chapter Twenty-Four

"What's wrong with you?" Gabi asked after our book club meeting the following night. "You hardly said a word all night."

"Nothing," I said.

She raised her eyebrows at me. "Liar."

We stopped at her car, but Gabi wasn't ready to let things drop. She crossed her arms over her chest and pinned me with her mom-of-a-teenager stare that usually worked. Not today. Today I was too confused to put words to my inner turmoil.

Thatcher came out of Hyperbole's and locked the door behind him.

"Thatch," Gabi called. "Come over here and help me with Lacey."

Thatcher strolled over and slung an arm around my shoulders. "What's going on?"

"Nothing's going on. I'm fine. I just want to go back to my apartment and sink into my newest books."

By the looks on their faces, something in my voice must have given me away.

"Methinks she doth protest too much." Thatcher squeezed my

shoulder and steered me away from Gabi's car. "This calls for chocolate."

Gabi checked the time. "I have thirty minutes before I have to get Shane from practice." Not waiting for us, she strode down the sidewalk toward Frenchie's Chocolate Shop. She opened the door and ushered us inside. "Find somewhere to sit. I'll get the usual."

Thatcher turned to look at her. "No—"

"White chocolate," Gabi said, interrupting him as she turned for the counter. "I know."

The scent of cocoa and caramel made my mouth water. I'd walked dogs during dinner, and I couldn't remember what I had for lunch. Over the last week, I'd taken on as many dog-walking clients as I could handle. Whenever I had an idle moment, I obsessed over Beckett. It was better to stay busy.

Thatcher led me to a booth under a chandelier shaped like an octopus. Tiny paper hearts hung from the glass tentacles. Just in time for Valentine's Day. I should get Beckett a pair of socks in honor of the holiday. Where would I find a pair of crazy socks?

Tears welled in my eyes. I blinked them back with a snort. "I don't know why I'm crying."

Thatcher grabbed a chair from a nearby table and dragged it to the booth. He turned it around backward and straddled it, leaning forward on the table. His blue eyes settled on mine, calm in the wake of my storm.

"Does this have anything to do with a certain author?" he asked.

My jaw fell open. "What are you talking about?"

"Summer let it slip about her uncle."

I glanced around to make sure no one was listening. "Jesus, Thatcher! No one is supposed to know. He wouldn't be happy that Summer is telling people."

Thatcher gave me a hurt look. "I'm people now, huh?"

I waved a hand at him. "This isn't about you. Beckett is private about his writing. You haven't said anything to anyone, have you?"

"No. Why would I? It's none of my business. I know how to respect a man's privacy. And she made me swear not to tell."

"You just told me."

"I figured you already knew." He stood as Gabi approached the table. "I figured right, didn't I?"

I grabbed his sleeve. "Don't say anything, okay?"

"Don't worry. My lips are sealed."

Tears welled behind my eyes, and I struggled to blink them away.

"Tell me what's going on in that head of yours." He leaned across the table. "You're not planning on taking off, are you?"

That was the problem. I hadn't even thought about leaving Mossy Oak. Beckett wanted me to be his. He'd said the word "mine" with the same passion I'd cried out his name. I should be packing up my life in anticipation of my next move, but I hadn't even picked up any boxes.

I hung my head in my hands, tears of frustration leaking from my eyes.

"What the hell, Thatcher?" Gabi slapped a box of chocolates on the table. "What did you do?"

"It's not my fault," he said. "She's in love."

I lowered my hands to glare at Thatcher. "I am not."

Gabi selected a chocolate and took a bite, smiling as she chewed. "I thought I recognized that glow."

"I am not in love." My cheeks heated, and my heart squeezed. *Was I?*

"Definitely in love." Thatcher grabbed a piece of chocolate and popped it into his mouth. "Look at that blush."

I hated it when people pointed out my embarrassment. Didn't they know that only made it worse? I cursed my pale skin that always gave away my thoughts.

"Spill," Gabi said. "Is it Sloane's boss? The one who punched the pervert?"

"His name is Beckett," I said, feeling my temperature rise as his name tripped over my tongue. "And Xan is not a pervert."

"How does Boss Man feel about you?" Gabi asked.

I shrugged. My friends exchanged a long look, then both broke out in smiles.

"Stop," I said, holding up a hand as they both started speaking at once. "This is all too good to be true." Beckett was too good. Too tall. Too handsome. Too everything. "You should have seen the date he took me on. It was something straight out of a Miranda Lockhart novel." I wiped my eyes, thinking back to the most perfect date I'd ever been on. "There was a sleigh ride—" I took a breath in and out, pushing back the emotion. "And snow, and—" Another long inhale and exhale. "Magic cider, for crying out loud."

I knew how to breathe mindfully from taking Kennedy's yoga classes. I tried to count to five on my inhales and let my breath out to the same count. Deep, ujjayi breaths. Deep inhales. Deep exhales. Long inhales that didn't do anything to calm my racing heart. Long exhales that didn't make me want to stop throwing up one bit less.

"He shouldn't exist." Thoughts of Beckett Vinroot shot my breathing to hell. "He's Heathcliff. He's William Darcy," I said, leaning my forehead on my fist. "He's Almanzo Wilder."

Beckett was mysterious, engaging, and romantic. He was all of my favorite romance heroes rolled into one—and he scared the hell out of me.

Gabi nudged my elbow, and I raised my head to look at her. "But is he Christian Grey?" she asked.

"I don't know." I sighed.

"Ah!" Gabi wiggled her eyebrows. "That's the problem." She had a knowing gleam in her eye. "You're not in love. You just need to get laid."

"One-track mind." Thatcher gestured at Gabi, rolling his eyes.

"It's true," Gabi insisted. "Go to bed with him, and you'll find out pretty quickly he's not as perfect as he seems." Gabi bit into another piece of chocolate. "He probably has a Tic Tac penis, or he refuses to go down on you, or he finishes before you've even gotten started..." Gabi trailed off shaking her head. "Or all of the above."

"He doesn't have a Tic Tac penis," I said. I'd been in his lap in the back of the limo long enough to know that.

"Please don't ever say that phrase again in my presence,"

Thatcher begged. "It's offensive to every man alive."

"Relax," Gabi said. "Everyone knows we aren't talking about you."

Thatcher had been featured in a Mossy Oak calendar of eligible bachelors for a charity. In his underwear. There wasn't much hiding anything in the boxer briefs he'd worn.

"Get your head out of the gutter, Mrs. Salinger," Thatcher said. "Sex isn't the answer to everything."

Gabi's mouth dropped open. "Get out your wallet."

"Why?"

"I'm taking your man card." Her eyes flashed over him. "If you still even have it."

Thatcher turned toward me. "You don't need to get laid," he said. "Maybe you need the opposite. You need distance. Take a break from him. Then you'll see if you miss him."

"That's the worst advice I've ever heard," Gabi said. "Don't listen to Thatcher. Go over to his house and jump his bones."

"He's in New York."

"That's a problem."

"That's perfect," Thatcher insisted. "Take a breather." He nodded for emphasis. "Everything will become clear."

I closed my eyes with a sigh and leaned my head back against the booth. I had a strong feeling sex with Beckett was only going to make it harder to deny him. I wasn't even sure I wanted to resist him, but I was too scared to find out. My heart might not be able to take it.

"You should go to Kennedy's next yoga retreat." Thatcher said. "Get away for the weekend."

"After you bone him," Gabi said.

Thatcher sighed loudly. "Whatever you do, don't run away."

"I'm not running away."

Thatcher covered my hand with his and squeezed. "You'll figure it out. I have faith in you." He transferred his attention to Gabi. "Now, can we talk about you, Mrs. Salinger? How's your love life?"

It was Gabi's turn to squirm, and I sat back to watch.

Chapter Twenty-Five

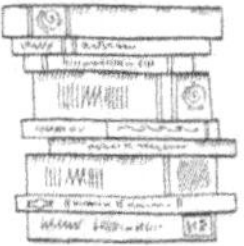

A few days later, I let myself into Beckett's house to walk Aslan. As soon as I walked into the house, Aslan bounded across the floor. He skidded to a halt just shy of my ankles.

I bent down to pet him. "What are you doing on the loose?" I straightened and walked through the foyer into the white living room. One glance told me that Aslan had behaved himself. The only color in the room was in the paintings hanging on the walls.

Although everything was in place, I sensed something different. My heart froze and then tripped to life as I noticed Beckett's brief-case on the kitchen counter. A shiver ran down my spine as I spotted his camel-hair coat tossed over a stool.

I dropped my purse and hurried down the hall. Aslan chased me, then ran ahead of me to the staircase leading down to Beckett's bedroom. Aslan leaped down the stairs two at a time; I followed on his heels.

Chills danced along my skin as I heard the low murmur of Beckett's voice.

Did he have on a suit? Or maybe he was wearing faded jeans and one of those insanely soft sweaters? I thought about pressing my cheek to his chest and inhaling his spicy scent.

I didn't care what he was doing. I only wanted to see him, to throw my arms around him, to tell him...

Beckett's laugh sounded low and sensual. My belly tightened and my sex throbbed, humming in anticipation of his hands on me.

But first, we needed to talk.

I stepped into his room and saw Beckett sitting at his desk with his phone to his ear. He removed his glasses and placed them on his desk in what had become a familiar gesture, and my pulse raced.

I stood watching him, frozen. I couldn't breathe as my eyes raked from the top of his head over his broad shoulders. Suddenly, he spun around in his chair, squinting across the room.

He saw it was me, and his face changed. His mouth went from stern to smiling. His dimples popped, and my body ached for him.

"I'll call you back," Beckett said into the phone.

Without waiting for an answer, he tapped the screen and tossed the phone to the desk. He grabbed his glasses and set them on his face as he rose from the chair. His smile grew as his eyes blazed over me, devouring me like a long-awaited new release.

Any other man would have looked tired and rumpled after a long day of traveling, but not Beckett. Square jaw, thick hair styled to perfection—Beckett looked like a magazine ad for men's cologne. The scent would be cedar, and spice, and very, very expensive.

His energy filled the room, enveloping me in its sizzling embrace. His smile curved as he finished his slow perusal of my appearance. He looked gorgeous and sexy and... hungry.

In two long-legged strides, he reached for me. His arms closed around me, and his lips crashed down on mine.

I couldn't think. I couldn't stop the moan of pleasure that pushed past my lips. His hands slid down my back, molding me to every inch of his iron-hard body.

I clutched his shirt front and stretched higher on my toes, unable to get close enough to satisfy my craving of him. His taste. His smell. The feel of his smoothly shaved cheek rubbing against mine. I wanted more of him. I wanted everything.

Beckett shifted his lips from mine, and I protested by clinging tighter. He reached past me and shut the door on Aslan's curious face, then both his hands were back on me. He backed me up, and then his mouth was on mine again.

I wound my arms around his neck and brushed my fingers over the crisply clipped hair at the nape of his neck. The soft bristles undulated under my touch. The skin below was silky smooth. My busy fingers trailed down his collar and around his throat to the first button.

Beckett stepped back before I could work the button free. He dropped to his knees in front of me and reached up to encircle my waist. His eyes flashed up, and I could see the desire pulsing through him. A thrill raced through me as his thumb slipped under the waistband of my jeans.

He'd told me he wanted me to belong to him. I'd meant to tell him I didn't belong to him, or anyone. But I couldn't find the words. I wanted his mouth. We'd talk later. We'd work everything out. I would say I didn't want a relationship. I didn't do romance. He would understand.

My thoughts went hazy as Beckett unclasped the button on my jeans and dragged down my zipper. His eyes stayed on mine the entire time he pushed my jeans over my hips, burning through me, seeing everything. Could he tell how terrified I was? Could he hear the thoughts banging around inside my head?

He lowered his eyes to look at me, and the noise he made —somewhere between a growl and a moan—melted me. His eyes devoured the delicate lace that covered my sex, then shot up to mine, hot and hungry. The panties were one of my favorites. A purple lace thong embroidered with bright orange flowers, it plunged low in the front, covering only the essentials. A tiny bow at the top of the low V added a touch of sweetness.

Beckett's eyes snapped up to mine. "Can I kiss you?"

The rasp in his voice made my knees quake. The first words spoken between us since my arrival scorched through me. The memory of Beckett's promise echoed in my head. Once he put his mouth on me, it would be the same as a brand searing my heart. It would mark me as his woman.

The hot pads of his fingers eased under the elastic band at my hips. My skin sizzled from his touch. I could feel the puff of his breath against my thigh, so close to my center, but not nearly close enough. I wanted his mouth on me—yes. But was I ready to give my heart? Not a chance.

I braced my hands on his shoulders and felt the flex of his muscles as he spread his hands over my hips to cup my bare cheeks. His eyes were on mine, smoky hot beneath inky lashes. I couldn't take the heat of his gaze. I reached up and pulled off his glasses, afraid they would spontaneously combust from the fire in his eyes.

Beckett kneaded my soft flesh, one hand tracing along the elastic band up and over my hip. He flicked the bow on my panties. I shivered, and he grinned up at me.

"You want me to kiss you?" He slid his thumb under the lace at the inside of my thigh. "You want my mouth on you?"

"Yes." I wanted it. I needed it. I was on fire for it. "But..." I leaned my head against the door and watched from slitted eyes as Beckett hooked his finger under the scrap of lace and tugged it aside. His warm breath brought chills to my skin.

"Let me give you what you want." He scraped his chin against my inner thigh. He was so close that I could feel his lips move when he spoke. "Let me inside that big beautiful heart," he said against my skin. "Let me give you everything you need."

My heart thundered so hard in my chest I thought it would burst. I let Beckett's glasses slip to the floor and threaded my fingers in his hair.

"Yes?" Beckett asked, teeth nipping at my thigh.

I nodded and squeezed my eyes shut as he brushed kisses across my belly.

"Not good enough, Princess," he said in a tightly coiled growl. "I need your words." He nudged the delicate lace of my panties aside, his breath stirring my mound of blonde curls.

A frantic spasm of need tore through me. "Yes." The word burst from my mouth, ending on a desperate hiss.

As soon as the word ripped from my mouth, I had what I wanted—Beckett's mouth trailing fire over my skin. His tongue lapped at the inside of my thigh. I bucked my hips against his face, desperately wanting more. The sound Beckett made was just short of feral as he hooked his fingers around the thin lace and yanked. The elastic snapped, and the lace fell away.

My blood roared in my ears as Beckett spread my thighs apart. He grabbed my hips, tilting me up like a dessert he couldn't wait to devour. My breath came in hot little pants as he spread me wider. His fingers stroked over me, sliding through my wetness. His thumb brushed over my tight bundle of nerves, and I whipped my head back. Pain ricocheted through me as my skull banged on the hard wood and then pleasure flooded me when Beckett pushed a finger inside.

I clutched his shoulders as his velvet tongue licked up my seam. He eased me closer, burying his face against me as he sucked and probed and did things with his tongue that I didn't think possible.

A riot of sensations built inside me as he swirled his tongue over my sensitive flesh, nibbling, sucking, gently biting...

I writhed against him, losing all sense of shame as I rode the waves of pleasure on his magic tongue.

"Yes." The word tore from my throat, ragged and wild.

Beckett groaned against me. The added vibration was my undoing. A savage orgasm crashed over me. I didn't have time to fight it. I had no choice but to surrender and let myself tumble into the thrilling abyss. Beckett's arms tightened around me. He hitched my leg up higher, catching me as I fell.

* * *

Words scrambled over each other in my head, struggling to form a story. One name kept repeating over and over, trying to break past my lips.

Beckett. Beckett. Beckett.

He grabbed his glasses from the floor and rose to tower over me. My hands trailed from his shoulders to his chest where I felt his heat radiating under the soft cotton of his shirt.

"Beckett..." I gave in to the overwhelming need to say his name.

I realized it was one of the few words I'd spoken since I'd walked into his bedroom. And now, I had to go. I'd only come to pick up Aslan. It didn't feel right to leave after what he'd just done, but Aslan was waiting.

I dropped my hands from his chest.

"I have to go," I told him, pulling up my jeans. My panties were ruined, lying on the floor at our feet.

What he'd done with his mouth shouldn't have been possible. He'd done things—and made me feel things—that I'd only read about. I knew now that it was actually possible to see stars. A whole galaxy of them.

I dropped my hands to the front of his chest, then lower... over his belt, and then along the zipper of his pants. Beckett froze as I flattened my palm over the hard length of him. He sucked in a sharp breath.

"I didn't do that for anything in return," he said, voice full of gravel. "I just wanted to. I needed to."

"I know." I squeezed his impressive length, eager to drive him as crazy as he'd driven me.

Beckett inched away from my exploring hand. "There's nothing I want better than to do exactly what you're thinking." His words faded into a growl as I reached for him again. He grabbed my hand, trapping it between us. "But, not now. I won't rush this with you."

"We didn't get a chance to talk before..."

He squinted down at me, eyes hot and soft at the same time. "Before I made you come on my tongue?"

My cheeks burned at the image. "I'm not ready for this."

His eyebrows drew together. "I told you we would take it slow. We have time."

"I'm not talking about sex," I said. "I'm talking about us. What if we don't have time? I don't even know where I will be in a few months. My lease is almost up."

Taking my shoulders in his hands, Beckett gently separated us. His eyes found mine, probing deeply behind the lenses of his glasses. "You're thinking of moving?"

I nodded. My throat ached. "It's what I do."

Beckett's jaw clenched. "It doesn't have to be."

My chest ached, and my blood ran cold. I didn't let myself get attached to people. I usually took off long before I got anywhere near this close. "It's the only way I know." I could barely push the words through my tight throat.

Beckett wrapped me in his arms and rested his chin on top of my head. I resisted for a single heartbeat and then melted into him, linking my arms around his waist. "We can find a new way."

"We haven't even started yet. It's easier this way."

Beckett curled his hand around my low ponytail and tugged until I looked up and met his eyes. "We started the moment we met." His voice was steady, confident, and sure. A touch arrogant. He bent his head and kissed me. I tasted myself, and my body thrummed with desire. He thrust his magic tongue against mine, kissing me until we were both breathless.

"Beckett..." I pulled back.

"We can talk more tonight," he said. "I've got meetings all afternoon, so it might be late."

"I don't want anything fancy," I said. "No limos. No sleighs. No barns with five-star restaurants."

"You have a lot of rules." He smiled down at me, making those dimples pop. If I'd been wearing panties, they'd be soaked.

He tugged my hair again, and I turned my face up for one last kiss. My head and other parts of my body seemed to be at war. My head was losing, especially when he dipped his tongue between my lips.

Chapter Twenty-Six

The Carolina blue sky stretched for miles without a cloud. If only my mind was that clear. I walked through the park in a daze, letting the dogs pull me wherever they liked. I didn't hear the laughter or smell the blooming crocuses. I didn't notice the bikers whizzing past or the chill in the air.

My skin was still warm from Beckett's touch.

My phone jangled, and I shifted the leashes to one hand to fish it from the pocket of my coat.

"What's up, Sloane?"

"I'm at the Inn. She's here!"

"What?" My mind was still replaying Beckett kneeling between my legs, his tongue doing wicked things, my hands tangled in his hair.

"She checked in under a fake name, but it's her." Sloane's voice dropped to a whisper. "I'm following her down the hall right now!"

I jerked Aslan's leash as he attempted to chase a squirrel. "Who?"

"Miranda Lockhart."

My body went rigid, frozen to the spot on the trail. The dogs pulled on the leashes, confused by my erratic behavior. I'd nearly forgotten about Miranda Lockhart. That's what Beckett had done to me.

"I'm looking at her right now," Sloane whispered.

The dogs yanked me forward. "What does she look like?" Miranda Lockhart on paper was sophisticated and sexy with every shiny hair in place. Was she that perfect in person?

"Gorgeous." Sloane was breathing hard, as if she'd been running. "She's wearing Diane von Furstenburg and Jimmy Choo." There was a pause as Sloane said something to someone else. "She's getting in the elevator," she reported, breathless. "When can you get up here?"

I checked my watch. I could finish up my walk, run home for a quick shower, and drive to the Inn. "Give me an hour."

"She has to come out of her room sometime." The smile in Sloane's voice could be heard clear to my end of the line. "And when she does, we'll be waiting."

* * *

It was hour three of our stakeout. My butt was sore from sitting on the barstool, but I wasn't budging until I laid eyes on Miranda Lockhart.

"She has to come out eventually." Sloane rested her chin on her fist and fixed her eyes on the lobby. "She can't stay in her room all night."

It was Friday night, and the hotel bar at the Inn was busy. The last time I'd been in here, it hadn't ended well for me. But it had brought me closer to Beckett, so... there was that.

Sloane and I trained our eyes on the lobby. Guests flowed in and out while we munched on peanuts and sipped water.

"Maybe she's writing." I popped a peanut into my mouth and crunched.

Sloane groaned. "Don't say that."

"The food is excellent. I'm sure her room is comfortable. She has everything she needs to stay in her room until the event." I glanced down at the book on the counter. A contemporary romance about best friends who became lovers, *Heaven on Earth* was my favorite Miranda Lockhart book. I imagined her signature on the title page and felt dizzy. Maybe someday it would sit on a shelf in my permanent residence. "I hope she's writing," I said. "I don't want to have to wait another year for her next release."

Sloane pushed the bowl of peanuts away from her. "Take these away from me. If I keep eating, I won't be hungry for dinner with Ben."

"I thought his name was Chris."

She winced. "I'm never going out with him again."

"What did he do?" Sloane had the worst track record with men.

"He brought his mother on our date."

I laughed. "Did you ever hear back from Marcus?"

Sloane shook her head. "I deleted his contact." She grabbed her phone and swiped her finger across the screen. "But I did save that video of Beckett carrying you off. Want to see it again?"

"No."

"I do." She tapped her screen. "It's *so romantic*. And I'm *so bored*."

Color rose to my cheeks as I thought of the whole disaster. The last thing I wanted to do was watch the video. Ever. I grabbed Sloane's phone and pressed delete before she could stop me.

"Hey! I was saving that for your rehearsal dinner," she said.

"We aren't even dating." One date, a half-dozen phone calls, and two mind-blowing orgasms didn't mean dating.

"If you two have kids, they are going to be good-looking and smart."

I choked on a peanut. "Hold on. You can't skip ahead to our wedding and future children."

"Time's ticking." Sloane tossed a peanut into her mouth.

"I'm only twenty-five."

Sloane cocked an eyebrow at me. "Exactly." Her eyes widened, and she stared at something over my shoulder. "Look!" She grabbed my wrist with an iron grip and jerked her chin at the lobby.

I followed her gaze and saw a woman gliding towards us. Dressed in slim jeans and a silk blouse, she exuded style and elegance. She was polished and sophisticated and...*Oh my God!* She was Miranda Lockhart.

I could hardly breathe as I watched my favorite author toss her hair over her shoulder and scan the lobby.

"How does she get her hair to shine like that?" Sloane wondered aloud.

I patted my wild tangle of curls, staring at Miranda's sleek mane with longing. Miranda had the kind of hair I'd always been envious of, the kind that flourished under a thorough brushing every night while sitting in front of a vanity. I didn't have hair like that, or even a vanity to sit at while brushing it. The only time I could get a comb through my curls was when they were wet.

I watched Miranda whip out her phone and tap it to life as she headed straight toward us. Every nerve in my body went on high alert as she neared. I caught a whiff of her expensive perfume and a snippet of her conversation as she strolled past.

"I'm at the bar," Miranda said into her phone. "Do you want your usual?"

I strained to listen to more of her conversation, but she chose a seat in a booth—too far away to eavesdrop.

"Now's your chance to meet her before she's swamped with fans," Sloane said, elbowing me.

"What about you?" I asked Sloane. "This was your idea."

Sloane shook her head. "I don't want to lose my job for harassing a guest," she said. "I've done all I can do."

"I don't think I can do it," I said. "I'm too nervous. And it sounded like she was meeting a date," I babbled. "I couldn't interrupt Miranda Lockhart on a date! There would be something incredibly wrong about that. It would be... sacrilegious."

"I know," Sloane said. "But try to remember that Miranda Lockhart is just a regular person. She's just like us."

I laughed. "She's hardly like us. Just look at her hair."

"We both have dates tonight. We aren't total losers. We're just fans. And I want to know where she got that top. It's gorgeous." Sloane pushed me until I eased off the stool. "Go. Don't let fear stop you."

"You sound like Kennedy." Our yoga guru friend was always spouting affirmations. "My fear is definitely stopping me."

Sloane picked up my copy of *Heaven on Earth* and handed it to me. "Don't forget your book."

My hands trembled as I took the book. "I can just wait until Sunday."

"When she's surrounded by other fans?" Sloane gave me a friendly shove. "Now's your chance."

I stumbled forward. Sloane was right. I would regret missing the chance to speak to Miranda one-on-one.

"What am I supposed to say?"

"We've been sitting here for three hours. You didn't come up with anything yet?"

"No."

She rolled her eyes. "Just be yourself. Now, go."

Sloane gave me another push, and this time once my feet were going I kept moving. I screwed up my courage, adjusted my hat, and walked over to the booth.

With each step that brought me closer, I rehearsed what to say. *Hello, I'm your biggest fan?* That wouldn't do. She'd probably heard it a million times. *I'm obsessed with you?* No way. Too creepy.

I stopped at Miranda's booth like a statue, too intimidated to speak. Up close, she was even more beautiful than in her author photo. Long brown hair, creamy skin, and perfectly symmetrical features—she looked exactly like the best-selling author she was.

My tongue tied in knots, and my throat closed up.

"Hello." She barely looked up from the menu. "I'll take a Dewars on the rocks, and do you have a wine list?"

A blush rose over my cheeks. Miranda thought I was a waitress. Did I look like a waitress? I was wearing a vintage velvet dress with a corseted bodice I'd found on consignment and a purple wool felt hat. It was a far cry from the crisp black uniforms the servers wore.

"I'm your biggest fan," I blurted.

Miranda eyes slowly raised from her menu to drop over me. "You're not the waitress?"

"No." I thrust my copy of *Heaven on Earth* at her. The dog-eared pages were wrinkled within the binding. I'd read the book so many times I had complete passages committed to memory.

"You want me to sign that for you?"

I tried to speak but was too afraid nothing wouldn't come out. I nodded instead.

"Come to the bookstore on Sunday. I'll be working then. Right now, I'm trying to get a drink." Her mouth lifted in a smile that didn't reach her eyes. "So, if you're not the waitress, go away."

The waitress came up beside me, and Miranda repeated her order and request for a wine list. I mumbled an apology and made my way back to the bar on watery knees.

"How'd it go?" Sloane asked when I stumbled up to the bar.

I shook my head, feeling the rush of tears. "Not good."

Sloane took one look at me and reached for a cocktail napkin. "What happened?"

I took the napkin and dabbed under my eyes. I felt like someone had just ripped the last chapter out of my favorite book. "She wouldn't sign it."

Sloane wrapped her arms around me, enveloping me in her fragrant embrace. "That bitch. Do you want me to take her out?"

I laughed. "Yeah. Kind of. But you can't risk your job."

Sloane pulled back. "I'll figure something else out." Sloane's eyes narrowed. "I can't believe we wasted all afternoon waiting around for that bitch."

I sniffed, refusing to cry over something as silly as being rejected by a celebrity. "At least I can go to the bathroom now."

I slid off the stool and headed to the bathroom. While washing my hands at the sink, I gave myself a pep talk. It wasn't the end of the world. So my favorite author was a snotty bitch. It didn't matter. She was still a literary genius. I would still buy her books.

Sloane was waiting for me in the lobby when I came out of the bathroom.

"I think we should go now," she said, shoving my copy of *Heaven on Earth* at my chest. Grabbing my arm, she spun me around so my back was to the bar. "Come on." Sloane gripped my wrist tightly and pulled me toward the exit. "Let's get out of here."

I glanced from the pained expression on Sloane's face toward the bar. "What happened?" I asked, suddenly suspicious. Sloane was acting funny.

"Her date showed up," she said.

"What's he like?" I craned my head to get a view of the booth. "I bet he's hot. Is he hot?"

Sloane's face blanched. "He's hot all right."

"What's wrong?"

"Lacey." She took me by the shoulders and looked me in the eyes. "Her date is Beckett Vinroot."

Chapter Twenty-Seven

"**M**y Beckett Vinroot? You're kidding."

"I wouldn't joke about something like that."

"Are you sure?" I could barely hear my voice over the sound of blood rushing between my ears.

"Tall, dark, and dressed like he just walked off a magazine shoot?" Sloane chewed her lip. "I think I know Beckett when I see him."

I tried to pull in a breath, but my chest was too tight to let in air. I clutched my book, fingers digging into the binding. There had to be an explanation. They were both authors. It could be work related. Beckett had said he had meetings. I'd been the one to assume it was for his day job.

"Maybe it's not a date," I said.

Sloane winced. "It looked like a date to me. I'm sorry, Lacey. I hate to say it, but I warned you about him."

Sloane hadn't been the only one. Pressly had advised me to steer clear of her brother too. I hadn't listened to either of them.

I side-stepped Sloane, determined to see for myself. If I didn't, my imagination would fill in the blanks, and it wouldn't be pretty. I strode through the lobby and into the bar.

My steps slowed when I heard a low male laugh coming from Miranda's booth. Beckett's laugh.

I took another step, and another laugh sounded. This one was high and light—Miranda's laugh.

A bitter taste flooded my mouth as I took the final step and rounded the corner of the booth. The first thing I noticed was that they were sitting on the same side of the booth together. The second thing I noticed was how comfortable they looked. Their dark heads were bent close. Beckett had one arm draped over the back of the bench seat, his other hand wrapped around the drink Miranda had ordered. His usual.

Heat burned my cheeks as I saw what they were looking at on the table: a book. Beckett lifted his hand from the glass and flipped a page.

My stomach heaved, and I felt dizzy. I blinked rapidly, hoping the intimate scene was just an illusion, but they didn't disappear. Beckett spoke softly, and Miranda laughed again. Neither one of them noticed me standing a few feet away.

Sloane came to my rescue. She grabbed my hand and tugged. I followed, stumbling blindly behind her.

Pressure built in my chest, making it impossible to breathe. Tears blurred my eyes. There was no mistaking that intimate scene for a business meeting.

"They were reading together." It was the ultimate betrayal.

Sloane put her arm around me. "I know."

I gasped, and tears burned the backs of my eyes. "They were sitting on the same side of the booth."

I sank into the softness of Sloane's hug as my mind reeled. All my insecurities reared their ugly heads. I wasn't Beckett's type, and Miranda was perfect for him. I was a dog walker, and Miranda was a best-selling author. Her hair was a soft wavy curtain. Mine? As twisted as the plot in a nail-biting thriller.

A sob escaped my mouth, but the tears didn't fall. My mind tripped over every detail of my relationship with Beckett. I'd suspected he was too good to be true, and now I knew I was right.

The validation sparked no happiness. It was a little like guessing the ending of a novel from the first chapter, even though I was glad to be right, I would rather have been surprised.

I felt calmer after a few deep breaths. It was almost a relief to give up on the dream of me and Beckett. Our relationship would never have worked.

"I'm so sorry, honey," Sloane said.

"It's okay."

And it really was. Everything would be okay. Beckett had never been mine to begin with. Letting him go made everything easier. I no longer had to risk my heart. I could bandage it up and seal it off before it was too late.

"I'm gonna go." I grabbed my purse and pulled on my coat. Saying the words out loud sparked the wanderlust that had been missing since I'd moved to Mossy Oak. It was time to leave this charming town. I would put Mossy Oak and Beckett in the rearview.

Sloane pulled me close for another hug, and I savored the feeling, knowing it might be one of our last.

"Are you sure?" she asked. "Do you want me to drive you?"

"I'm fine. Easy come, easy go." My throat constricted on the last word because it was exactly what I intended to do. "Don't you have a date tonight?"

"I can cancel."

"Don't you dare," I said. "He could be the one."

Sloane narrowed her eyes at me, her delicate brows arching together. "Are you sure you're okay?"

"I'm good." I shouldered my purse and started for the door.

"Don't forget your book," Sloane said, handing me my dog-eared copy of *Heaven on Earth*.

Chapter Twenty-Eight

It rained on the drive back to my apartment. The desolate winter night was the perfect setting for a good cry—the ugly kind that would leave me with puffy eyes and pale cheeks.

But I felt too empty to cry.

An eerie sense of calm spread through me as I drove along the steep hills and winding roads back to my loft apartment. I pulled onto my street and passed the charming bungalows and cottages of Frog Level until I reached my place.

I was going to miss it when I left. I'd been lucky to find my apartment above the garage. The cost of living was low in Mossy Oak, and my rent was dirt cheap.

I climbed the stairs in the pouring rain. There was no overhang above my door, so I was soaked by the time I unlocked it. I wouldn't miss getting soaked trying to unlock my door. Rain crept up quickly in the North Carolina mountains. The sky would be perfect one moment and black the next.

I went inside and tossed my wet hat on the breakfast table, shaking out my hair as I crossed straight to the sealed box by the wardrobe. Miranda Lockhart's works had traveled with me everywhere. I had dreamed about one day having a shelf to display them, but now I never wanted to see them again. I opened the box and piled all her books together.

I'd never read an author who could transport me to another place like Miranda did. And the characters she created? They were so real, I could imagine grabbing a mocha latte with them and walking among the cherry trees at Ginger Cake Acres. I'd lived and breathed her books, but I couldn't stand to look at them ever again.

I went into the kitchen and came back with a garbage bag. One by one, I tossed her masterpieces into the trash.

A sick feeling settled in my gut as I tied the trash bag. The feeling multiplied as I marched to the door, pulled it open, and threw the bag onto the stoop. I closed the door and leaned against it.

Tonight had been my best dream and my worst nightmare rolled into one. I'd met Miranda Lockhart, but the man I was falling for had betrayed me. He'd made me think about changing my ways and opening my heart to love again. I was glad I wasn't completely under Beckett's spell. It wasn't too late to come to my senses.

My stomach clenched as I imagined the rain seeping into the trash bag, soaking the words and flooding Miranda's imaginary towns. A storm of doubt swirled inside me until I pulled the door open, and grabbed the bag, and hauled it back inside.

Even though I knew I would never read another Miranda Lockhart novel again, I couldn't bear to throw them away. No matter what a cold-hearted bitch she was, the woman could write a whole-hearted love story. Her words didn't deserve to go in the trash.

I fished the books out and brushed them off. After thumbing through each of them one last time, I set them aside for donation.

Giving the books away was like breaking off a chunk of my soul. The tears I'd kept at bay finally fell down my cheeks. Saying good-bye to Miranda Lockhart was more painful than saying good-bye to Beckett.

Saying good-bye to Beckett would be a relief. I'd been dangerously close to falling in love with him. He'd saved us both a lot of trouble. Love in real life was messy and complicated. Love in a romance novel was much more ideal. When my emotions got too rough, I could always close the book.

My phone rang, and the happy ringtone startled me. It couldn't have been more at odds with the way I felt. Swiping the tears from my cheeks, I saw Beckett's name scroll across the screen. He must have finished his "meeting" with Miranda and was ready for me. Well, I wasn't ready for him. I tossed the phone on the table and shrugged out of my wet coat, then hung it over the back of a chair.

My phone buzzed with an incoming text message. I ignored it and walked across the room to my bedroom. I would miss this bed, set in the loft's alcove. It was cozy and bright with natural light, and the bed was big and soft. I'd fallen asleep here many nights with a book in my hands.

I went to the wardrobe that housed my clothes. Hopefully, my next apartment would have an actual closet. The thought brought a fresh crop of tears to my eyes. I'd lived in nearly a dozen places in the last seven years since graduating from high school, and none of them had felt like home as much as Mossy Oak. I'd loved it here, but it was ruined now. I didn't want to be here without Beckett, and the town wasn't big enough for both of us.

Beckett (8:10pm): Answer your phone

Beckett (8:10pm): Did you forget to charge your phone again?

Beckett (8:11pm): I'm coming over

Beckett (8:32pm): Answer. Your. Phone.

Beckett (8:32pm): I'm getting you a new phone ASAP. You need to join the twenty-first century. You probably aren't even seeing these texts. Are you?

* * *

A car pulled up in my driveway. I pushed the curtain away from the window and saw Beckett's sleek black car below. I pressed closer to the glass, feeling queasy as I watched him unfold himself from the car and hurry up the stairs. His footsteps pounded on the metal staircase outside the window. I let the curtain fall, and I jumped up when the knock sounded.

Beckett knocked again. My heart was angry with him, but other parts of my body hadn't gotten the message yet. It was safer to pretend I wasn't home until he went away. If I opened the door, I would want to invite him in. That would lead to touching and probably kissing and more.

"Let me in, will you? I'm getting soaked."

Beckett's voice shot a tingle of awareness down my spine. My heart didn't stand a chance as long as other parts of my body had a vote. I told myself to get it over with. I had to say good-bye at some point. I yanked open the door, and as soon as I saw Beckett's face, I knew I was in trouble. Trouble with a capital T. He was too damn good looking. Even with rain plastering his hair to his forehead, he looked like he'd walked straight off a movie set.

Beckett frowned down at me, his eyes intense behind the wet lenses of his glasses. "Are you going to let me in?"

I opened the door wider and allowed Beckett into my apartment. That was another mistake. I should never have let him in. The apartment was tiny to begin with, and it seemed to shrink when Beckett entered. He peeled off his wet jacket, filling the room with the scent of his woodsy aftershave and crisp winter rain. Ducking to miss hitting his head on the light fixture, he draped his coat on the chair next to mine.

"Is something wrong with your phone? I've been texting."

"My phone is fine."

His head whipped around at the tone of my voice. Tension pulsed in the air as his eyes roamed my face.

"Is something wrong with you?" he asked.

I glanced at the Miranda Lockhart novels on my counter, and

my blood turned to ice in my veins. It was easier to tap into my anger and ignore the pain. "I'm fine."

Beckett took a step toward me. "You don't sound fine. You don't look fine."

My muscles tensed under his scowl. "Why are you here?" I asked.

"We had a date, remember?"

I breezed by him into the kitchen, intent on putting the counter between us. Beckett's hand shot out to encircle my wrist, and he tugged me closer.

"You seemed fine the last time I saw you."

I closed my eyes against the image of Beckett on his knees, pinning me to the door with his mouth. I could feel the heat of his fingers penetrate my sleeve, burning my skin.

"Tell me, Princess." He pulled me into his arms, wrapping me tight in his hold where I felt ridiculously safe. His wet shirt dampened the front of my dress. He leaned down and rubbed his lips over my cheek. "Whatever it is, we can work it out."

Emotion welled inside me, and I couldn't hold it back. "I saw you. With Miranda."

Beckett smoothed my hair back, holding the curls prisoner as his eyes searched mine. "Is that what this is about?" he asked. "You saw me with Sally?"

My brows pulled together. "I saw you with Miranda Lockhart."

"Her real name is Sally."

<h1 style="text-align:center;">Chapter Twenty-Nine</h1>

My mind raced as I struggled to process Beckett's reaction. He wasn't even trying to deny it. I braced my hands on his chest and pushed. Beckett released me, and I stomped across the room. My apartment was too small to get very far away from him. He was too big to escape. I could feel the heat of his body and smell his scent from across the room. Beckett had a fragrance that stayed with me even when he was gone. I knew I'd remember it for years.

He crossed his arms over his chest, drawing the wet fabric of his shirt tightly over his biceps. "You assumed we were on a date," he said.

I wanted to rip the smug expression from his face. "You were sitting on the same side of the booth," I said. "You had your arm around her."

Beckett's mouth tightened, fine lines radiating from the corners. "I can explain."

"You were reading a book together. There's no explanation that can fix that."

Beckett walked over to stand on the opposite side of the counter from me. He picked up one of Miranda Lockhart's—Sally's—books and thumbed through it. I watched the emotions flicker across his face. Finally, he set the book down and looked up at me. He pushed his glasses up on his nose and leveled his eyes on me.

"I'm sorry," he said. "I can't imagine how I'd feel if I saw you with another man like that. But I know you have friends too. I wouldn't tell you not to have drinks with Thatcher."

The mention of my best guy friend raised my hackles. Thatcher might know my favorite drink and flavor of chocolate, but he wouldn't sit on the same side of the booth with me, sharing a book. We wouldn't laugh like that, as if we knew all each other's secrets.

A pang of guilt stabbed me. Would we? Thatcher and I had never been more than friends, but he had trusted me with details about his past he'd never told anyone, and I'd done the same with him.

Beckett had a point. Maybe I was overreacting. I'd let jealousy blind me. I'd been so star-struck and then devastated by Miranda that I had jumped to conclusions.

"I hate that I've hurt you," Beckett said. "I'm sorry."

The memory of Beckett and Miranda cozied up in a booth reading squeezed my heart like a fist. Tears blurred my vision. "You'll hurt me again." *Just like Julian.* "You'll keep hurting me."

Beckett nodded, his expression somber. "And you will hurt me. We will hurt each other."

He looked like a different version of himself. Gone was the cocky tilt to his head, the arrogant smile, the flashing dimples. This was a man with the weight of a library on his shoulders.

My heart softened as I looked into his green-brown eyes, as shy and vulnerable as I'd ever seen them.

He stepped around the counter into my tiny kitchen. "You're worth the pain." He took my hand and threaded our fingers together. "You're worth every ache." His eyes searched mine. "Am I worth it to you?"

The anguish in his voice gutted me. A chunk of my heart broke off, forever lost to Beckett. I sucked in a quick breath, bracing for the pain that would accompany the loss. But it didn't come. Losing a part of myself to Beckett didn't hurt nearly as bad as I'd thought it would.

Instead of pain, an exhilarated hum spread through my body. It was a lot like turning the page to find a plot twist you hadn't seen coming. Beckett kept hitting me with surprises, shocking my system. He wasn't hiding anything from me. It had been a misunderstanding. I breathed a sigh of relief that I'd rescued Miranda's books from the rain.

His thumb swept over the tender inside of my wrist, and my heart rate spiked, throbbing to meet his touch. He stroked the base of the tattoo on my wrist, brushing his fingers up the thin brown branch that circled my wrist and then wound up my forearm in a bloom of delicate white orchids. Beckett lifted my hand and bent to brush a velvet kiss over the pale petals.

"*Gossamer wings open in the dewy light,*" Beckett quoted, trailing his lips over my inked skin. "*Fragile shells prepare for flight.*"

My breath hitched, and I felt dizzy. The flowers tattooed on my arm were a nod to the orchids growing in the gardens of mythical Mooreland. Only a genuine fan could quote the book. Only Beckett would combine my favorite prose with soft kisses.

He pressed his mouth to my palm and then lifted his head to look at me. Glasses slightly crooked over intense green-brown eyes. Long, straight nose. Full, sensual mouth. I drank in his magnificent face, pleasure blooming through me at the sight of all that masculine beauty.

Beckett waited for my answer, his patience as tangible as the smell of rain on his skin. He didn't mind waiting, because he knew I was going to give in. He knew I couldn't resist him.

This love was going to hurt us both. Love always did. It was why I liked my boyfriends between the pages, where they were safe. I'd be a fool to believe I could survive an encounter with Beckett unscathed. I was going to end up broken, just like when Julian left me.

Am I worth it? Beckett's words echoed in my head. Getting hurt was inevitable, but maybe Beckett was worth it. He was everything

I'd ever wanted in a hero. I'd never thought I would get this close to a man again. Every time I'd started to get involved, I'd packed up my stuff and moved. It was nothing to me to start over in a new city, make new friends, and find a few jobs to keep my head above water.

But Mossy Oak had been different. From the start, the town had welcomed me. Mossy Oak collected outsiders like me and made us feel welcome. Mossy Oak felt like home. Beckett felt like home.

He was worth the risk.

I linked my arms around his neck and stretched into his kiss. Our bodies rocked together as we strained to get closer.

His shirt was cold and damp, soaking through my dress. I pulled back enough to reach between us and undid the buttons of his shirt without breaking our kiss. Beckett's hands spread up my back and then tugged at my zipper. A shiver spread along my spine as my dress gaped. I pried his buttons open.

The clang of warning bells in my head dimmed with each button I worked free. By the time I spread the shirt over the mountains of Beckett's shoulders, the bells were a distant memory, drowned out by roar of blood in my ears. His skin was molten lava under the damp chill of his shirt. My touch spread chills over his arms as I pushed the fabric down to catch at his wrists.

We stopped kissing long enough for Beckett to undo the buttons at his wrists and shove his shirt to the floor. My hands immediately found his skin again, pressing flat to the heat over his heart. I felt the frantic beat beneath my hands as our mouths locked on each other's again.

Kissing Beckett was like reading a favorite passage over and over. I discovered something different every time. The faint tang of whiskey on his tongue. The warm spice of his scent. The sensual caress of his tongue gliding over mine.

He spread my dress over my back, then slid it over my arms and down to my waist. I wiggled my hips, and the dress dropped to the floor to pool around my feet in soft waves.

Beckett's eyes darkened as he took in my matching lace underwear. When they rose back up to mine, his eyes were heavy, hooded with desire.

"Do you own any underwear that isn't designed to kill a man?"

I shivered at the raspy need in his voice.

Sexy underwear was my splurge. I worked two jobs in order to pay off my pile of debt, but I couldn't resist extravagant underwear. Whether I was walking dogs or stocking books, I liked knowing I wore something sexy under my clothes.

The matching bra and panty set in bold fuchsia had set me back half a paycheck, but the spark in Beckett's eye told me it had been worth every penny. The flimsy bra barely contained the swell of my breasts. My nipples peaked into hard pebbles under Beckett's lustful gaze, the pink areolas visible beneath the sheer lace.

Beckett looked at me like he wanted to devour me. I felt the same about him. I'd seen him shirtless before, but never this close and never in my apartment, where his masculinity was magnified by my feminine touches. Beckett's strong masculine chest, which could have been carved from a slab of granite, contrasted sharply with the pastel quilt draping my bed.

I reached for him, fingers fumbling to pry open his belt. Beckett gently pushed my fingers away so he could pop the button and lower the zipper.

He shed his pants, revealing black boxer briefs that left little to the imagination and a pair of black socks decorated with red and white baseballs.

"Do you own any socks that don't look like you bought them at a clown shop?"

Beckett grinned. Dimples winked. Ovaries may have exploded.

"Nope." He reached for me.

I wound my arms around his neck, coming up on tiptoe for his kiss. "You're too tall."

His hands cupped my ass, and he lifted me into his arms. "Maybe you're too short."

I hooked my legs around his hips, delighting in the advantage of not having to stretch to get to the level of his mouth. My tongue plunged between his lips, and he made a little noise of pleasure that had me grinding against him.

Beckett broke the kiss and swore softly as he set me down on my feet.

"I can't do this," he said.

Beckett was breathing fast, and an impressive hard-on strained against the cloth of his briefs. There was no way I could misinterpret the signs that he wanted me.

"What's the problem?" My stomach dropped.

Then he said the words that no half-naked woman in sexy underwear wants to hear.

"I have to tell you something."

My heart sank. "Okay."

"It's about Miranda Lockhart," he said.

My heart took another trip south, this time to land on the ground, ready to be stomped. I braced myself for his confession.

"Were you lying about her?"

"Not exactly."

I crossed my arms over my chest, suddenly conscious of my near nudity. This wasn't a conversation I wanted to have while dressed in skimpy underwear. I reached down and grabbed the nearest article of clothing I could find—Beckett's shirt. I shrugged it on and buttoned a few buttons, firing an angry glance at Beckett who was just standing there staring at me with a perplexed expression, as if he wasn't about to rip my heart out of my chest.

"Do you have any liquor?" he asked.

I glared at him. "You need a drink to tell me what happened with you and Miranda Lockhart?"

I didn't wait for him to answer as I marched into the kitchen and tore open the freezer door. I kept an emergency stash of chocolate and a bottle of vodka in there. I shoved up the sleeve on Beckett's shirt and reached for the bottle.

The shirt was another mistake. Buttery soft, slightly damp, and smelling deliciously of Beckett's aftershave, the shirt sent a shiver of longing down my spine. I wanted him even when I shouldn't, even when whatever he wanted to tell me required clothing and a shot of liquor.

I suddenly wished I'd never heard the name Miranda Lockhart. I took the bottle back to Beckett, not bothering with glasses.

He was sitting on the couch wearing only the tight briefs, a miserable expression on his face.

My belly fluttered at the sight of his tousled hair and flushed skin, and I forced myself to remember why I was carrying a bottle of vodka.

I handed him the bottle, but he shook his head. "It's more for you than me," he said.

He watched while I tossed back a healthy swig and swallowed with a hiss. I handed him the bottle, and he held it by the neck for a long moment before bringing it to his lips to drink.

"You're sleeping with her?" I asked.

He shook his head, choking on the vodka. "No."

"But you have slept with her."

He didn't deny it. "That's not the point," he said. "We've known each other a long time. When we first met, we hooked up a few times." He drank again, shuddering as he swallowed. "I met her at a party in college. We got a little drunk, and I told her about my writing."

My skin crawled, and I felt the sharp pang of jealousy. It didn't matter that it was years ago. It killed me to hear about Beckett sharing his biggest secret with another woman.

"Sally was interested in becoming a literary agent. She read my work, and we struck a deal."

"Before or after you slept with her?"

He winced. "After."

I bit my lip. "What was the deal?"

Beckett's mouth opened and then closed, forming a few sentences and then abandoning them as he changed his mind. His green-brown eyes focused on mine, even though I could tell he was dying to look anywhere else.

"We agreed to be partners." He sighed and looked down at his lap. "I wrote the books..."

I placed two fingers under his chin and forced his head up until he looked at me. "What did Sally do?"

Beckett grimaced. "She made all the appearances. Sally isn't Miranda Lockhart," he said. "I am."

Chapter Thirty

A bark of laughter escaped my mouth before I could stop it.

"You're what?" I asked, incredulous.

"Who," Beckett corrected my grammar.

I started to walk away, but Beckett grabbed my wrist.

"Wait. Do you believe me?"

I blew out a breath of frustration. "I don't know what to believe."

I broke away from his hold and paced a few steps to the kitchen. Had my apartment always been this small? I needed distance from him to clear my muddled thoughts. I leaned against the kitchen counter and grabbed one of Miranda Lockhart's novels from the bag.

I couldn't wrap my head around the fact that Miranda Lockhart wasn't the woman in the picture on the back of the book. Or that *she* was really a *he*.

I looked over at Beckett. He sat on the edge of my couch with his head in his hands. He'd taken off his glasses and was pressing the heels of his hands into his eyes. His shoulders slumped.

My anger mounted. I never understood pen names. It seemed like hiding to me. Gabi and I had this argument all the time. She wrote her reviews under the pen name Valentina. No last name, just

Valentina. Gabi insisted it was necessary because of her role as an elementary school principal, but I argued she shouldn't hide for any reason. There was nothing wrong with reading erotica. Erotica had been improving couples' sex lives for centuries.

"I saw your review of *Beneath the Stars,*" Beckett said. "It wasn't great."

My cheeks colored. I'd raked the book over the coals. "At least it was honest."

He groaned. "I didn't lie to you."

"You didn't tell me the truth."

"You knew I was a writer." He glared across the room, his eyes unfocused. "You knew I had pen names."

I sat on the stool at the counter, my mind spinning. "I can't believe you're Miranda Lockhart."

Beckett shoved his glasses back in place, got up, and stalked toward me. Beckett was better-looking than any book boyfriend I could conjure. I imagined him bent over his keyboard, crafting his story. This man created art out of thin air. How much sexier could he get?

"You don't believe me?" he asked. "You don't think a man can write romance?"

I hopped off the stool. "Of course I think men can write romance. Just like I think women can write horror. What I don't get is why you can't own your work. Why do you have to hide?"

Beckett laughed. "You think they would welcome me at RomantiCon?"

"Why not?" RomantiCon was the most popular book convention for romance readers. Every year in Las Vegas, readers flocked to the convention from around the world.

"Have you been to RomantiCon?" he asked.

I shook my head. I never had enough money after I finished paying bills.

"The only men there are cover models," Beckett said.

"What about those three brothers? The Luckys?"

Andrew, Charles, and Matthew Lucky had conquered the subgenres of military, western, and rock star romance. They were famous examples of men who were breaking the romance industry's stereotypes.

Beckett laughed. "Is that the best you can do?"

"I'm sure there are more examples, but my brain is a little fried right now.

"The Luckys aren't men," Beckett said. "Nor are they siblings. They are three women hoping to capitalize on a novelty." Beckett pushed his glasses up on his nose. "No thanks. I'd rather be anonymous."

I was stunned to find out that the Luckys weren't male or even related. I felt betrayed.

"Why can't everyone just be themselves?" I wondered.

"It's not so easy for everyone," Beckett said. "I've been groomed for a role in my family's company since I was eleven years old. I'm expected to work for the family, not write novels. Romance or otherwise."

"What about what you want?" I asked.

Beckett shook his head. "It doesn't matter. My grandfather would turn over in his grave if he knew I wrote books. Especially those." He pointed at the stack on my counter. "My mother would never look at me the same way again. Even Peppy doesn't know, and she's my favorite sister."

Beckett's voice rang out in my small apartment, full of anguish. The last of his words died away, resonating deeply within me. I knew what it was like to have a family who didn't approve of you.

"Beckett," I said, reaching for his hand. "I'm sorry."

He looked startled for a moment, eyes flashing down at me as if he'd just surfaced from his rant. "What?"

"I'm sorry."

"Why?"

"You shouldn't have to lie or pretend. You should be proud of everything you've accomplished. You should claim your work."

Beckett frowned, and he shook his head vehemently. "Never."

"Why not?"

"I can't tell anyone," he said. His eyes avoided mine, staring down at our joined fingers. "I can't believe I told you," he said. "But I couldn't take our relationship to the next level without telling you the truth."

My heart squeezed.

"You don't hate the idea, do you?" Beckett asked. "Think less of me?"

"My head is spinning," I admitted. "I don't know what to think." I remembered the poignant passages in some of my favorite Miranda Lockhart novels. Beckett had written those words. My blood heated as I pictured him creating those scenes. "I think it's incredibly sexy that you wrote those books."

Beckett's eyes shot up to mine. "You do?"

I looped my arms around his neck and hugged him fiercely. His arms tightened around my back, gathering me close. I felt some of his stress melt away.

"I was so afraid to tell you," he said. "But I knew I had to."

A thought occurred to me. "What happened to John in *Tangled Up in You*?"

Beckett's eyebrows knitted, and he pushed his glasses up his nose. "Mary Lou's brother?"

I nodded.

"He dies in Vietnam."

In the book, John had enlisted in the United States Army straight out of high school. He'd been shipped off to war and never mentioned again. I'd always wondered what had happened to him and hoped that maybe he'd return in another book.

"John's dead?" I asked, feeling as sorry as if I'd really known him.

"Yeah," Beckett said, his voice gruff. "John wasn't meant to be a leading man. I only wrote him in to demonstrate Lou's loneliness within her family."

"You really are Miranda Lockhart."

"I really am."

"What about your other books? You said you had more than

one pen name. Do you have other people you team up with? Other women?"

Beckett raised one eyebrow. "You don't need to be jealous of Sally. She and I are long over."

I thought of Sally's tinkling laugh and the way she'd ordered Beckett's drink as if she were ordering for a lover. "Does she know that?"

Beckett nodded. "She does."

"You seemed awfully cozy with her."

"It wasn't like that."

"I asked her to sign my book," I complained. "She refused." My anger mounted. "Bitch."

"I wish I could be like you," Beckett said, his voice raw and pained. "So unapologetically you. It's so brave."

"I'm not brave."

I'd been planning an escape not long ago, intent on ditching Mossy Oak in favor of avoiding my feelings. How brave was that? I'd been ready to give up the life I'd made—my book club friends, Pressly, Summer, Aslan. I'd been ready to run.

Beckett's hand cupped my chin, and he tilted my face up to his.

"You're so strong and independent. You don't care what anyone thinks about you. I've never met anyone like you. It's one of the reasons you inspire me so much. One of the reasons I want you to be mine." He brushed his lips over mine. I'd never felt his mouth so hesitant. "You are mine, aren't you?"

Tears filled my eyes. "I meant to tell you no."

He frowned down at me. "Lacey, please..."

I cinched my arms around his waist. "Okay," I said.

"Okay, what?"

"Okay, you're Miranda. I get it. I respect it. I don't agree with the secrecy, but that's entirely your business."

"You can't tell anyone." His mouth thinned, and his face turned grim.

"Of course not."

"That means you're my girl, right?" His hand drifted down my back, his tone teasing. "My woman. My muse. My—"

"Yes. Okay," I said, interrupting him before he could come up with any other possessive noun for me.

Beckett laughed and squeezed my butt. "My Princess," he said.

I groaned, still not entirely comfortable with the nickname. "Anything else you want to tell me?" I asked.

His fingers slipped under the hem of my shirt, pushing it up my thighs.

"You look really sexy in my shirt." His voice was thick and gravelly. "But I like you even better without it."

Chapter Thirty-One

Beckett undid the buttons and stripped off the shirt, then bent to lift me into his arms. In two long strides, he crossed the room to my bed.

I clung to his shoulders, pulling him with me as he put me down on the bed. I reached up and stripped off his glasses, then tossed them toward the nightstand. He braced his hands on either side of my face and leaned down to kiss me long and deep.

"I'll be right back," he said.

I came up on my elbows, watching him squint and stumble his way across the room. Poor thing couldn't see five feet in front of him without his glasses. It was adorable. He pulled his wallet out of his pants and plucked out a condom.

I wasn't sure how to feel about that. On one hand, it was good —safety first. On the other hand, I wondered if it meant this was a regular thing for Beckett. This definitely wasn't a regular thing for me, not at all.

"You came prepared," I said.

"That's me."

He walked back to the bed, tripping over a pair of shoes and landing on the bed next to me.

"You really can't see a thing without your glasses."

He raised up on one elbow and skimmed his fingers up my ribs, stopping just below the swell of my breast. "I can see plenty."

I ached for him to inch his hand higher. Then, he was kissing my mouth again, taking over, dominating. His kiss was fire, but it still couldn't distract me from the fact that I needed his hand on my breast. Beckett teased me with featherlight touches just under the lace of my bra.

When he finally stroked along the curve of my breast, his fingers barely a whisper, I nearly cried out. His thumb grazed over my nipple and I bucked my hips.

The throb in my belly spread lower, filling me with dizzying need. Beckett wedged his knee between mine, and I lifted my hips, shamelessly riding his thigh in an attempt to quell the hunger inside me. He slid the lace down over my nipple, fingers pinching. I writhed against him.

Two could play at this game.

I flattened my palms against his broad chest. My fingers brushed over the soft curling hairs across his pecs and then lower along his ribs where his skin was silky smooth. Then lower to the rippling muscles of his abs. Even though I loved Beckett's writing, I was very appreciative of how much time he'd spent in his home gym not writing.

His body was perfect.

I shoved both hands under the waistband of his briefs and filled my hands with his perfect ass.

Beckett hooked his fingers under the strings of my panties and tugged at them. I lifted my hips, and he peeled them off slowly and carefully.

"I'm sorry I ruined your pretty panties earlier," he said. "I'll buy you a new pair."

Showing none of the patience he'd shown me, I shoved his briefs down over his hips. When I saw Beckett for the first time, I felt like it was Christmas morning and I'd saved the best gift for last.

On a scale of one to ten, Beckett was a solid fifty-five.

"Wow," I said.

Beckett burst out laughing. "I can't believe you just said that." He cupped my face for a kiss.

I rolled over, reaching for the condom he'd dropped on the bed. I hadn't seen a man's cock in a long time. I'd read about them plenty of times, but even I had to admit that in this case, reading wasn't the same thing as seeing.

Beckett was beautiful. Standing stiff and demanding, he was long and thick. Built for pleasure. I reached for him, wrapping my fingers around the base of his erection. I'd never thought a dick could be elegant, but Beckett's was.

The noise he made was not.

He let out a guttural groan as I encircled him and squeezed. I watched his eyes glaze over.

"You know that scene in *Heaven on Earth* when Kate and Eric are at that fundraiser for dog toys?" I asked, my voice husky as I thought about one of my favorite scenes.

"Mmm-hmmm."

I gripped him harder, loving how he stiffened to steel under my touch.

"You remember the part where Kate gets on her knees under the table?"

"Yes," Beckett hissed through clenched teeth. "I wrote it."

"I've read it a hundred times," I whispered. "The pages are wrinkled. The binding is cracked." I stroked and squeezed, just like Kate had done to Eric.

Beckett growled and captured my mouth in a bruising kiss. Fire burned through me as his tongue filled my mouth.

I was making out with Miranda Lockhart.

The thought made me feel feverish. The heat was too much. I was on fire.

Beckett ran his hand along the valley between my breasts and down my belly to cup my sex. My hips lifted to grind against his palm. Flares of heat shot down my spine as he dipped one finger inside.

Swallowing my moan with his kiss, he eased another finger in, stretching me wide.

My heart punched in my chest as I rode his hand, and I felt my muscles quiver.

"No," I said, breaking the kiss and releasing my grip on his hard cock.

Beckett blinked down at me, startled.

"What's wrong?" he asked, his voice raw. "You don't like it?"

"I like it too much."

"There's no such thing."

I handed Beckett the condom. "I need you."

Beckett's eyes blazed as he took the condom, tore it open with his teeth, and rolled it on. I curled my hands around his neck and pulled his mouth to mine.

Our tongues met as he guided himself inside me. He did it slowly, with the infinite patience that I was beginning to understand Beckett used in all things. Beckett never lost control. He was deliberate in every movement, keeping himself in check the whole time as he sank farther into me.

My body burned with too much heat as he filled me. I breathed in the scent of his skin—clean spice and winter rain. When he pushed deeper, all the way inside, there was a moment so intense I squeezed my eyes shut.

"You okay?" Beckett asked, going very still. His voice was strained, and I could feel the tension pulsing through him. The beat of his heart filled me.

"Yeah." I pulled in a deep breath. "It's been a while."

"How long?"

Unable to trust my voice, I shook my head. It had been a long time since I'd been interested in a man. My books, my dogs, and my travels fulfilled me. I didn't need a man. I didn't even want one. I hadn't had a man since... well, since Cincinnati. I'd gone to bed with a man called Owen, but I hadn't even liked him that much. Didn't even remember his last name. I'd slept with him, then a few weeks later, I'd moved to Mossy Oak.

Beckett wasn't just any man. He was special. He was an artist who'd written the most beautiful stories I'd ever read. He was a genius who could create something legendary out of thin air.

Beckett's hand came to my face and caressed my cheek. "Look at me."

I hadn't realized my eyes were closed. I opened them, blinking up into those incredible brown eyes flecked with sparks of emerald. Tears swam in my eyes.

"It's okay," he said.

I nodded, searching for something to say to make this moment less poignant. "You're too big," I said, smiling slyly.

His eyes flared. "Maybe you're too small."

He shifted his hips, moving just a little, and I gasped at the pleasure it caused. His lips brushed mine, and I could feel the smile on his mouth. I lifted my hips, and he sucked in a moan. I kissed him deeper, sliding my tongue into his open mouth.

He started to move faster. Fire streaked through me. I might have cried out. I might have lost my mind.

I looked up at his eyes burning through me. They'd lost focus and had turned a hazy brown. Desire stamped his features, but I sensed the iron grip of his restraint as he held himself back.

Curving an arm under my shoulders, he let his elbow take his weight while his other hand moved to my hip, pinning me to the mattress.

He rocked into me slowly, letting our bodies adjust to each other. My mind dropped away, and my body took over. I hooked my legs around his hips and wound my arms around his neck.

Beckett set the pace, driving into me with a hard, fast rhythm. He was good at this, so good.

"I can't believe I'm having sex with Miranda Lockhart."

Beckett leaned back, eyes connecting with mine. "Don't say that."

"Why not?" I asked, pulling his mouth down for a kiss.

"This is me," he said. "Us. I don't want you thinking of anyone else."

For the first time I understood what a toll his dual life had taken on him. He'd separated himself into pieces.

"I want every part of you."

I watched Beckett's eyes change as I said the words. He blinked, and I swear I witnessed the moment he let go, allowing me to see all the way to his soul. There was nothing left to hide.

He kissed me tenderly. When he pulled back, his eyes held mine, telling a story that I could read as clearly as if it was written on paper.

Planting his hands on either side of my head, he buried himself deep, moving with exquisite slowness. I could feel every pulse of his heart echo through me. His mouth came down to claim mine, branding me as his own.

Us.

No one else.

Beckett stroked into me, each movement deliberately meant to drive me wild. I writhed on the sheets, a delectable burn streaking through me as he plunged deeper with every slow stroke.

Each thrust brought me closer to a fire that threatened to destroy me. Wave after wave of pleasure surged through me until I couldn't hold back anymore. I cried out, and Beckett fastened his mouth on mine, claiming my pleasure in a searing kiss.

I clamped down tightly on him, the ripples of my orgasm making his cock throb inside me. He tore his mouth from mine and threw his head back. The corded muscles in his neck strained, his mouth fell open, and a groan tore from his throat.

My blood raged through me, hot and wild as Beckett pulsed inside me, finally letting go of the iron grip of his control.

A moment later, he collapsed against me, warm and heavy, solid and already so familiar. I wrapped my arms tighter around his back and raked my fingernails over his fevered skin.

Finally, Beckett pushed up on his elbows to claim my mouth in another long kiss. When he pulled back to look at me, his green-brown eyes were intense as always, searing through me. His eyes roamed over my face, and I knew he was taking in my swollen lips, my heavy-lidded eyes, and the flush on my cheeks—all the signs of a satisfied woman. One corner of his beautiful mouth lifted in a cocky grin. He pushed aside a stray curl and kissed my cheek.

"One more thing I should tell you," he murmured, lips teasing the corner of my mouth.

"Hmmm?" I asked, my voice sounding just as sex-addled as I felt.

"I'm falling in love with you, Lacey," he said.

Chapter Thirty-Two

My eyes snapped open. "What did you say?"

He kissed the other corner of my mouth. "That cider really worked." The rush of his breath caressing my lips. "I'm totally gone for you."

"Beckett."

He dragged his lips along my jaw to nibble at my ear. "Lacey," he whispered, sending a bolt of lust straight through me.

His mouth felt so nice on my sensitive flesh. My name on his lips sent a rippling swell of pleasure through me, almost like another mini orgasm. Heat flooded my body.

No, Lacey. Focus...

I braced my hands on Beckett's chest, trying not to be distracted by the warm velvet of his skin and the slabs of muscle underneath and pushed, but Beckett barely moved. His solid weight pinned me to the bed.

"You can't say things like that," I said, using my sternest voice—the one I usually reserved for misbehaving dogs.

"Why not?" He nuzzled my neck, beard stubble catching strands of my wayward hair.

I steeled myself and pushed harder against his chest. "Because you're still inside me," I said. "Everyone knows you don't tell someone you love them during—or right after—sex."

"Okay." Beckett pulled back to brush his lips over mine with finality. "You're right." He eased back, sat up, and scooted to the side of the bed. Reaching for his glasses, he set them on his face and turned to look at me. He smiled, dimples winking. "Yep, still in love with you, and I'm at least a foot away."

My stomach quivered, and not in the good way it usually did when Beckett was around. "Why are you telling me this?"

His brows furrowed. "Not the response I was hoping for," he said.

"I'm sorry." I rolled over to face him. "That was just really good sex," I said. "Not love."

"Just really good?"

"Fine. Fantastic sex. But it's just endorphins. It's not love."

A confident smile played on his lips as Beckett leaned down to kiss my cheek. "I've been writing love stories for the last seven years," he said. "I think I know what love is. Besides, I knew it before we had sex, or I wouldn't have told you about Miranda. I just happened to be inside you when I said it."

My heart swelled a little at that news, but I didn't know what to say in return. I hadn't thought Beckett could throw me for any more loops, but this was BIG. Possibly bigger than Miranda Lockhart BIG.

"Be right back." Beckett got up from the bed and strolled into the bathroom, uncaring that I was staring at his naked ass, or maybe thinking it was to his advantage.

Which it definitely was. The man had a fine ass. The other parts were just as nice. And he looked just as good walking away as he did coming toward me.

Aware that I was possibly falling into a trap, I raised up on my elbow to watch. Each step made muscles ripple all over his body. Sparks ignited in my core where they should have been satiated. I thanked God for writer's block if it was the cause of Beckett's buff body.

When he closed the bathroom door, I collapsed against the pillow. I felt entirely too warm and cozy. Maybe I was drunk. But was I tipsy from that shot of vodka? Or was I drunk on Beckett?

His body enticed me. His mind fascinated me. But, love? Real romantic love? Not the kind I had for Aslan or Hyperbole's Bookshop or a new favorite bra-and-panty set, but the kind between a man and woman? Nah! That was impossible. Love only happened in fiction.

Love wasn't real.

Authors like Beckett wrote beautiful stories about love, but they were just that—stories.

I heard the toilet flush and the faucet turn on and off, and I propped myself on my side in anticipation of his return. I pulled the quilt up to my chin and curled my knees to my chest, waiting for the door to open. Selfishly, I hoped Beckett couldn't locate a towel. I wanted to see him—all of him—again.

Beckett stepped out of the bathroom, fully naked. My heart flip-flopped as I took him in. His body was perfect. Sinuous torso, narrow hips, powerful thighs. He strode toward me, unaffected by my curious gaze.

Ducking under the rafter just in time, he narrowly missed hitting his head. He leaned over me, his warmth already invading my space.

"Is it okay if I crash here tonight?" he asked. "I don't think I can stay awake long enough to drive home."

My eyes flashed up from his rock-hard abs to his face. His hair was adorably disheveled. Behind his spectacles, his eyes were bloodshot. Dark circles had taken up residence under his eyes, and his skin was pale. I remembered that the last time Beckett had lain his head down was hundreds of miles away. Knowing what I knew about his demanding schedule, it was possible that he hadn't slept since London. He might look just like a sexy Clark Kent, but he wasn't Superman. Beckett needed sleep.

But there was a problem. I didn't do sleepovers. I'd lived in Mossy Oak for almost a year, and I'd never even had a man—besides

Thatcher, who didn't count—in my apartment. But Beckett was different. He wasn't just any man. He was also Miranda. And he was exhausted.

My heart softened, and I scooted over. Beckett lifted the quilt and nestled in beside me.

The bed, a white-spindled Jenny Lind that squeaked just enough to make me glad my downstairs neighbor was a Chevy Impala, wasn't built for a man like Beckett. I laughed when his feet hung over the mattress. He solved the problem by curling onto his side and pulling me against him. I stiffened at the feel of his hard chest behind me. My naked back against his heated skin was fuel for fantasies. The curve of my ass flush against his groin made me want round two. His big hand spread over my ribcage and then cupped my breast possessively. I felt the heat of his palm branding me just as his tongue had done earlier.

I scooted back against him, seeking more of his warmth. He stiffened, flexing his hand over my breast. "If you don't stop wiggling that sexy ass, neither one of us is going to get any sleep."

Now, I was wide awake, mind whirling with possibilities. I shifted toward him for a hot, slow kiss. "Sorry, I know you need sleep."

"S'okay." Beckett sank deeper into the pillow we shared.

His weight made a dent in the center of the mattress that I fell right into. Beckett's front was all smooth skin and hard muscle. I didn't want to move, not even if my apartment was on fire.

My body melted into his, but my mind wouldn't stop spinning. Beckett's words, both those he'd said and those he'd written, crowded my thoughts.

When I could tell he was asleep by the sound of his breathing, I whispered, "You don't know me well enough to love me."

Beckett stirred and pressed a kiss between my shoulder blades. "You love dogs and books," he said. "What else matters?"

"Beckett..."

"Can we talk about this in the morning?" he asked, sounding very drowsy.

"Okay."

We fell silent. Beckett kissed the crease of my neck and whispered, "Love you."

The words had barely dropped from his lips before he fell asleep.

It wasn't so easy for me. I lay awake for a long time, listening to the rain drum on the roof and Beckett's peaceful breathing. It should have been enough to lull me into Dreamland, but there was an odd tightness in my chest that made it hard to breathe and impossible to sleep.

Chapter Thirty-Three

I woke up at the crack of dawn to an empty apartment. I rolled over in my bed, instantly noting the absence of the hard male body that had been wrapped around me all night long.

A tremor shook my body. Not again.

I got up and went into the bathroom where the evidence of Beckett was right there on the floor. His feet had left wet impressions on the fluffy pink bathmat. Size thirteen from the looks of them. Beckett must have used my shower before leaving. My eyes were on the footprints, but my mind was back in Milwaukee on the morning of my eighteenth birthday.

I'd shown up at our spot on Lake Michigan. I'd waited for hours until the sun was high in the sky and my skin turned pink. Julian never came.

He was supposed to come straight from the train station to meet me, and my mind instantly went on tragedy alert. What if the train derailed? What if he'd been in an accident on his way to meet me?

With thoughts of fiery passenger cars and flashing emergency lights in my head, I'd rushed to Julian's house. His mom had answered the door. After assuring me that Julian wasn't dead or dying in a hospital bed, she'd told me he wasn't coming home as planned. She had taken pleasure in delivering the news that Julian had gotten a girl pregnant. He was going to marry her, and he was breaking up with me. She'd told me all this on the front porch of her house. She hadn't even bothered to invite me in and deliver the news over a beverage. Mrs. Ambrose had never liked me.

Ever since that day, Julian was gone from my life.

I gaped at the fading footprints on my bathmat, wondering if that was all that was left of Beckett. The tightness in my chest that had kept me awake last night was back with a vengeance. I wandered to the kitchen counter and picked up my copy of *Heaven on Earth*. I flipped it open to see that Beckett had signed it for me. I dropped the book and picked up another one. He'd signed it too. And now, he was gone.

I went back to the bed and slipped under the covers, jerking them up to my neck.

Beckett had just proven me right. I'd never been so sorry to be right.

For a hot second I'd thought maybe love did exist outside of romance novels, but Beckett's absence punched a hole in that theory.

I sucked in a deep breath, trying to focus. Maybe this was a good thing.

I didn't have room for a man like Beckett in my life. He was too massive, too consuming.

And he was a cuddler. I hated cuddling. The only thing I cuddled up with in my bed was a book.

Last night Beckett had clamped his big hand around my waist and trapped me against his hard chest, his muscular thighs wedged behind mine. He'd even drifted into my dreams after I'd finally fallen to sleep.

I hadn't been able to move all night. And now I was sore all over, cramped from being tucked inside Beckett's big spoon.

Now that he was gone, I could finally breathe. I spread my heavy arms and legs across the bed and stretched, only to discover that I was sore in other places too. There was an ache between my thighs and a throb in my chest.

He'd made me believe him last night. I'd lain there, surrounded by his warmth, reluctantly accepting his gift of love, only to have it snatched away at first light.

I choked on a sob. Beckett was gone, and I was going to have to accept it. But this time I'd put on my big girl panties and deal with it. This time, I would not run. I might not have Beckett, but I had Mossy Oak. I didn't have to give up Mossy Oak. This town had Aslan, the Blue Ridge Book Club, and the best damn bookshop in the world. For the first time in years, wanderlust didn't breathe down my neck. I would stay here and thrive. I wouldn't give in to fear and run.

Heavy footsteps sounded on the metal stairs outside my apartment, and a moment later, the doorknob rattled. The door swung open, and Beckett pushed inside carrying a drink tray. He had a paper bag with a grease stain spreading across the bottom clamped in his mouth. His eyes lit up when he saw me, and he pulled the bag from his mouth.

"Mocha latte, right?" he asked.

They were the sweetest words I'd ever heard.

Even though his hair was a little rumpled and he was wearing last night's clothes, Beckett managed to look like he'd just strolled out of a casual business meeting.

"I brought muffins, and something that looks sort of like a crushed ear, but she swore it was—," He stopped abruptly, bracing himself as I launched myself at him.

I crushed my mouth to his, unable to contain my enthusiasm. "You came back," I said.

Beckett dropped the bag and wrapped his free arm around me, the coffee tray balanced precariously in his outstretched hand. "What'd you expect?" he asked between kisses. "I'm not going anywhere."

I threaded my fingers through his hair and pulled him close, kissing him with a hunger that threatened to consume us both. He kissed me back, matching my eagerness. He walked me into the kitchen and put the drink tray down so he could put both arms around me.

I pulled back to look at him, completely overwhelmed by my feelings. I needed space. I needed time. I needed... I reached up for his mouth.

I needed Beckett.

Chapter Thirty-Four

We lay on our backs in my bed, staring up at the ceiling. Beckett's arm was under my head, his thick bicep the perfect pillow. His fingers toyed with mine, typing softly across from my thumb to my pinky and back. I dozed in and out of a satisfied sleep.

"Are you going to the event at Hyperbole's tomorrow?" I turned to face him and ran my fingers through the hair at the back of his neck.

"No." He curved his hand around my hip and bent to kiss the crook of my neck. He hadn't shaved yet this morning, and the scruff of his beard was rough against my skin.

"Why not?"

"I never go to those things." He nibbled my neck, lips moving up to my ear.

I shivered and pulled away. "Don't you want to meet your fans?"

"Nope."

"Why not?"

He sighed and leaned back to look at me. "I don't write for my fans. I write for me." He rubbed his thumb over my bottom lip, swollen from his kisses. "What would you say if Miranda Lockhart retired?"

Every nerve in my body went rigid as I tried not to panic. A world without Miranda Lockhart wasn't one I wanted to live in.

"Don't joke about that." I stiffened in his arms and pulled away. "It's not funny."

"I'm not joking. What do you think Sally and I were talking about last night? It's why I wanted to meet with her. I planned the event in Mossy Oak to get her down here on my turf."

"No." I felt dizzy just thinking about it. "You can't."

"I can." He pulled me back into his arms. "Sally's gotten too full of herself. She thinks she's Miranda Lockhart, for Christ's sake."

I felt a sly satisfaction that Sally was getting the boot, but it wasn't enough to make it okay for Miranda to retire. I couldn't imagine never reading another Miranda Lockhart novel again. A thought took hold in my mind. Beckett's latest novel was dark and gritty. While it had elements of romance, it belonged in the thriller aisle.

"What name are you going to use for your new novel?" I asked.

"Definitely not Miranda. Maybe Perry can be salvaged. My last couple of books were duds. Only die-hard fans stuck with me. Then, I saw you on that ladder..."

"Wait!" I shoved Beckett in the chest. His big body didn't budge, so I did it again. He moved about an inch, and my hand hurt. "You don't mean Perry Griffin?"

A pink blush spread over his cheeks. "Yeah. Sorry about *Woven Uprising*. I know it was a disappointment."

"Oh. My. God. Beckett!" I slapped his chest, hurting my hand again. "You're Perry Griffin?! I always thought he was an older man who looks like Santa." Perry Griffin was notorious for being a recluse who took forever between novels.

Beckett blushed from his neck to his toes. "Those are photos of the mailroom manager at my publishing house," he said.

"How the hell do you do it?" I demanded. "How do you have

time to fly all over the world fixing companies *and* publish best-selling novels?”

He yawned. “I don’t sleep.”

I rolled on top of him and covered his face with sloppy kisses. “You *are* a genius!”

His big hands encircled my waist. I felt his cock stiffen against my thigh and my kisses grew more urgent. “I love your work so much. I would read anything you wrote,” I told him. “Even your stupid limericks.”

“My limericks are not stupid.” His arm snaked around my waist, and he rolled over so he was on top of me. He braced his elbows on either side of me and looked into my eyes, suddenly serious. “This new book terrifies me,” he said.

“It’s dark,” I agreed, looking into his naked eyes. His glasses were on my nightstand, and although I knew he couldn’t see much, I loved looking into his mossy eyes with no barrier between us. “But it’s so beautiful. It’s your masterpiece.”

His eyes sparked. “Because of you. I was burned out until I saw you...”

“I know, standing on the ladder in my good-butt jeans.”

A smile ghosted Beckett’s lips. “Thank God for good-butt jeans.” He tucked a curl behind my ear. “This book is my entire soul spilled out on paper. I’ve never been so scared in my life.”

I went still as I processed his words. I couldn’t imagine what it would feel like to put my secrets out there for anyone to devour. I never considered how brave he was, and it made my heart ache for him. I shifted and kissed him with a tenderness I hadn’t known I possessed, hoping to show him how deeply he’d moved me with his stories.

“Your soul is perfect.” Tears clogged my throat making it difficult to speak.

He leaned down to bury his face in my neck. “I don’t know if I can do it,” he said into my hair.

“If you don’t, you’ll regret it,” I said. “You can’t let fear control you.”

My words echoed in my head. I should be taking that advice, not giving it. My first reaction to seeing Beckett and Sally was to run. And when Beckett told me he loved me, I'd hidden behind my walls instead of admitting that maybe, just maybe, I loved him a little bit too.

"I'm scared too," I said.

He eased back and met my eyes. "Why?" he asked, brushing my hair away from his face.

I thought about the simple question for a long time. Confronting the memories of rejection and betrayal wasn't easy. "I haven't let myself get this close to anyone in a long time," I said. "I haven't let myself believe in love."

"And now?"

Beckett hung on my words. It was the perfect opportunity to tell him I loved him, but I was still too scared. "Love doesn't last," I said instead.

The gleam in his eye disappeared. "What happened to you? Who broke your heart?"

I took a page from Beckett's book and changed the subject. I sat up and swung my feet over the bed. "I'm starving. What kind of muffins did you bring?"

"Nope," he said, wrapping an arm around my waist. "You're not getting away that easily. I trusted you with my deepest secret. Tell me yours."

"I really am starving," I said.

Beckett scooted up against the headboard and sat with his hands folded over the sheet in his lap. "Blueberry and chocolate chip." His voice dripped with patience.

I pulled on a T-shirt and walked into the kitchen. Beckett put on his glasses and watched me open the bag. I pulled out the chocolate chip muffin.

"You want some?" I asked.

He shook his head. I broke off a piece of chocolate-chip muffin and chewed slowly, trying to gather my thoughts. Beckett waited patiently on the bed for me to speak.

"It was a long time ago," I said.

Beckett tilted his head, watching me.

"In high school I thought I had my life planned out," I admitted, the bitterness in my voice overriding the sweetness of the chocolate. "I was top ten in my graduating class. I had a scholarship to DePaul University, where I was going to join my high school boyfriend." I stopped talking as the pain washed over me again. I remembered the sneer on Julian's mother's face as she stood on her front porch, not inviting me inside. "And then he dumped me."

Beckett's eyebrows rose as he waited for more. But there wasn't any more. That was my big heartbreak—the reason I didn't believe in love. I'd been nurturing the pain of Julian breaking up with me via his mother for so long that it had become monstrous in my mind. But now that I'd said it out loud, it lost significance. It seemed almost silly.

"What about college?" Beckett asked.

My throat burned as the memories came flooding back. "I didn't go," I admitted. My parents had threatened me. My friends had pleaded with me. I was ruining my life. I was throwing away a golden ticket.

"Why not?" Beckett asked. Steepling his fingers in his lap, he studied me with an intensity that made me squirm.

My stomach clenched. It was a simple question with a complicated answer. "At first I didn't want to go to school with him, where I might see him on campus or in the city."

"Chicago has a couple million people."

"I know."

"So what's the real reason?"

I thought about my answer for a long moment. "I was never really a school person," I admitted. "I made good grades because my parents kept me on a tight leash. I never even wanted to go to college. I was only doing it to be with my boyfriend and because my dad threatened to disown me if I didn't go."

I spoke in a rush. Getting all the words out felt good. My chest felt empty, relieved of an oppressing weight.

"And did he?" Beckett asked. "Disown you?"

"Yeah." I struggled to keep the nonchalance in my voice. I remembered my dad's face turning purple as he screamed at me, spit flying from his mouth and spraying me in the face. He'd called me a coward, a loser, a freeloader, and more. "He kicked me out," I said. "I bounced around for a while, staying with friends until I could figure out what to do with my messed-up life. A few months later Dad tracked me down." I paused to tear off a chunk of the muffin and crumble it between my fingers, leaving a mess on the kitchen counter.

"Did he take you back?" Beckett asked, watching me destroy the muffin.

I laughed, and the noise sounded just as hollow as I felt. "No. He presented me with a bill for $200,000, demanding I repay him for my expensive private school education."

"I thought you didn't go to school."

I scoffed. "The bill started from kindergarten."

"Damn," Beckett said. "And I thought my family was ruthless."

I remembered the article I'd seen on Gabi's phone about Vinroot Enterprises and their hostile takeovers.

"Then what happened?" Beckett asked.

I chewed my lip. "I'm still paying him back," I said.

Beckett scoffed. "I'm sure you didn't ask for an expensive education when you went to kindergarten. You shouldn't have to pay for your parents' decision."

I shrugged. Beckett was right, but it didn't matter. I was paying it back on principle. The sooner I sent that last check, the better.

"If only I didn't have such a weakness for expensive underwear and mocha lattes, I would have paid more of it off by now," I said.

"I'm a big fan of your underwear collection," Beckett said. "But I think your issues with love have more to do with Daddy Dearest than the asshole who dumped you."

"Actually, his mother dumped me," I said, laughing. I'd never spoken to Julian again. I'd never even Googled him.

"That's rich," Beckett said. His eyes suddenly skittered past me, as if he was chasing an idea.

"That's going to end up in a book someday, isn't it?" I asked.

Beckett's gaze snapped back to mine. "Sorry," he said, clearly embarrassed to have been caught plotting. "Not if you don't want it to."

My chest tightened, then I exhaled, letting Julian and his mother go. "It doesn't matter. Maybe you're right. Maybe my issues are with my dad, not Julian."

"I can't even tell my dad I'm a writer," Beckett said. "We're quite a pair."

I liked the sight of Beckett in my bed. His torso was bare, and his broad shoulders blocked most of the headboard. He took up too much space in the bed... my apartment... my life.

I took a deep breath and then sipped a little more air until my lungs were full. As I slowly let the breath go, I made room for Beckett. I let him invade my heart.

"Are you done eating?" he asked, eyes sparking at me from behind his crooked glasses.

I nodded, pushing aside the remains of the abused muffin.

He patted the mattress beside him. "Then come back to bed."

* * *

A few hours later, Beckett disentangled himself from my sheets and scrambled out of bed. Standing up too fast, he hit his head on the low rafter. "Oof," he groaned. "You should really get that fixed."

"Where are you going?"

"I have to go..."

He searched the floor for his clothes, stepping into his pants without bothering with underwear. He zipped his pants but didn't button them and reached for his shirt.

I watched his tantalizing chest disappear as he pulled on the shirt and did half the buttons before leaning over the bed to kiss me again. He leaned into me, kissing me long and deep. His beard scruff scraped against my cheek as he slanted his head to deepen the kiss. His tongue filled my mouth, and I threaded my hands through his hair.

Once we started kissing, we couldn't stop. Beckett's moan filled my mouth as he finally broke away.

"Come with me." His hand curled around the back of my neck, holding me in place.

"Where?" But I already knew I was going. *Anywhere.*

"To my place," he said. "I have a book to finish. But..." He kissed me again. "I need you too."

His words shattered my resolve. I should have told him I needed him just as much, but the words wouldn't come. The idea of needing him—needing anyone—was still too foreign.

"But what will I do? I don't want to distract you from writing."

"You won't. Do whatever you want," he said. "Walk Aslan, take a nap, order food. Just come with me. Be with me."

Beckett was allowing me a peek inside his creative process. The thought thrilled me almost as much as the press of his firm lips against mine. I hopped up out of the bed and lunged for my clothes so fast that a laugh exploded from Beckett's mouth. But I didn't let it slow me down. I couldn't afford to give him a chance to change his mind. I gave Beckett one last kiss and hustled him out the door.

SERVING MOSSY OAK SINCE 1958

like us on facebook

Kirsty	Register 2
Mocha Latte LARGE	1 @ 4.75
Coffee of the Day LARGE	1 @ 1.75
Espresso shot	2 @ 2.75
Muffin	2 @ 3.99
subtotal	19.98
tax	1.40
total	21.38

Thank
you!

Lacey.

I think I should give you a warning.
Whether the night is placid or storming.
I'll love you all night. and keep holding you tight.
And I won't let go 'til the morning.

Love. Beckett

Chapter Thirty-Five

"You work too much." Beckett grabbed me around the waist before I could roll out of bed, and he pulled me against him.

"Look who's talking. You were up until 3:00 a.m."

He fit me snugly against him so that the heat of his chest warmed my naked back. "We could be in Littlecloud right now." He scraped my neck with his beard scruff, and a shiver ran down my spine.

"You would have still been up until 3:00 a.m." Beckett had moved his office to his bedroom last night. While I'd slept, he'd typed furiously on his laptop.

"Yeah, but you wouldn't be escaping my bed." He pushed my hair aside to kiss my ear.

My body melted against his. "I wish I didn't have to go." There was no joy in going to the book tour now that I knew Sally wasn't Miranda, but I was scheduled to work and couldn't let Thatcher down.

Beckett's mouth slid from my ear to my neck. He swept aside my hair and pressed kisses across my shoulder. His teeth nipped my skin. "So, don't go." His hand moved up my ribcage to cup my breast. "Stay here with me."

My nipple hardened against his palm. An ache grew inside me that only Beckett could ease. His thumb stroked my nipple, and I arched into him. My body burned for him again, even though he'd just been inside me a few hours ago.

I wanted to stay with him. I didn't want to leave this bed with these thousand-thread-count sheets that felt like layers of clouds and this man who woke me in the middle of the night with his mouth, who could make a volcano of sensations erupt inside me with a flick of his tongue.

"Beckett..." I gasped as he rolled my nipple between his thumb and finger, gently tugging.

"Hmm?" His voice was full of gravel. He pinched my nipple harder, then turned his attention to my left breast, squeezing and massaging until I squirmed against him. "What do you want, Princess?"

He nudged my legs apart with his knee, and I felt the heaviness of his erection pressing against the back of my thigh. Heat flashed through me. I was instantly wet and aching for him.

I shifted and found his mouth with mine. His body curled around mine, hand cupping my breast possessively. He tasted of the espresso he'd been drinking to stay awake.

"Tell me what you want." He turned me in his arms so that we faced each other.

My heart slammed in my chest as Beckett skimmed his teeth over my jaw. He inched his hand up my leg and hooked my knee over his hip. His thigh wedged between mine, and I felt him, hot and hard, close to my entrance.

"Are you too sore?" he asked. We hadn't been gentle with each other. "Do you want my mouth?"

The thought of Beckett's talented mouth doing wicked things to my body sent a wave of longing through me. I moaned and opened my mouth to his kiss.

His mouth left mine, and he kissed down my chest. After teasing one nipple and then the other, he moved down my ribcage to kiss my belly. I threaded my fingers in his hair and tugged. He stopped kissing me and looked up, eyes hooded with desire.

"I really have to go." I trailed my hands down his neck and over his broad shoulders. His muscles rippled under my touch, causing a ball of tension to coil in my belly. Beckett made me crave things I hadn't known I wanted. "You could come with me," I said.

Beckett rolled off me and sat up, swinging his feet to the floor. "No thanks. The last thing I want to do right now is deal with Sally," he said. "You want to grab a shower before you go?"

"Tempting," I said. "But if I get in the shower with you, I know what will happen."

"I know what I'd like to happen."

His sexy voice sent a streak of lust through me. "You're too good to be true. Like some sort of unicorn or something."

Beckett glanced down at his lap. He was completely naked and still hard. "Is that a penis joke?"

I laughed. "No. And no, I'm not joining you in the shower. I have to go."

"Next time?"

I hesitated. Beckett assumed there would be a next time that I slept over here. A next time that we woke up in each other's arms. I could hardly blame him. I'd willingly come home with him. I'd spent the night in his bed. But that didn't mean I was ready for a next time. This was moving at a lightning pace, too fast for me.

I sat up and pulled the sheet up to my neck. I opened my mouth to tell Beckett I wasn't ready to talk about next time, but the words wouldn't come out. My eyes raked over him, taking in his disheveled hair, the shadow of beard darkening his jaw, the soft fullness of his mouth. A red mark stood out against the pale skin of his shoulder. My heart leaped to my throat as I remembered sinking my teeth into his collarbone while he'd plunged inside me earlier this morning.

Beckett leaned over me, placing one hand on either side of my hips. "What's going on in that head of yours?"

I blinked and looked away from his probing eyes. Even without his glasses, his gaze was intense, burning through me.

"Nothing." I forced a smile. "I just need to get out of here before you distract me any more. I've got dogs to walk before I go to Hyperbole's to meet Fake Miranda."

Beckett frowned. He leaned forward and curled his hand around my neck, fingers sliding into the hair at my nape. "I'm not going to push you, yet," he said. "It scared me at first too." He kissed my jaw. "But I've had more time to get used to the idea of us. I knew from the moment I saw you that I wanted to make you mine." His mouth claimed mine, and he kissed me with barely restrained passion. "I'll give you whatever you want," he said when we parted. "My heart. My soul." He grinned, making those delicious dimples pop. "My words."

My pulse raced as he stood, grabbed his glasses off the nightstand, and started toward the bathroom. I watched the sinuous muscles in his back ripple with each step. He turned around and caught me staring.

"By the way—" One eyebrow cocked over the black frames of his glasses. "I finished."

"Huh?" I was concentrating so hard on keeping my eyes on his face instead of dipping down to devour the rest of him in his naked glory that I couldn't think straight.

"I finished the book last night while you were sleeping."

"Oh!" My skin flushed with excitement. "When can I read it?"

"It's in my editor's hands right now." He leaned an arm against the doorframe, and my eyes wandered down the length of his body. "But if you come get in the shower with me, I might consider letting you read the first draft early." He casually fisted the base of his cock. It was one of the sexiest things I'd ever seen. "You gonna leave me to take care of this by myself?"

The temptation of Beckett's gorgeous body and the luxurious shower was too much. I couldn't resist. I was already slick from wanting him, and watching him slowly stroke up and down made flames of desire heat my blood. I threw off the sheet and climbed out of the bed. What the hell? I needed a shower before work anyway.

Chapter Thirty-Six

"**G**ood morning!" Thatcher called as I passed his office.

I peeked in the open door to see him running a comb through his damp hair. He whistled a tune as he finished tucking his shirt into his jeans.

"Why are you so cheerful this morning?"

He raised an eyebrow at me. "Late night?"

My cheeks heated as I thought back on the previous two nights. I'd spent both of them with Beckett and hadn't done much sleeping.

Thatcher read my mind. "How's the boyfriend?"

My cheeks burned hotter. "He's not my boyfriend."

"Tell that to Summer." Thatcher came out from behind his desk. "She says her uncle is a lot less grouchy now."

My cheeks were going to catch fire. "Since when are you hanging out with nine-year-olds?" I asked.

"She likes to read in the nook. What am I supposed to do? Kick her out?"

"She's cutting dance class to come here and read," I said. "Pressly's gonna freak when she finds out."

"So don't tell her," Thatcher suggested. "Geez, Lacey, when did you turn into such a stick-in-the-mud?"

"I'm not..."

"Let the kid read, will you? The only good things in her life are Aslan and reading. And you. She's obsessed with you." He grabbed my arm and steered me down the hall. "She wants to be you when she grows up. Tattoos, nose ring, and everything."

I pushed open the door to the café, pointing at Thatcher. "You have a tattoo." Tweety Bird rode high on his right shoulder.

Thatcher glared at me. "You know that's only because I lost a bet."

"I need coffee," I said.

The café bustled with employees getting ready for the day. Thatcher grabbed mugs and helped himself. He loaded mine with sugar and cream, just the way I liked it.

"I thought you'd be more enthusiastic today."

"Hmmph." I took a sip of the hot coffee and hissed as it burned my mouth.

"Easy." He watched me over the rim of his mug. "You do know your favorite author is due in the store in less than an hour."

We walked into the main floor of the shop where the first customers of the day perused the aisles. A line had already formed around Miranda Lockhart's table. A flare of anger shot through me as I realized everyone in line thought they were meeting the author today.

"Why can't everyone just be themselves?" I muttered.

"What?" Thatcher turned to look at me, eyebrows raised.

I shook my head. "Never mind." My feelings were irrational. Lots of writers had pen names. I wasn't mad at Perry Griffin, was I? Then again, Perry Griffin wasn't a glamorous brunette with perfect hair who'd known Beckett since college.

It made me feel marginally better to know that Sally would not be the first to read Beckett's latest work. This novel was his best yet. Even though it wasn't romance, true Miranda fans wouldn't be surprised to know the same person who'd written *Heaven on Earth* had penned it. Beckett had a way with prose that made even the mundane seem spectacular. His settings pulsed with life. His characters sauntered into your life like an old friend. And the sex scenes? Panty melting.

I realized I was already composing the five-star review in my head, and I hadn't even read the ending. Was Perry Griffin going to get the credit for Beckett's new novel, or would he create a new name?

It was a genre of its own, and it was going to be a groundbreaking hit.

"Help me get some more books from the storeroom." Thatcher eyed the crowd forming around Miranda's books. "This is going to be great for business."

I glared at the cardboard cutout of Sally and the handsome man covered in red kiss marks. If looks could kill, the cardboard would have spontaneously combusted.

"I could hardly believe it when Miranda's agent reached out to arrange a book tour," Thatcher said. "Is something wrong with your eye? It's twitching."

"I didn't get much sleep the past few nights."

"Join the club. Painting isn't as easy as it looks." He opened the door to the storeroom. "It took four cans of paint to do the living room. I think I got three on the floor and one on the walls. I spent half the night cleaning up."

"Hmm."

"Okay, what the hell is wrong with you? You were jumping out of your skin a month ago when I told you Miranda was coming, and now that she's due any minute, you look like you're plotting a murder."

I sat on a box of books and peered into my coffee mug as if it had all the answers. "I'm thinking about something else."

Thatcher chuckled. "More like someone else. If Beckett can get your mind off Miranda Lockhart, you must have it bad."

Even before I'd known Beckett's secret identity, he'd distracted me. Now, he was all I could think about. "I've tried to tell him I don't want a relationship, but he refuses to listen."

Thatcher sipped his coffee. "Why are you so sure you don't want a relationship?"

I scoffed. "I don't do relationships. You know that."

"That was the past," he said. "Things change. You're not the same person you were when you started working here a year ago. First of all, you're still here."

I stood and paced across the room. I remembered warning Thatcher that I wanted to work at Hyperbole's temporarily. I'd told him I never stayed put for long.

Was Thatcher right? Had I changed? I blamed Mossy Oak. The fine weather, the clear Carolina sky, the ease of small-town life where everyone had a greeting and a kind word for a neighbor—all of them combined to make me want to stay in Mossy Oak forever.

I'd never wanted forever before. I had a perpetual wanderlust that only relocating could satisfy.

But I'd never been anywhere like Mossy Oak before. The town seemed to collect people like me—outsiders who didn't really fit in anywhere—and bring them together.

Mossy Oak had everything I wanted—the best bookshop in the world, the closest friends I'd ever made, weather that hardly ever kept me from doing what I wanted, and Beckett Vinroot.

My heart beat faster just thinking about his green-brown eyes twinkling at me.

I took another gulp of coffee. The sugar and caffeine made my brain buzz.

"What does Beckett want?" Thatcher asked.

I sighed. "He says we're made for each other. But we're total opposites. He has the worst taste in music, and he doesn't sleep. He's so smart he wired his entire house to be electronic. He drinks whiskey and drives a Maserati... and his closet is bigger than my entire apartment. Do you know how many pairs of glasses he owns?"

Thatcher winced, watching as I gestured wildly with my coffee cup. "Not a clue," he said.

"Loads. He has a whole drawer full of them." I took a giant sip of sugar-laced coffee. "And he wears the most adorable socks."

Thatcher finished his coffee, picked up a box of books, and handed it to me. "You've got it bad."

I nodded. "I know."

"It's about damn time." He grabbed two more boxes, and we headed back into the bookshop.

The line of people at Miranda's table had grown. It was almost time for her to arrive.

"I'm going to take these books up to the register." Thatcher nodded toward the front of the store. "Will you put those out on the table? And try to remember how much you've been looking forward to this day. You'll figure things out with Beckett. He's not going anywhere, Lacey. He'll be there after you meet Miranda."

If only Thatcher knew how true his words were.

I watched him walk away and then made my way through the line of fans to the signing table. I gave the cutout of Sally and her kiss-marked boyfriend a blistering glare as I placed copies of *Beneath the Stars* on the table.

The thought of Sally signing all those books, pretending she'd been the one to write them, made my skin crawl.

I slammed the last book on the table and scanned the crowd of fans. These women had no idea they were being scammed. Every one of them thought they were getting a book signed by their favorite author, but Sally was nothing but a fake. I sent the cutout another poisonous glare, and I noticed a man standing in the group of women. I couldn't see his face, but I knew who he was by the pile of black hair pulled into a messy bun at the back of his head.

Chapter Thirty-Seven

I hadn't seen Xan since that day at the park a month ago. As promised, he hadn't called or texted. I realized I hadn't given him much thought. My mind had been stuck on someone else.

"Hey, Xan."

His head popped up. When his eyes lit on me, a big smile transformed his face. It was like watching the sun come out from behind a cloud.

"Hey! You work here?"

I pointed at my Hyperbole's T-shirt. I'd modified it by cutting off the sleeves and ripping out the shoulder seams, which were now held together with oversized yellow safety pins. "Nah, I just like the uniform." I glanced down at the copy of *Beneath the Stars* he clutched. "Are you a fan?"

Xan blushed. "Nope. It's for my mom." He stepped out of line to grab a book off a nearby shelf. "This is a little more my speed."

I walked over and looked at the book he'd chosen. It was a guide to the best mountain trails in the area. "That's a good one. It has all the best hikes."

Xan flipped through the pages, nodding. "I think this is what I need." He pointed at a picture of bikers grinding their way up a trail.

"Looks brutal," I said.

"Pretty much." He grinned, then snapped the book shut. He seemed oblivious to the fact that every woman in the vicinity was checking him out. "How've you been? Cause anymore bike accidents at the park?"

"Not lately. I haven't seen you around the park."

"I qualified for Celtman." His eyes sparked with enthusiasm. "I've spent all my free time training."

"Celtman? What's that?"

"It's an endurance triathlon in Scotland with an attrition rate of fifty-eight percent." His voice rang with pride. "You have to qualify to compete."

"Attrition rate?" I asked.

"The drop-out rate."

"You mean more than half the competitors drop out?"

"Yup." He nodded happily. "It's a three-point-eight-kilometer swim, a two-hundred-kilometer bike, and a forty-two-kilometer run over two Munros to finish."

I wasn't sure what a Munro was, but the whole thing sounded terrifying. "That's a lot of kilometers," I said. "What's the prize?"

"A T-shirt." He laughed. "And bragging rights."

A commotion at the front door drew our attention. Sally strode in on three-inch heels, every hair in place. A buzz of excitement rippled through the line of fans.

Seeing Sally's face triggered a waterfall of emotions. I'd thought of her as my favorite author for years, but now I thought of her as the woman who had a piece of Beckett. A pretender who had everyone in this line fooled.

"My mom is her biggest fan," Xan said, following Sally with his eyes.

The crowd parted to allow Sally to glide through. She smiled at her fans, her lips shining with her signature red shade. A wave of nausea rolled over me as I watched her toss her perfect hair over her shoulder. From the top of her glossy head to the toe of her Louboutins, Sally was the picture of what a best-selling romance author should look like. But it was all a lie. She'd probably written nothing longer than an email.

"My mom is going to flip when I get a book signed for her. Hopefully, she will be so happy with me that she'll forget I'm her last unmarried son." He laughed. "At least for a day or two."

Rage welled up inside me as I glowered at Sally. "She's a fake."

"What?"

My anger spilled over, an unleashed volcano. "She's not the real Miranda Lockhart."

I hadn't realized I'd said the words out loud until I noticed a few people in the crowd had turned to look at me. Sally tossed her head in my direction, and I steeled myself not to quiver under her inspection.

Feeling my cheeks flush, I pressed my lips together. I hadn't meant to say those words, but now that they were out in the open, I felt an enormous sense of relief. Sally wasn't Miranda Lockhart, the author who I had admired for years. She was just a regular woman with a gorgeous head of hair.

"She's not the real Miranda Lockhart?" Xan asked in a loud voice.

Someone in the crowd gasped, and everyone turned to eye Sally. Her smile dimmed, and her eyes shot daggers across the room—straight at me. She came out from behind the table and strode toward me.

"Do you work here?" she asked.

I glanced down at my T-shirt and then raised my eyes to her. "Yes."

Sally's eyes flicked over me, taking in every detail of my appearance. "I need to speak to your manager."

"Is there something I can help you find?" I asked. *Like maybe the exit?*

"Just get the manager."

I wasn't quite sure how I got there, but suddenly I was in Sally's personal space. I jutted my chin, meeting her eye.

"I don't take orders from you."

Xan leaned closer and cupped my elbow. "Hey," he hissed under his breath. "What's your problem?"

Sally's nostrils flared as if she smelled something rotten. "You're that waitress from the bar. Still upset that I wouldn't sign your book?"

I smirked. "I got my books signed by the *real* author."

I had the pleasure of seeing the color drain from Sally's face, but then I noticed the crowd. The fans who'd been surrounding Miranda Lockhart's table swarmed around us. A few of them had their phones out, aimed at us.

The euphoria of exposing Sally was short-lived as I realized what I'd just done. I'd betrayed Beckett.

Xan came to my rescue. Stepping between me and the gaping crowd, he flashed a smile that drew all eyes to him.

"Just kidding around here." He laughed heartily. "You can put away your phones. Nothing to see."

Sally turned to her fans. "There's a little misunderstanding with the store," she said. "Give us just a minute to fix it."

Sally clamped a hand on my elbow and towed me behind the golden Eiffel Tower where no one could see us.

"You're Lacey." Sally pronounced my name like an insult.

"That's right." I threw back my shoulders. I may have been four inches shorter than her, but I felt like I could take her. I was ready to fight dirty, and she looked like the type who didn't want to mess up her manicure or smear her lipstick unless it was on a man's cheek.

She gave me a pitying look. "Beckett told me about you."

I lifted my chin. "He told me about you too."

Sally raised an eyebrow in sympathy. "He got to you, didn't he?"

My stomach rolled, and I felt dizzy.

"You probably think Beckett is in love with you." Her voice dripped with false compassion. "I've seen so many muses come and go, I've lost count." She made the word muse sound like whore.

"Maybe he is in love with you." She shook her head, making her hair cascade in a waterfall over her shoulder. "That man falls in love every time he writes a new book." Her mouth thinned. "He falls out of love just as quickly. The only thing that remains the same is me." She took a step closer to me, pointing at her chest. "I'm here to stay. That little exposé of yours didn't cost me anything. My readers will eat it up. They love drama. But you? You just wrecked things with Beckett for good." She whipped out her phone, a snarky smile on her glossy lips as she tapped the screen. "There," she said. "Congratulations. You just went viral."

Chapter Thirty-Eight

Over Sally's shoulder, I saw Xan handling the group of fans who'd been recording our little performance. He looked to have them wrapped around his little finger. The tinkling sound of their laughter floated across the aisle. Xan's eyes flashed up to mine, full of concern. I shook my head slightly, feeling my stomach churn.

I didn't have to be an expert on social media to know what Sally was doing. By now, the whole World Wide Web knew Sally wasn't Miranda Lockhart. I'd spilled the secret Beckett had entrusted to me.

I realized Sally had just outed herself for the sake of ruining my relationship with Beckett.

"Why are you doing this?" I asked. "You just ruined your career."

She gestured back toward the table where her fans had circled Xan as if he were one of the cover models. "That's my face on the cardboard cutout. No one will believe some jealous clerk at a backwoods bookshop over me."

No one except for the most important person—Beckett.

Sally glanced to her fans, then back at me. "Don't worry," she said. "Beckett will probably give you something really nice when he breaks your heart. He's very generous and has excellent taste in jewelry." She fingered a sapphire necklace that hung around her neck.

Tears blurred my vision as I watched Sally walk away. Suddenly, I couldn't breathe. I couldn't move. Xan came over and put an arm around my waist. He guided me to a private spot between the aisles and pushed me into an armchair. Squatting in front of me, he offered me the handkerchief from his vest pocket.

"Thanks." I crushed the handkerchief in my fist. I would not cry in public. I pulled in a lungful of air and straightened my back, hoping it would make breathing easier. It didn't. A lump lodged in my throat, and I couldn't seem to get enough air.

Xan's dark eyes searched mine. "What the hell was that all about?"

I cringed, shaking my head. Squeezing the handkerchief, I sucked in fresh tears. How could I have been so thoughtless?

Xan's phone rang, and he stood to pull it from his back pocket. His brows drew together, and he frowned. "It's my mom." He swiped his finger across the screen and held the phone to his ear. "Hey, Ma."

I could hear the high-pitched squeal from a foot away. "Alexandah!"

Xan winced and held his phone away from his ear. "What's wrong, Ma?" He paced a few steps and then glanced back at me. "No, she's not my girlfriend," he said. "I don't have to work today." He rolled his eyes. "No," he said. "Don't do that, Ma. Ma?" He sighed and winced again, holding the phone away from his ear. "Ma? I gotta go. Yeah, I'm coming for dinner. No." He glanced back at me, gave me a quick smile. "I'm hanging up now." He ended the call and shoved the phone back in his pocket. "You want to explain why my mom just saw a video of me on Facebook?"

I hung my head and pressed the balled-up handkerchief to my eyes.

"I should have never taught my mom how to use Facebook," Xan said.

Xan's mom had seen me tell Beckett's biggest secret to the world. Rage built inside me, pulsing in my head loud enough to make me want to scream. Some of my anger was directed at Sally, but the majority pointed in my own direction.

Xan crouched in front of me and placed his hands on the arms of the chair. "Are you gonna tell me what that was all about?"

"What did your mom say?"

Xan smiled, his eyes going soft. "She's a typical Filipina mother."

I shook my head, at a loss. "What does that mean?"

He sighed and sat back on his heels. "Her biggest goal in life is to see her children happily married. She saw us on Facebook together, and now she thinks we're getting married. She wanted to make sure I invited you to come to our family dinner this Sunday."

"What did she say about Miranda Lockhart?" I steered him back toward the source of my pain.

"I told you she was a fan?" he asked.

I nodded. That was one of the last things I remembered before everything happened.

"My mom knows everything Miranda Lockhart does. She's in a bunch of Facebook groups that stalk the poor woman."

My eyes narrowed at the description of Sally as a poor woman.

"Ma only wanted to talk about my impending nuptials. She didn't say anything about..." He paused, obviously at a loss for words.

I pressed my knuckles to my eyes, wishing I could take back what had just happened.

Xan reached up to pry my hands away from my face. "Don't worry about it too much. Something else will happen and everyone will forget about that... whatever it was."

If only I could dismiss it as easily as Xan, but I couldn't.

"You might not realize it, but that was a pretty big deal. I did something horrible. Something I can never take back."

Xan grasped my hands and gave them a gentle squeeze. "Did you commit a crime?"

I shook my head. "I betrayed someone."

"Let me guess... That someone is a stuck-up suit with a killer right hook." Xan grimaced.

I nodded. "Beckett." Just saying his name made me feel like I'd been the one to get punched.

Xan's eyes lit up as he put the pieces together. His mouth dropped open, his eyes went wide, and his fingers tightened on mine. "No way," he said.

I nodded, feeling miserable. "It's true."

"So that wasn't the real Miranda Lockhart?" He glanced around and dropped his voice. We were quite alone in the self-help aisle. The rest of the store was gathered in Romance. "That lady was not the one who wrote those books my mom's obsessed with?"

"No," I said. "She's just a front."

"No way."

"Way."

Xan's eyes went round as the truth finally hit home. "That dude that hit me writes romance novels..." He said each word slowly, as if testing the theory.

A loud noise at the end of the aisle drew our attention. I looked over to see Beckett standing a few feet away. The noise had been him dropping his briefcase on the floor. Feet planted wide apart, arms crossed over his chest, broad body taking up the whole aisle, Beckett looked like a volcano ready to erupt.

"It's 'who,'" he said, a murderous look in his eye. "That dude *who* hit you writes romance novels."

Xan dropped my hands, and I scrambled to my feet.

"What are you doing here?" I asked Beckett.

His eyes flicked from Xan to me, shooting daggers. "I came to see you. I have to leave, and I wanted to say goodbye."

"I'll let you two talk." Xan rose to his feet and stepped aside. I tried to give him back his handkerchief, but he pressed in against my palm. "Keep it." He wisely slipped past Beckett and disappeared around the end of the aisle.

When Xan was gone, Beckett jerked his chin at me. "Let's talk."

I thought nothing could cut me deeper than the injured look on his face, but the sound of his pained voice pierced me to the bone.

"Beckett..."

"Not here."

Although we were alone in the aisle, anyone could walk around the corner at any moment—as Beckett had just proven. I'd already revealed too much to the public. I didn't want to advertise our private conversation all over the internet too.

I got up and walked across the main floor, through the café, and to Thatcher's office. Beckett followed me and closed the door behind us. There was only one chair in the room, and neither of us took it. I forced myself to look up at Beckett. I wished I could slip my arms around his waist and bury my face against his chest. I wished I could go back in time and stay in bed with him this morning instead of coming in to work.

"I'm sorry." As soon as the words left my mouth, I knew they were wrong. They weren't enough, not for what I'd done.

"I can't believe it." Beckett looked at me as if I'd just spoiled the ending of his favorite book.

"I didn't know anyone was filming," I said. "I didn't realize..."

"Have you been talking to him this whole time?"

I frowned up at him. "What?"

Beckett's presence was enormous in the tiny office. He stalked two steps forward and was nearly on top of me. He placed his hands on the desk on either side of my hips, trapping me in place. "Answer me."

My poor brain struggled to keep up. "Wait." I pulled in a breath, my eyes flashing up to his. "What?"

"Are you seeing him?"

"What are you talking about?"

Beckett made a noise in his throat that sounded more animal than man. He bent his head, and his hair flopped onto his forehead. He seemed so much bigger than me. So broad and intimidating. So intense. "Tell me the truth," he growled.

I couldn't resist touching him. I lifted my hand to trace the hard flex of his jaw, but he jerked away. He paced a few feet to the door, giving me his back.

"I said I was sorry. I would take it back if I could. I would take back this entire day." Well, except the shower. "I didn't mean to expose your secret."

Beckett turned back to look at me. His face was pale except for the two bright splotches that colored his cheeks. "I was willing to wait for you to come around," he said. "I thought deep down you loved me, and you would realize it." He pulled off his glasses and pinched the bridge of his nose. "You're always saying I should be authentic, pushing me to own my work. But you're the one who has been lying to me."

"What?" I took a step towards him, but he raised a hand as if to ward me off. I laced my fingers together to keep from touching him, heart beating frantically in my chest. "I never lied to you."

"That scene I walked in on was..." He shook his head, glaring at me.

"What scene?" My mind struggled to keep up. Beckett wasn't making sense. "Me and Xan?" The angry look on Beckett's face helped me piece things together. "You're jealous of Xan?"

Beckett's mouth thinned to a line. "Don't say his name."

I stepped closer. If I could just touch him, maybe he would feel how much I meant it. I was horrible with words. I wasn't a writer like him. I couldn't bend words to make them sound pretty. I couldn't even find the right ones to express my feelings.

"How could you even talk to him after what he did to you?"

"I told you that was a misunderstanding." Frustration burst inside me. "Xan didn't drug me."

Beckett threw his hands up in the air. "I swear if you say his name one more time, I'm going to lose my mind." He turned and paced one step to the other end of the room, ripping off his glasses to rub his eyes with his balled-up fists.

I came up behind him and touched his shoulder. His muscles stiffened beneath my hand, but he didn't pull away. "I'm so sorry. I didn't mean to tell your secret. I was so angry..."

He shrugged my hand away from his shoulder. "How can you have this power over me? You've just ripped my heart out and I still want you. I still love you with everything I am."

Tears ran down my cheeks. I didn't bother to wipe them away. I hugged my arms across my chest to keep my emotions inside. "Beckett..." My heart slammed against my ribs. Why was love so much easier in novels? The real thing was messy and scary, and there were no guaranteed happy endings. "I'm sorry."

"You just told my secret to the one man I hoped never to see again, and you think an apology is going to fix it?"

"I don't know what else to say."

"How about you love me too? How about you want to be in a relationship with me?" His glare was glacial, causing chills to run down my spine.

Anger pulsed between us. He accused me of lying, but I'd never been anything but truthful. He and Sally were the ones lying to the world. I shook my head. I knew I had been wrong to tell his secret when he'd trusted me, but part of me wasn't sorry to have revealed his identity. Didn't he know how much he deserved to be recognized?

"Maybe now that the secret is out you can finally be yourself."

Beckett's dark eyes heated, scorching me from across the room. "You don't get to make that decision," he said, his voice as sharp as a blade.

My heart raced as the tension filled the room. "Maybe it's for the best. You don't have to hide your talent."

Beckett's throat worked as if he was trying to form words. He moved suddenly. Crossing the room in a single stride, he hooked me around the waist and hauled me against his chest. His mouth crashed down on mine, taking me like a fierce predator. Fire exploded between us. His mouth was hard, branding my lips. After a moment, I responded with a demand of my own. I leaned into him just as he let me go.

His arms dropped so abruptly I nearly lost my balance. He stalked to the door and put his hand on the doorknob. I'll never forget the look of desolation on Beckett's face as he glanced back at me.

"Good-bye, Lacey."

I pressed my fingers to my mouth, still feeling the sting of his kiss as he walked away.

Chapter Thirty-Nine

For the rest of my shift, I was like a robot. I stacked books, gave recommendations, and helped with directions, all with a frozen smile. By the time I got off work, I was numb.

I drove home and parked in the driveway, but didn't get out. I turned off the engine and rested my head on the steering wheel as a highlight reel of my relationship with Beckett flashed before my eyes.

His pink socks the first time I saw him.

His moss-brown eyes looking up at me from the bottom of the bookshop ladder.

His dark hair glittering with snow on our first date.

His dimples popping the first time he'd told me he loved me.

I wanted to cry, but I was too mad for tears. I slapped the steering wheel in frustration. I had screwed up, but he hadn't even given me a chance to explain.

My phone rang, and I reached over and grabbed it. The bubble of hope in my chest burst when I saw Thatcher's name scroll across the screen.

I flipped open the phone. "What?" I barked.

"What are you doing?" he asked.

"Sitting in my car," I said, voice dripping with misery.

"I know," he said. "I'm in your driveway."

I looked up and saw headlights cutting through the rain into my front seat.

I winced. Was Thatcher going to fire me? Was that why he was here? I had been too numb to check in with him when I left. I'd caused a scene in his bookshop that was probably going viral on the internet.

I was so fired.

"You saw the video?" I asked, shrinking inside my jacket. I hadn't thought my heart could squeeze anymore, but the thought of losing Hyperbole's...

"Yeah," he said. "Thanks for the free publicity."

"I'm not fired?" I asked, biting the inside of my cheek.

"No," he said. "Of course you're not fired. You're the best employee I've ever had. You care more about books than anyone I've ever known. I'd be a fool to fire you."

I sighed and glanced up in my rearview mirror. Thatcher's Jeep sat behind me in the driveway.

"What are you doing here?" I asked, staring at his car in the rearview mirror.

"Wanna go for a ride?"

"No."

"A drink?"

"No."

"Come on," Thatcher said. "Get in the Jeep." Rain drummed on the roof of my car. "I have books."

Any other time, that would have been enough. Not now. Not after what I'd done to ruin things with Beckett. "I don't want books right now. I can't even think about reading."

"That's really bad."

"It's not a joke."

"Get in my car." Thatcher's voice rang in my ear. "Or you're fired, Lacey. I mean it. And I will make sure no other bookshop in the state hires you. You will be untouchable. If you don't think I can do it, just watch me. I'm hanging up now. If you are not in my Jeep in thirty seconds, I will call the first shop on my list."

"You wouldn't."

"Hanging up now."

And he was gone. The dial tone sounded in my ear. I glared at Thatcher in my rearview mirror. The rain made it difficult to see, but I knew he was staring at me.

Huffing a deep sigh, I got out of the car and splashed through the rain to Thatcher's Jeep. I snatched open the passenger door and threw myself inside. Thatcher caught me in an awkward, one-armed hug and hauled me across the console to his chest. His dog, a Labrador named Daisy, nuzzled my hair.

"I can't believe you fell for that load of bullshit." His laugh vibrated against my chest.

I sucked back tears, determined not to cry, and buried my head in the armpit of Thatcher's canvas jacket. "I've ruined everything."

Thatcher patted my back and muttered condolences. Rain drummed on the roof of the Jeep. Daisy licked my cheek. I don't know how much time passed before Thatcher finally spoke again.

"Uh, Lacey... I can't feel my arm," he said.

I let go of Thatcher and leaned back to my side of the car. Thatcher flexed his arm and rolled his shoulder. The tears wouldn't stop. I needed to fix this. But how?

"I can't believe I messed up so badly."

Thatcher reached over and covered my hand with his. "Something else will happen, and the internet will forget all about you screaming in Miranda Lockhart's face."

I stiffened. "I didn't scream in Miranda Lockhart's face."

Thatcher patted my hand. "I saw the video. You were screaming."

"Bitch," I muttered, thinking about the way Sally had fingered that sapphire hanging around her neck. Had it really been a gift from Beckett? There was so much I didn't know.

Thatcher's eyebrows shot up. "What the hell, Lacey?"

I buried my head in my hands, Sally's words echoing in my head. Was I just another muse to Beckett?

I hated Sally for planting the thought in my mind, where it lodged and festered. But what if it was true? What if Beckett fell in love every time he wrote a book, and then out of it just as quickly?

I choked on a sob.

Thatcher pried my hands from my face. "It can't be that bad," he said, his face pinched with concern.

I remembered the atrocities of war Thatcher had witnessed in Africa and felt a stab of guilt. My love life was insignificant compared to the horrors he'd seen.

"I really messed things up with Beckett," I said.

"This isn't about Miranda Lockhart?" he asked, thoroughly confused.

I shook my head.

"Do you love him?"

I hesitated. I hadn't been able to tell Beckett, even though he'd practically begged. "I don't know. I think so. Maybe. Yes."

Thatcher laughed. "I hope you didn't tell him like that. Men are fragile creatures."

I peered down at my lap. "I haven't told him at all. And now I can't."

"Does he love you?"

I frowned. "He used to, although I don't know why."

"Only one way to find out if he still does," Thatcher said. "Ask him."

I cringed. "I can't."

Thatcher threw the Jeep in reverse so fast my head flew forward. "You can." Thatcher flashed me a grin and threw his arm over the seat, gesturing for Daisy to get down. "Buckle up," he said.

* * *

Thatcher pulled up to the gate at Beckett's house and stopped. "Code please," he said.

"This is a terrible idea," I said. "I can't just barge in there and tell him I love him. At this point, three little words won't make a difference."

"Code. Please."

"I'm a mess," I said. "My hair is…"

"Do you want to get out here and walk up to the house?"

He gave me a look that said he wasn't kidding, and I leaned over him to punch in the gate code. The gate didn't budge.

"Entry is incorrect," said the automated voice. "You have two remaining tries."

"Beckett changed the code." I slumped back into my seat. "It's too late."

"Bullshit. It's not too late."

"Trust me, when that alarm goes off, you don't want to be anywhere near here."

"Call Pressly." Thatcher scrubbed a hand over his beard scruff. "She'll give you the code."

It felt a lot like cracking my chest open to call Pressly and ask her for the code, but I did it anyway. Pressly gave me the code, no questions asked, and the gate rolled open.

I watched Thatcher's jaw drop as Beckett's house came into view.

The rain had finally stopped, and a fine layer of mist rose like fairy dust from the wet ground. Beckett's house seemed to be sitting on a silver cloud. All shimmering glass, shining metal, and slick rock, the modern masterpiece stood out against the darkened sky.

"Jesus. This place is unreal." Thatcher craned his neck to get a better look.

Behind him, Daisy pressed her nose to the window, seeming equally impressed. Thatcher pulled to a stop in the driveway and stopped the car. He straightened his shoulders, and a steely glint came into his eyes.

Recalling Thatcher's history with Pressly, I wondered what he was thinking. I'd been so self-centered that I hadn't considered what it meant for Thatcher to see Pressly. The Jeep was filled with his nervous energy. Daisy felt it too. She nudged her head between the front seats and gazed up at Thatcher. He reached down to give Daisy's ears a scratch.

He looked over the dog's head at me. "You ready to do this?"

He tried to flash a smile, but it fell short, looking more like a grimace. I was dying to comfort my friend, but I could hardly tell him I knew about his teenage romance with Pressly.

I inhaled a deep breath as if courage was in the air. "Thanks for making me do this," I said.

Thatcher nodded briskly. "Life is short."

"Can you walk up with me?"

He turned and pointed at Daisy. "Stay here, girl. We have a relationship to fix."

Thatcher took my arm, and we walked to the front door together. Through the glass door, we could see straight through the foyer to the view of the mountains behind the house. A spiral chandelier threw sparks of golden light from the two-story ceiling, illuminating the stark white interior.

It felt strange to use the doorbell when I was used to letting myself in without permission. I pressed the button and listened to the low tone of bells ringing on the other side of the glass.

Aslan appeared, barking as he skidded to a halt at the door. A moment later, Summer came into the foyer. Her face lit with a smile, and she hurried to open the door.

"Hi, Winter," Thatcher said.

Summer smiled up at him like he was the hero in one of her fantasy novels.

"Summer!" Pressly's voice came from around the corner. "You know better than to open the door."

"But it's Miss Lacey and Thatcher," Summer protested.

Pressly came into view wearing a pair of pink leggings and a baggy sweatshirt. Her shoulder-length hair was half tied up in a messy ponytail, half falling around her neck in limp strands. Her cheeks were gaunt, and bags puffed under her eyes. It was a shock to see Pressly looking so undone. I'd never seen her look anything less than perfect. Her makeup was always impeccable, her nails manicured, and her hair sprayed into a sleek flipped-up-at-the-ends bob.

Pressly froze when she saw us standing at the door. Her eyes lit on Thatcher, and the color drained from her face. Her mouth hung open, and her hand fluttered to her hair then dropped to tug at her sweatshirt.

I glanced at Thatcher and saw a glimmer of apprehension in his eyes before he straightened his posture.

"It's Mr. Hayes, Summer," Pressly corrected, her tone frosty.

"Sorry, Mr. Hayes," Summer said, her lip poking out.

"It's okay," Thatcher said.

An awkward silence descended on the four of us and then Aslan broke the ice with a bark. I bent and patted his head.

My heart lodged in my throat. "Is Beckett here?" I asked.

Pressly tore her eyes from Thatcher to look at me. "No."

"Do you know where he went?" Thatcher asked.

"I assume he's flying." She touched her hair again, then crossed her arms over her chest.

"Where?" I asked, my voice barely above a whisper.

"I honestly don't know." Pressly gave me a sympathetic glance. "He wasn't here when I got home, and he has his phone turned off."

A wave of despair washed over me. I hadn't thought I wanted to confront Beckett, but now I wanted desperately to see him. Even if he hated me, I needed to see him.

"Do you want to see my room?" Summer asked, looking up at Thatcher.

"Mr. Hayes is a grown man. He doesn't want to see your room."

Summer glared up at her mother. "He loves Warrior Clan as much as I do. He would want to see my collection."

Thatcher's face looked pained as he glanced from mother to daughter. "Maybe some other time. Okay?"

Summer's face fell, and she turned and ran from the foyer. Her footsteps receded down the hall, followed by the loud slam of her bedroom door. Pressly's cheeks blazed, and she aimed a murderous glare at Thatcher.

The air between them crackled with tension.

"Will you tell Beckett I need to talk to him?" I asked.

Pressly's eyes flicked to me. "I thought things were good with you and Beckett."

My face flushed. "I messed up."

Pressly smiled, her face softening. "You're not the first."

Thatcher winced as if she'd punched him. "Love is messy. Sometimes people get hurt. But if they care enough, they pick up the phone and call the other person, even if they are falling apart."

Pressly glared at Thatcher. "Phones work in both directions."

"But he loves her." Thatcher's voice rang out in the night.

Pressly's face cracked. "If I hear from him, I'll let you know." She stepped back and closed the door, then disappeared around the corner.

Thatcher sighed audibly, watching her go. He caught me staring and schooled his expression. "Don't give up, okay?"

I wasn't sure if Thatcher was talking to himself or me. My heart was breaking, but I knew Thatcher was right. I couldn't give up. I'd never believed romance could be real, but Beckett had blindsided me with it, and now I didn't want to live without it.

I had to fight for him.

Lacey,

It's crazy how much I miss
the touch of your sweet lips.
And, when I get home,
I won't need my phone
To make you cry out in bliss.

All my love, Beckett

Lacey Donovan
138 1/2 Eabenezer Ave
Mossy Oak, NC
28802

Book Review of "The Big Mistake" by Allison Ashley

BY LACEY DONOVAN, BLUERIDGEBOOKCLUB.COM

O STARS —DNF—

5 FIRE EXTINGUISHERS

O BOOK BOYFRIEND BOW TIES

DEAR READERS,

Will this book slump ever end? Have I done something to aggravate the romance novel gods? I can't seem to find a book that has decent characters, a love story, or even much of a plot.

I've heard wonderful things about Allison Ashley. She's a new-to-me author who came highly recommended. Her previous books have glowing, gushing reviews, which makes me wonder, is it just me?

After a few pages, I wondered if the wrong book had been inserted between the binding. Was that the "big mistake" to which Ms. Ashley was referring? The cover was a cute picture of a man and a woman holding hands on the beach. Between the pages was a completely different story.

PLOT OVERVIEW:

I have no idea, I quit reading at chapter five.

PROS:

- Trope: Older man, younger woman. I'm a sucker for this trope!

Cons:

- Meet Cute: No one wants to meet their future lover on the examining table at the gynecologist. Can you say GROSS?
- Sex: There was way too much of it. By the fifth chapter, I'd already read three scenes. I'm no prude Goldilocks, but there's a tipping point into erotica that may have been crossed by chapter five.
- Book Boyfriend: The gynecologist leading man (I don't even remember his name) was the first to score zero bow ties and arrows on the book boyfriend chart.

The Final Word:

I hated this book! It was a train wreck, totally unenjoyable, and unfortunately I can't cleanse my mind of the cringe-worthy meet cute. If you like slutty heroines, pervy heroes, and unrealistic plots, this book is for you. If you like books with at least a little bit of substance and maybe a likable character or two, don't make a BIG MISTAKE in wasting your money on this book.

Love,

Chapter Forty

Fighting for Beckett proved harder than I'd thought. I called, texted, and left messages. Either he was somewhere he couldn't get calls, or he didn't want to talk to me.

It served me right that my sheets smelled like him, and that two days after he disappeared, I got a postcard in the mail from him with a naughty limerick scrawled on the back.

On the fifth day of Beckett's absence, Gabi called and threatened my life if I didn't come over to Thatcher's and meet the rest of the book club for drinks.

When that didn't work, she said, "Thatcher said if you're not here in ten minutes, then you're fired.

"He already tried that threat. It didn't work then either."

"So does that mean you're not coming?"

"I'd just be a drag."

Gabi sighed. "Don't you want to see Thatcher's new cabinets?"

Cabinets made me think of Beckett. It had taken me forever to figure out how to open them. "Not really."

"Fine. But you have one more week to wallow in pity, and then I am kidnapping you. Mia said she won't pursue a case against me if I do."

We hung up and I went back to wallowing. A few minutes later, my phone rang again. I lunged for it, hoping it was Beckett, but it was his sister.

"I found him," Pressly said when I answered.

"Where?"

"He's royally pissed because I had to get our mom involved," she said.

I could barely hear her over the thunder of my heart. "Where?"

"New York."

"You think I should go? You said he was pissed. What if he doesn't want to see me?" My words came out in a tumbling rush.

"You said you wanted to fix things."

"I do."

"Well, then why wait? You can't fix them from here, and I don't know when Beckett will be back. So what if he's pissed? That's Beckett eighty percent of the time, and somehow you still like him."

I more than liked him. "He's not that bad."

"If you looked up 'brooding asshole' in the dictionary, there would be a picture of my little brother. He didn't become remotely tolerable until he met you. So, please, for the sake of all of us, fix this mess."

"What if he doesn't want to fix it?"

"He does," she said. "Trust me."

Pressly gave me Beckett's New York address and the private code to the elevator, but she couldn't guarantee he wouldn't change it by the time I got there.

"I need to do something to show him how sorry I am." I chewed my fingernail, thinking.

"What exactly did you do?"

"You don't know?"

"Beckett doesn't tell me anything. It took me a week to track him down, and I live in his house."

"It's better if he tells you," I said. "But I need your help. I have an idea about a present for him."

"Sexy lingerie? That always worked on Jeff."

"Not exactly. I was thinking socks."

Pressly laughed. "I know the perfect place."

* * *

The next afternoon, I caught a cab outside La Guardia and headed to Beckett's Chelsea apartment.

I began to panic on the drive. What if the unicorn socks weren't enough? They were socks for crying out loud; they were nothing special. He might not even get the joke. After my betrayal, I needed to do something bigger, something really grand. Something that would hook him like he'd hooked me.

I thought of the limericks he left for me, and an idea took shape. I rummaged in my bag until I found a pen and paper. I would write him a limerick to show him how much I cared. I scribbled a few lines, then crossed them out. I crumpled the paper and found another. I started over but soon grew frustrated.

Writing limericks was no joke. How did Beckett do this?

He made it look easy, churning out the rhyming poems with little effort. The only thing I'd ever penned was a book review. I regretted teasing Beckett about his dumb limericks as I struggled with the first line.

There once was a girl named Lacey…

We passed Madison Square Park, and I knew time was running out. I exhaled with enough force to draw the eye of my cab driver.

"You don't happen to know any limericks, do you?" I asked her.

She spared a glance at me in the rearview mirror, her eyes narrowed with suspicion. "Those silly poems?" she asked in a strong Caribbean accent that took me straight to blue skies and cerulean seas.

"Yeah."

"Sorry, my baby, I'm just tryna ta drive."

Traffic was heavy. We were right in the middle of rush hour. My driver was doing her best to avoid getting in a pileup. I was on my own with my limerick. I tried again, grateful for the slow-moving traffic that allowed me more time to get creative. By the time we arrived in front of Beckett's building, I'd scribbled a limerick that would show him how much I loved him. Or at least I hoped it would.

Thanks to Pressly, the doorman was expecting me. He allowed me inside the industrial-chic building, offered me a cup of water, and let me know that Mr. Vinroot had left about twenty minutes ago. I could wait in the lobby or go up to his apartment if I had the code. I wasn't sure if I had the correct code. Beckett changed them so often it was possible Pressly's was outdated.

I wouldn't mind freshening up before I went upstairs. "Is there a bathroom I can..." I patted my flyaway hair.

The doorman pointed me down a long hall. "You look beautiful, young lady. If I was twenty years younger, I might try to steal you for myself."

I smiled at the older gentleman, thinking it was more like fifty years. He could have been my grandfather. But I would take the compliment. In the bathroom, I fixed my hair and straightened my clothes. My outfit made me look more confident than I felt. The off-the-shoulder dress in deep wine featured a steel-boned corset top that cinched my waist and displayed my cleavage. The skirt fell in soft folds to my ankles. The three-inch heels on my boots gave me a boost of confidence and would make it easier to reach Beckett's mouth.

I could only hope I got the chance to kiss him. He might take one look at me and order me to leave. I wiped my damp palms on a paper towel. What if he slammed the door in my face? Worse, what if he acted like everything was fine? That we were friends, and there were no hard feelings. No feelings at all.

I might die if Beckett was unaffected by me. Down deep, I couldn't believe he'd intended that good-bye kiss to be our last.

My heart climbed into my throat as I left the bathroom, clutching the paper with the elevator code in my clammy hands. As I walked down the hall, I heard the doorman call hello, and then a familiar voice. An icy feeling of dread spread through my chest as I recognized the woman's voice. I would know that snarky tone anywhere.

"No, he's not expecting me," said Sally.

I turned the corner into the lobby, and my fears were confirmed. Sally stood next to the elevator, her hand poised to push the button.

My high-heeled boots clicked on the tile, announcing my arrival. Sally's head snapped up. When she saw me, her eyes went round and then narrowed suspiciously. "What are you doing here?"

"The same as you."

"Beckett doesn't want to see you." She turned toward me, blocking the elevator.

I felt dizzy, remembering that day so long ago when Julian's mother stood on her front porch—a guard refusing to let me in. History was repeating itself. Another woman was telling me I'd been dumped. Tears burned behind my eyes, but I'd be damned before I let a single one fall in front of Fake Miranda.

Her eyes thinned to slits as she looked me over. "You should do yourself a favor and leave before he gets here. He won't be happy to see you."

Humiliation burned my throat and behind my eyes, but I was no longer the young girl whose heart could be broken by a third party. If Beckett truly didn't love me, he would have to say it to my face. I wasn't going to accept a relayed message. Not this time.

I turned my back on Sally and sat on a chair in the lobby.

Sally followed me. "What are you doing?"

I pulled open a book, not sparing her a glance. "I'm reading."

"You can't stay here," she said.

"I'm not going anywhere," I said, raising my eyes to glare in her direction. "Maybe you're the one who should leave."

"Beckett doesn't want anything to do with you. He's over you." Her hand moved to her neck, and she slid the diamond-encrusted sapphire along the silver chain. "I don't know what he saw in you in the first place. You're not even his type."

My muscles tensed, but I refused to respond. She wasn't telling me anything I didn't already know. So what if Beckett and I weren't each other's types? It hadn't seemed to put a damper on our fireworks.

"I'm calling him right now." She brandished her phone in the air.

"Go ahead."

"Is everything okay here, ladies?" the doorman asked.

Sally ignored him and cocked her chin at me, radiating superiority. "He ended things with you. You don't belong here."

A little cloud of doubt sailed over my blue skies. *What if Beckett didn't love me? What if Sally was right? What if Beckett had already moved on, forgotten me?*

I gritted my teeth. "I thought Beckett fired you."

Color swept up her neck to her cheeks. "Beckett would never fire me. He needs me."

"You think very highly of yourself."

"Beckett and I are a team."

I bristled, anger flaring in my chest. This woman had been the face of Miranda Lockhart for too long. "What exactly do you contribute to the team? Beckett has the talent, the drive, the passion. He's the genius. You're only the face."

Sally sneered at me, raising her phone to her ear. "He couldn't publish without me."

Neither one of us had heard the faint click of shoes on the tile, but there was no mistaking the ringing of the phone from a few feet away.

Sally's face fell, her smug smile slipping away as we both turned to see Beckett coming down the hall, ringing phone in his hand.

His eyes swept over us, flashing furiously behind the black frames of his glasses. The room pulsed with tension as Beckett's ringtone continued to blast. He frowned down at the phone and swiped the screen. Silence filled the air.

"You want to say that to my face, Sally?"

"Thank God you're here." She rushed over to him. "Can you get her out of here? I can't work with her around."

Beckett shoved his phone in his pocket. A vein pulsed in his forehead as he reached up and pulled off his glasses. "Your work is done."

Sally tossed her hair over her shoulder, undaunted by Beckett's rejection. "You don't mean it."

Color rose on his face, but his naked eyes were cold and hard. "You're fired, Sally."

"You can't do that. You need me."

Beckett's hand trembled as he replaced his glasses. My chest ached for him. I sent a silent message that I hoped he could hear, telling him I believed in him.

Beckett's eyes found mine. I silently pleaded with him to tell her to go to hell. I concentrated so hard that sweat broke out on my brow. *When was Beckett going to own his talent?* I jumped up from the chair and flew across the lobby. He caught me as I launched myself at him. I grabbed him by the collar of his jacket and shook him hard.

"You don't need her!" My voice rang out, echoing to the tall ceilings of the lobby. "You're good enough on your own!" Tears clogged my throat, choking my voice.

The doorman stepped up to us. "Mr. Vinroot? Do you want me to escort these ladies out?"

Beckett gripped my waist and looked down at me. His glasses were skewed from me jumping him, and his cheeks were bright red. "Get her out of here," he said, jerking his chin at Sally.

"What about the other one?" the doorman asked, eyeing me warily.

I clung to Beckett's lapels, uncaring if I looked like a fool. I'd come all this way to tell him I loved him, and I wasn't leaving until I said the words. If I could just force them past my lips...

Beckett hooked an arm around my waist and towed me to the elevator. "She's coming with me."

Chapter Forty-One

The elevator doors closed on us, and Beckett released his grip on my waist. He pressed the button for the top floor and then typed the code into the keypad. The elevator began the long rise to the penthouse, but my stomach stayed on the ground.

Beckett crossed his arms over his chest and glowered at me from behind round tortoiseshell glasses. "Why are you here?"

A wave of dizziness passed over me that had nothing to do with the rising elevator and everything to do with Beckett's energy pulsing through the small space. I sucked in a breath that smelled like Beckett's aftershave—cedar and spice and everything nice. God, I had missed that smell. I wanted to leap into his arms and bury my face against his neck, breathe in his tantalizing scent.

I gripped the handrail behind me so I wouldn't throw myself at him. He looked delicious in a pair of dark jeans, a blue button-down shirt open at the throat, and a gray blazer. His hair swept back from his face, and his jaw was shaved smooth.

One eyebrow ticked up over the frames of his glasses. "Are you going to answer me, or just stare at me?"

I couldn't breathe with the weight sitting on my chest. My

knees trembled, and I leaned heavily on the railing, gripping it with sweaty palms. "You smell really good," I blurted.

Beckett's other eyebrow rose, and he cocked his head to the side to study me as if trying to gauge the truth in my words.

"You came all the way to New York to tell me I smell good?"

The elevator stopped, and my stomach pitched. I wanted to throw up. My mouth went dry, and my pulse hammered in my throat.

"You wouldn't answer your phone."

"I was busy."

The elevator door opened to reveal the polished concrete hallway of Beckett's penthouse apartment. The Empire State Building shone in the afternoon light from the far window.

Beckett stepped into the foyer and turned to look at me. His eyes narrowed, and his mouth thinned. "You coming?"

"Is that an invitation?"

The sensual lines of his mouth hardened, and he reached out to snag my wrist. He pulled me out of the elevator and straight into his arms. "You're as stubborn as that damn dog you brought into my house." His arm hooked around my waist. "Do you think I would have given Peppy the code if I didn't want you here? I practically dragged you into the elevator. I can't be in the same room with you without wanting to touch you." He cinched me tighter in his arms. "It's a fucking invitation, Lacey."

I shivered at the savagery in his voice. "Don't cuss me," I said.

The elevator door closed, barely stirring the air.

His fingers dug into my waist. "Don't get in the goddamn elevator with me and fucking tell me I smell good." His eyes narrowed. "I've been going crazy without you, and you walk into my building looking like pure sex and sweetness and tell me I smell good?"

I grabbed the lapels of his blazer and pulled his mouth to mine. I was terrible with words, but I could use my mouth in other ways. I poured my heart, soul, and body into the kiss.

Beckett remained stiff. His sensual mouth didn't open under

mine. His tongue didn't plunge between my lips. I slanted my head, kissing his full top lip before turning my attention to the plump bottom. He stood like a statue, allowing me to kiss him but not participating or giving back.

I pressed against him, flattening my breasts against his chest, tangling my hands in his hair. Still no response. It was maddening, especially since we were standing so close that I could feel the bulge in his jeans. I knew he wanted me.

His mouth ticked up in the corner, and he reached up and pushed his glasses up his nose.

"Frustrating, isn't it?" His voice was smooth as velvet, unaffected by me. "When you give someone everything and they don't reciprocate?"

He pried my arms from around his neck and took a few steps back. The air between us vibrated with heat, but Beckett's eyes were ice cold.

My throat constricted, and my palms went damp. Our eyes clashed, and the words crashed inside my head. Three words. I knew the ones I should say. I knew Beckett wanted them. If I said them, this would be real. It was like flinging myself from a cliff. A soft landing was impossible.

"I've given you all of me. I told you my secret, and you told the world."

His words sliced through me. A chill ran down my spine. His voice was so cold, so empty. I'd done that, and I couldn't take it back. Nor did I want to. The world deserved to know Beckett's talents. He'd left that door to his office open for a reason. He wanted me to know.

I straightened my shoulders and found my voice. It came out soft but steady. "I'm not sorry."

Beckett's eyes went wide.

I took a step closer and grasped another thread of courage. "I was wrong to tell your secret, but I'm glad I did." Another step. "Because I believe in you." Another thread. "I'm in awe of you." The final step. "I'm in love with you."

Beckett's hands came to my shoulders. He yanked me to his chest so fast that the air whooshed from my lungs. His mouth crashed down on mine with a force that made our teeth clash. He punished me with his mouth, claiming me with a kiss so electric I felt like I'd been struck by lightning.

He used his tongue ruthlessly, plunging against mine in an ancient rhythm that made my blood heat and my belly flutter. His hands spread over my back, caressing and molding my body to his.

I hooked my leg around his thigh, my long dress rucking up around us. I wound my arms around his neck and climbed him shamelessly.

When we came up for air, our panting breaths echoed down the long hallway. Beckett's glasses rode crookedly on his nose. I reached up to fix them.

"I'm sorry I didn't tell you earlier." I brushed a hank of dark hair back from his face. "I should have told you sooner. I wanted to tell you, but I was afraid. I thought if I said the words aloud, then everything would change. That—"

He fisted the hair at the nape of my neck and gave a sharp tug. "Say it again."

"I'm sorry."

"Not that."

I cupped his face, blinking back tears. "I love you."

A smug smile crept over his mouth. "I knew you'd come."

"You're not angry with me?"

"Hell yeah, I am. I hated you for about twenty-four hours, and then I realized I still loved you. There's no one like you on this Earth. No one who cares as much as you do about ugly mutts and melancholy girls and books." He cupped my cheek. "No one who listens to me like you do, who's sweet and naïve and trusting. I can't stop loving you. Believe me, I tried." He bent to kiss me.

I pressed my finger to his lips, stopping him. "Wait." There was something I needed to know. "What about the necklace?"

His eyebrows drew together. "You want a necklace?"

"Sally said you gave it to her as a parting gift. That I'd be getting one too. When you dump me."

He backed me up against the hard wall and pressed his body into mine. "Does it feel like I'm dumping you?" His erection strained against his jeans, hot steel encased in denim.

"Did you give it to her?"

He nodded. "After we hit the USA Today Best Seller list for the first time."

I bristled. "That was you hitting the list. All you."

He pressed closer, trapping me against the wall. "Any other questions, Lacey?"

I glanced over his shoulder at the view of New York City. "Can I see the rest of the apartment?"

Beckett's grin widened. "Sure." He slipped his hands under me and cupped my ass, lifting me off the ground. "We'll start with the bedroom."

Chapter Forty-Two

"Your boots," Beckett muttered against my mouth.

"What about them?" Glancing over his shoulder, I saw the spiked heels of my boots digging into his jeans. "Oh! Sorry." I relaxed my legs and let them slide to the floor.

Once I was on my feet, Beckett dropped to the floor and began unlacing my boots. He took forever working all the laces of my calf-high boots free. I stepped out of one, and he started on the other. I placed my hands on his shoulders for balance and watched him patiently unhook the laces.

He glanced up and caught me staring. "What kind of shoes are these?"

"Sexy ones."

Beckett's green-brown eyes flared, and he freed my foot from the high-heeled boot. "You don't need anything extra to make you sexy."

Once both my feet were on the ground, Beckett rose to his full height. My hands drifted down his shirt to explore across his chest. His muscles strained under my touch.

A thrill ran down my spine at the sheer size of him. Without my shoes on, Beckett towered over me. I enjoyed being small next to him; it made me feel protected. I knew the sentiment was as outdated as the stone tablet, but it was still sexy as hell.

I stretched up on my toes and placed a kiss to his throat, then pushed his blazer over his shoulders. The blazer dropped to the floor, and I began undoing the buttons of his shirt. I kissed where the fabric gaped, feeling his pulse jump against my mouth.

Beckett pulled me closer, trapping my hands between our bodies. His eyes fired at me, the flecks of green shining emerald. "This is real, Lacey. It isn't a romance novel. You can't just close the book when you're done with me."

"I know that."

He lowered his mouth to mine and kissed me with such tender sensuality that it took me a moment to remember my quest to get him naked. I fumbled with the remaining buttons of his shirt until it hung wide open. He undid the buttons at his wrist, and I pushed the shirt over his shoulders to the ground.

Beckett's chest was gloriously naked, and I was reveling in the feel of his smooth skin under my fingers when he gripped my waist and spun me around so my back was to him. His fingers found the zipper on my dress and pulled; then I felt his mouth on my back. My skin tingled where his lips trailed up my neck to my ear.

Beckett eased the zipper down to the small of my back and then stepped away, taking his heat with him. I shivered as he pushed my dress down over my hips. Then, his warmth was back as he wrapped his arms around my waist. I felt his bare flesh against my back—hot, hard, and solid as a wall. He kissed across my shoulders, his skilled fingers prying the pins from my hair and tossing them to the ground.

When my hair fell down my back, he turned me to face him and took my mouth with a fierce kiss. The heat between us was enough to make my skin prickle with sweat.

Beckett stroked a hand down the center of my chest, fingers brushing over the burgundy lace of my strapless bra. "Have I told you I have a deep, abiding affection for your lingerie collection?" He bent his head to brush his lips over the swells of my breasts. "But I still like you best in my T-shirt."

I slid my hand back to his chest, brushing my fingers over the rippling muscles of his abdomen. His breath caught as I flipped open the button on his jeans and slipped my hand under the waistband of his boxers. I felt the silk of his skin, so supple under my fingers. Then I lost my train of thought as Beckett pushed down my bra and swirled his tongue over my nipple.

Thunder pounded between my ears as he sucked the sensitive peak into his mouth. A rush of sweltering heat shot straight from my aching breasts to the juncture between my thighs, and I cinched my leg around him. I clasped one hand behind his head, holding him in place. I slid my other hand to the silken crown of his erection, and he moaned against my breast.

Even though I loved what Beckett's mouth was doing to my breast, I was suddenly desperate to have his lips back on mine. I needed to taste him again, to stroke his tongue with mine. Tugging his hair, I pulled him up so I could kiss his mouth, share his breath.

Our kiss became urgent—edgy and unrated. Beckett hooked an arm around my back and lifted me off my feet, hauling me into the bedroom. I glimpsed the Hudson River through the windows as we fell onto the bed. Beckett ripped off his glasses and stretched over me to slap them on the nightstand. He came back to my mouth, settling his thighs between my legs. I wrenched his jeans over his hips, filling my hands with the round perfection of his ass. Beckett single-handedly unhooked my bra as he kicked off his shoes.

"Socks," I said between frantic kisses.

"What?" He shoved his jeans down his thighs.

"What socks are you wearing?"

He laughed. "I have no idea."

He rolled over in the enormous bed, pulling me on top of him. Gripping my hips, he slid me up his body. I straddled him and bent down for a kiss.

"I brought you something."

"Other than this hot body?"

Nerves made me tremble. "It's in my purse." I hopped up before he could stop me and ran lightly through the hall to where I'd dropped my purse in the foyer. I grabbed the box of socks and the limerick and went back to the bedroom.

My breath caught in my throat as I saw Beckett lying on his bed. He sat propped against the headboard, wearing only a pair of boxer briefs and a pair of yellow socks decorated with smiley emojis. Light streamed in from the wraparound windows that overlooked the Chelsea neighborhood. His hair gleamed russet, contrasting with the stark-white headboard. He reached for his phone and tapped the screen, and the shades were lowered over the view of Manhattan.

Beckett tossed his phone aside and then squinted at me, waiting for me to come closer so he could see what I'd brought. I went to his side, feasting on the sight of his rippling muscles and smooth skin. Beckett was sexier than any book boyfriend I could conjure.

He snagged my wrist and pulled me to the bed. "What did you bring me?"

I handed him the box. "It's nothing fancy."

Beckett's laugh rumbled as he opened the box and saw the lavender-and-pink socks emblazoned with unicorns. He raised the socks closer to his face to read the thought bubble above the unicorn. "I'm a special unicorn," he read, laughing.

"You get it?"

"I get it." He reached for the folded paper in my hand, but I jerked it away.

"I'll read it for you." There were so many lines scribbled and crossed out, I was afraid he couldn't make sense of it. I cleared my throat, and my cheeks burned with embarrassment. "There once was a girl from Wisconsin. Who didn't think love was an option. Then she met a man, who knew his that from his who, and she fell for his wit, charm, and Johnson."

Beckett choked on a laugh. "That has to be the worst limerick ever written." He pulled me into his lap. "God, I missed you." He rolled so that I was underneath him and nuzzled my neck. "Have I told you how much I love you?"

"Not in the last minute or so."

Beckett arched off the bed, reaching for his nightstand. "I love you madly." He fumbled with the drawer and came back with a condom.

"Always prepared," I mumbled. Jealousy flared as I contemplated why he had a box of condoms right next to his bed.

Beckett, sensing my discomfort, pinned my wrists to the bed, shifting over me. His eyes seared through me. "These are for us." He rattled the foil packet.

"Pretty confident, aren't you?"

"I knew you'd find me. Just like you knew I would forgive you. Because I love you."

Guilt pricked my chest. Beckett and I still had a lot of landmines buried between us. They could go off at any time. I had to be willing to risk getting hurt in order to have him.

Beckett was worth it.

"You know what?" I grabbed the condom from him and ripped it open.

"What?"

"I'm really glad I drank that cider."

Beckett's laugh filled me up, shining a light into all the dark places I'd kept hidden for so long.

Epilogue

One month later

I dropped the cardboard box of advance releases onto the coffee table and stood back as the members of The Blue Ridge Book Club pounced.

Ever-practical Gabi used her Swiss Army knife to cut the tape. She'd barely put the knife away before Sloane tore open the box and greedily sifted through the contents.

"Here's yours," she said to Kennedy, who floated into the reading nook just in time to catch the 700-page tome with her chest.

"Oof." Kennedy groaned, collapsing back on the sofa with the heavy book.

"That's mine." Mia shoved Sloane out of the way to grab her book.

Brandishing the new crime thriller overhead with enough enthusiasm to dislodge her signature chignon, Mia sank onto the sofa beside Kennedy and kicked off her high heels.

"Don't judge me," she said, catching my eye as she cracked open the book like a junkie with her drug. "I've been waiting for this for two years."

I laughed. "I'm not judging." After all, I'd once felt that way about Miranda Lockhart books.

Sloane took her books from the box and perched on the arm of a club chair.

Gabi sighed as she pulled her books from the box and tossed them aside with a grunt.

"What's wrong?" I asked Gabi.

Sloane glanced at Gabi's pile. "I thought you loved those alpha bears."

Gabi grabbed the top book from the stack and half-heartedly flipped it over to read the description. "I have to fire Mr. Morales," she said.

"The hot Spanish teacher? What happened?"

Two splotches of color burst to life on Gabi's cheeks. "I walked in on him getting a blow job from some busty bimbo."

My eyes bugged.

"What exactly did you see?" Sloane asked.

"Everything." Gabi fanned her flaming cheeks. She closed her eyes and shook her head. "I can't unsee it." Her entire face burned with color. "It was like watching live porn. It was..." She shook her head, unable to finish.

Mia glanced up from her book, eyeing Gabi with a knowing smile. "Looks like you don't want to forget it."

Gabi glared at Mia. "It was extremely unprofessional. Right there on his desk." She fanned her face more aggressively. "He had his legs spread, and she was on her knees."

Mia laughed. "You're picturing it right now, aren't you?"

"Of course I am." Gabi buried her face in her hands. "I need a distraction." She peeked through her fingers. "What books did you get, Lacey?"

I dug in the box. Moving aside a biography of a famous astronaut, which must be Thatcher's, I saw that the box was empty. "They must be in a different shipment."

I'd been hoping for something fantastic. I was desperate for a new author to replace Miranda Lockhart.

When Thatcher strolled into the reading nook a few minutes later, he was empty handed.

"Where are the rest of the books?"

Thatcher lifted the biography and flipped through the pages, not meeting my eye.

"Thatcher?" I waved a hand in front of his face to get his attention. "Where are my books?"

"Not here yet."

"Are you still mad because I switched around the non-fiction section?"

Ever since Thatcher had promoted me to assistant manager, I'd been trying to implement improvements. Sometimes Thatcher didn't agree, and we ended up butting heads.

Thatcher's eyes met mine briefly, and he shook his head. "No. I'm not mad. Be right back."

Dropping the book to the coffee table, he hurried into the heart of the store, disappearing behind the tall shelves.

"What's he up to?"

"Beats me." Kennedy came up for air from her book. "He was acting strange at yoga class earlier. He kept leaving the room. When I asked him what he was doing, he told me I'd find out soon enough."

We didn't have to wait long before Thatcher rejoined us. Summer trailed behind him. I was getting used to seeing Summer in Thatcher's shadow. She spent all her free time at Hyperbole's. I could hardly blame her. If I'd had a bookstore like Hyperbole's when I was her age, they would have had to kick me out too. Pressly didn't like it, but she wanted Summer happy, and Hyperbole's made everyone happy.

"Do we have a new book club member?" I asked, smiling at Summer. "Maybe we could do some children's reviews."

Summer gazed up at Thatcher with wide eyes. "Can we?"

Thatcher dropped his hand to her head and mussed her hair playfully. "I can add it to the website. It'll be fun." Thatcher looked back at me, his eyes gleaming mischievously. "You already noticed I don't have any books for you," he said.

I cocked my head at him, studying the spark in his eyes. It wasn't like Thatcher to be so mysterious.

"I noticed."

Thatcher cleared his throat and stuck his hands in his pockets. He rocked back and forth, smirking at me. "We have a special guest author tonight."

Summer's gaze shifted behind me, and a smile lit her face, giving me a glimpse of the beauty she was sure to become. I turned to see what she was beaming about and saw Beckett striding toward our reading nook with a box in his hands. Wearing a charcoal-gray suit with a white shirt and striped tie, he looked good enough to eat. One glance at him, and my stomach filled with butterflies. Was it possible that he got more handsome every time I saw him?

I ran down the aisle toward him and jumped into his arms. Beckett laughed and dropped the box to catch me.

"Hello, Princess."

I hugged his neck, inhaling his spicy scent. "Missed you."

"Missed you too."

His big hand curled around my neck, and his mouth descended onto mine. I forgot our audience as Beckett kissed me. One hand spread up my back, the other cradled my head, and we were the only two people in the world.

My heart rate kicked into high gear, and stars burst behind my eyes.

Slowly, the sounds of the book club penetrated my ears. Thatcher cleared his throat, Summer giggled, and Kennedy whooped her approval. I laughed as Beckett released me, keeping one arm pinned around my waist.

"Ladies, you all know Beckett Vinroot?" Thatcher asked.

My friends nodded. Kennedy and Mia had only met Beckett a

few times, and they stared at him as if they were in the presence of a celebrity. I caught Kennedy's eye and made a face. She realized she was gawking and forced a smile.

"Summer's going to tell everyone why her uncle is crashing our book club meeting tonight," Thatcher said.

Summer looked around the group with wide eyes and stepped closer to Thatcher. Her eyes lit on Beckett, and he nodded, prompting her.

"Uncle Kit is a writer." She beamed with pride.

A murmur erupted through the club members, and everyone stared at us. My mouth dropped open, and my gaze sliced to Beckett. He didn't seem surprised. He smiled, giving me a wink.

"What's going on?" I asked.

"Show her, Uncle Kit!" Summer could barely contain her excitement.

Beckett placed a hand on the small of my back and urged me toward the club chair opposite Gabi. "Sit down."

Beckett chewed his lip, and I realized he was nervous. I did as he asked, sinking into the chair. I stared at him as he placed the box he carried on the table. Time seemed to crawl as he pried off the tape and opened the box.

My heart thudded in my chest as Beckett handed me one of the books. He knelt in front of my chair so that our eyes were level. "What do you think?"

I glanced down at the book. *Crave* by B. A. Vinroot.

"It's beautiful." My eyes blurred with tears. "So beautiful."

Beckett knew I wasn't talking about the cover; I was talking about his courage. He pushed his glasses up his nose, eyes sparkling behind the lenses. "Read the dedication."

I tore my eyes from his and flipped past the title page to the dedication.

For Lacey Lynne Donovan—my muse, who was brave enough to drink the cider. All my love, Beckett.

My vision blurred. I closed the book, set it aside, and wound my arms around Beckett's neck. Holding back tears, I kissed my favorite author. He kissed me back.

THE END

WANT MORE BECKETT AND LACEY?

Sign up for Jill's Newsletter and receive a bonus scene written from Beckett's point of view.

Acknowledgments

Thank you to all my readers! I love hearing from you guys! This job is already the stuff of dreams, but hearing from my readers makes it even better! Feel free to hit me up on social media or drop me an email through my website.

Thanks to my long-suffering family. To Grace, who discussed plot on long walks. To Michael, who encouraged me not to sit in the same chair ALL day. To Drew, who made all my dreams possible. To my biggest fan, otherwise known as Mom, for always liking everything I write. To Jana, for being my first reader.

Thanks to my editors—Kristen and Cyndi who made sure I didn't have thousands of dialog tags, Miranda with red hair in a few scenes, and limited how many times I used the word "delve." Gotta love that word, though!

And a huge thanks to our dog Mickey, the best companion a writer could ask for.

About the Author

Jill Brashear is a hopeless romantic and author of swoon-worthy contemporary romances that will leave you breathless. With a pen in her hand and a heart full of love, Jill weaves tales of passion, longing, and happily-ever-afters that will make your heart skip a beat.